THE BATTER'S BOX

Casey Morales

Casey Morales

One

COOPER

Creating a pleasant, welcoming office environment always made sense to me—similar to how a foreign secretary might say, "That isn't helpful," rather than "Bite my country's ass," when addressing a frustrating adversary. But I've always been baffled by the desire of many of my office mates to turn working relationships into personal ones.

I rarely allowed personal ones to be, well, personal.

Alas, a willow must bend with the wind.

I only hesitated a second before opening the kitchen door, desperate for my second cup of morning salvation, to find Dennis and Marjorie huddled about the coffeemaker, their voices low and conspiratorial.

". . . got a rose. I bet they did it. You could see it in her eyes when he stepped up," Marge said.

"Come on, do you really think—" Dennis's head snapped up faster than a zombie hearing a human in *The Walking Dead*, and with a frightening similarity in facial expression. "Oh, hey, Cooper."

I gave him a coffee mug salute. "Good morning."

The coffeemaker's offensive line was well positioned, and I paused, my gaze darting between them.

Dennis squared his Sketchers and glared. Marge pretended to take a sip, but was only smothering a giggle. Her eyes *clearly* giggled. I wondered if that hurt.

"Need something?" asked Dennis, now a fourteen-year-old bully on our office playground.

Dennis was junior to me in every conceivable way. We started working for our monster hospital chain's headquarters on the same day, and, after only three years, I already outranked him by several levels. I was two years older and a solid thirty pounds thicker. He was basically a walking toothpick with patchy, carroty facial hair and the complexion of a thirteen-year-old. Mind you, my hair's waves flowed blond-brown with a dayglow of rouge. I hand no qualms with gingers in general, only this one in particular.

More important than any coiffure, he was mediocre at his job—on his best day. And not just a little mediocre. He excelled at his mediocrity in ways that made me wonder if he could actually be decent if he put as much effort into working rather than fiddling off all day. He was a professional-level fiddler. Charlie Daniels would be proud.

The whole whatever-it-was between us confounded me. I had only ever tried to help the man, but he continued to repay my assistance with folded arms and pursed lips.

Why was I so intimidated by him?

Yet there I stood, clutching a frustratingly empty mug like it was the bloody holy grail, my eyes flirting with his feet, then drifting up to his strumming fingers.

"I'd like some coffee. I'm thirsty and it's really early and I need to wake up or I won't perform well and we have a meeting with Raj and I've been working on these spreadsheets and reports for days but they all blend together in the mornings until I've had a second cup and coffee would really make me feel better, perhaps with some cream, and possibly Splenda, definitely Splenda. I need a lot of cream and more Splenda. All of that. I need it, really. Please step aside?"

I didn't know why he made me so nervous, but I had the sudden urge I was about to pee. I really didn't need to, but it felt that way, and I could almost do a pee-pee dance right there, but we were in the break room and that would've looked silly.

Then, I remembered to breathe.

Marge choked out a snicker that sounded like a cat coughing up a fur ball.

Dennis grinned, crossed his spindly arms, and raised one rusty brow. "Well, go ahead, Rain Man. We're just chatting."

Intellectually, I knew he meant the moniker as an insult, but I couldn't help taking pride in the comparison to a character with such amazing recall, even if he may have had a shrimp problem. I mean, the shrimp thing was more endearing than troublesome. I could've lived with that. Then it hit me that that was the wrong movie and I was suddenly very uncomfortable with his name calling.

I glanced at Marge, who gave me her best *he's right, you know* shrug without removing her mug from her upturned lips.

"Dennis, entering your personal space would be inappropriate. At the very least, it would be uncomfortable."

"I hereby waive any HR action to which I might be entitled. Invade away."

An awkward moment passed before Marge's mug finally clanked against the countertop behind me.

"Come on, Coop. Get your coffee." She stepped aside and tapped her single bedazzled fingernail against the machine. Dennis, never one for détente, remained a statue, forcing me to push my glasses back up my nose with my forefinger, as it was the only correct finger with which to upright one's lenses, then reach around him with my mug and fiddle the buttons by memory.

The whole encounter forced me perilously deep into enemy territory.

I ducked my head to avoid getting near his face, but when he blew out a breath, humid air laden with Columbian Supreme and vanilla syrup battered my senses. We were so close I could even smell a hint of pot he'd likely smoked in the parking lot before clocking in, clinging to his shirt with its tiny five-fingered hands. That tangy, pungent scent made me think of a skunk, which made cartoon reruns of Pepé Le Pew race through my head, except it was Dennis's head on the skunk's body as it darted about, shooting pot poop out of its white-striped ass.

A giggle slipped out of my mouth and tumbled onto his shoulder.

"Hey—" He hopped away, banging his head into the fridge.

My giggle grew.

Marge snorted.

Pepé's face morphed into Yosemite Sam as his fists balled and slammed into his hips in the universal teapot pose—or is that a sugar bowl, since both fists were planted?—eliciting another round of merriment from the peanut gallery, but thankfully not requiring additional conversation.

Before he could gather his wits, the machine huffed; I snatched my mug and fled to the relative safety of my cubicle.

"See you in the staff meeting in five. Hope you're ready," Dennis called out as the door swung shut behind me.

Great. Dennis was likely planning some sort of sneak attack in front of our team. I doubt they would take him seriously, but the back-and-forth rivalry between us that had somehow grown horns and teeth was wearing thin on our boss. The last thing I wanted was for a jealous child like Dennis to hold me back. I liked my job.

Every day reminded me of going to the dentist. No, not the icky stick of the needle or scraping of the teeth; the comfy, clean feeling you get as your tongue teases across freshly polished enamel that still tastes of bubblegum-flavored paste. God, what could be better? Perfectly clean, orderly teeth, everything as it should be and tasting . . . happy. Yeah, that's the taste of bubblegum paste.

Happy.

And that's how my work made me feel, all bubblegummy.

Okay, maybe days in the office weren't quite that Disneyesque, but I enjoyed the work.

"Cooper, are you ready? You're up first."

My boss's face peered down from above the muddy fabric wall. Well, his nose and everything above it did. He wasn't tall enough for anything else. The nostril cam was zoomed in tight, revealing nearly as many hairs as the bushy things crawling above his eyes.

"Uh, hi, Raj. Yes, I am pressing print—"

He'd vanished before I could finish my sentence.

I fast-walked to the printer. There were no pages in the bin, and an angry red light was blinking. I opened and closed every drawer and door I could find, but nothing appeared stuck, so I double-checked the paper feeder, then shut its drawer, stepped back and stared, as if assessing a stubborn rhinoceros at the zoo. I have no idea why the copier made me think it was a horny beast, but in that moment, it did.

I was officially late.

Raj would thank me for "joining the *afternoon* meeting" as I entered, then remind everyone about the importance of punctuality by regaling us with an ancient Indian legend about a beetle that couldn't fly, or something equally obscure. It never made sense, but we all nodded like he was Yoda. Or a wise man who lived in a cave. Or a crazy one.

"Here, let me help you, hon."

I turned from the beast to find Marge approaching. Without her wonder twin, she was actually a very nice lady, something of the office mom. She even had the mom bun, sort of like Princess Leia, except gray, and only the one positioned on top. Maybe it was more like a powdered-sugar-coated dough crown than a bun.

The dance with Dennis had ruined my chance to eat. I was hungry.

Three beeps, two opens and closes, and one hip slam later, the copier was purring like a rhino-sized kitten that'd eaten a tree and was now spewing legal-length sheets. Thankfully, those sheets contained my report rather than oversized cat puke, so rhino-kitty was alright by me.

"Thank you, Marjorie," I said.

She smiled and patted my arm. "Anytime, sugar. You're late, you know."

I nodded and snatched my copies, then Usain Bolted my way down the cube aisle toward the conference room.

"Ah, good *afternoon*, Mr. Hawk." Raj tapped his watch and frowned like a disappointed father who'd caught his son stealing Goobers at the drug store. "Don't sit. We were about to skip you on the agenda, but since you decided to join us after all, you may as well give your report."

My collar itched and my glasses slipped down my nose but my hands were full and there was nowhere to sit and Raj was staring at me while everyone else in the room stared and Dennis was grinning and all I wanted was to crawl under the mahogany slab and hide.

On the outside, I said, "Everyone, please take a copy and pass the rest. As you see in the executive summary at the top of page one, this month was strong. Gross revenues for our division rose by one point three percent, outpacing the zero point four percent growth in the same month, prior year. We were, however, three-tenths of a point below our all-time monthly record, so there is room for improvement . . ."

My portion of the meeting normally lasted twenty minutes. Dennis decided that wasn't nearly enough stage time and peppered me with queries challenging my assumptions or questioning my math.

Thou shalt *not* question my math. Ever.

I hadn't been named valedictorian of my graduating class at Gonzaga while double-majoring in statistical analysis and business management for nothing. Dennis was wading in a pool far too deep for his bony little arms to dog paddle out of.

I heard a metaphorical bell ring when Raj stepped in and called the bout. It hadn't been close. Dennis's scant reputation lay on the shining surface of the conference table, bloodied and barely breathing. I smothered a smile, not wanting to appear too much like a vanquishing hero, you know, with a sword held high and cape snapping in the breeze. Raj must've sensed my burgeoning pride, because his next words yanked the superhero cape right off my shoulders. "Thank you, Cooper.

Excellent report, as usual, even if you wasted the team's time with your tardiness."

"Uh, thank you, sir, and sorry, again, sir," I mumbled as I finally sat and stacked my remaining copies, straightening them with my fingertips before aligning my pen and pencil in the precise center of the page.

Raj timed the remaining reports and slammed his leather folio shut at precisely eleven o'clock. He nodded crisply to no one in particular, then rose and strode out of the room without so much as a, "You're dismissed," or "Good meeting, everyone," or "I can't take you people anymore. I'm leaving."

I might've been projecting on that last one. The subconscious mind is a funny thing.

When I returned to my desk, the message light was blinking on my telephone. That was odd. No one ever called me at work—not even Raj. I was the guy everyone depended on for accurate reports, analysis, and recommendations based on statistical modeling and unbiased testing and assessment. I would like to think they respected the mental challenge and immense weight of my responsibility, but the truth was likely closer to something Dennis had once said:

"Everyone hates statistics, even nerds. You're beyond weird."

I might be fastidious, but I certainly was *not* weird.

One of my pens had rolled out of alignment with its brothers, and my fingers couldn't fly fast enough to save it from embarrassment, nestling it back into blessed harmony while pressing the play button on my phone with my other hand.

"Hello," the voice of a scrupulously professional-sounding woman drifted through the speaker. "I'm calling for Cooper Hawk. This is Bethany Sands at Whisker and Riley, attorneys at law."

I snatched up the receiver and banged it painfully against my ear, then glanced around to see if anyone was near enough to have heard me receive a message from a law firm. I was a lone island in a sea of cubes, so I rewound and pressed play again.

"There is an important matter we need to discuss. I'll be in the office all day, likely working late. Please call as soon as you get this message."

Unexpected calls from lawyers were never good, right? They're like going to the dentist, but without the bubblegum paste.

I scribbled the number she left, then stared at my realigned pens a moment before reluctantly dialing the woman's number.

Two

COOPER

I grabbed a pen, scattering the others, and began tapping it rapidly against my desk.

"Bethany Sands," the voice from the message answered, somehow sounding both reasonably pleasant and incredibly busy.

"Uh, hi. This is Cooper Hawk. You just called me. I mean, you called me twenty minutes ago. Twenty-two, actually."

"Mr. Hawk, thank you for calling me back. First, please accept my deepest condolences—"

"Wait. What are you talking about? Condolences for what?"

"Oh dear." In those two words, her voice lost its professional edge. She paused a beat. "Mr. Hawk, I'm so sorry you're hearing this from me, but Marjorie Polk passed away yesterday."

I stopped tapping.

"Grammy . . . died?"

Another pause, this one several beats.

"I'm *so* sorry."

I tossed my pen down, then a flush of panic flooded my chest before I could level it with the others. My OCD knew no bounds, not even in the midst of a familial crisis.

And then an ocean swell slammed into my chest, and breathing became a frustratingly difficult act.

"Mr. Hawk? Are you still there?"

"Yeah," I squeaked. "Sorry, I'm just . . . it's . . . you kind of caught me—"

"It's alright. Take your time." The compassion lacing her voice caused the waves to roil and froth. I was sure they would spill from my eyes at any moment.

I tried to speak.

I really tried.

When a moment—or ten—passed, she tossed me a preserver. "Mr. Hawk, I know this must be very difficult, and I'm truly sorry for your loss, but Mr. Whisker, the senior partner in our firm, needs to see you as soon as you can visit our office."

The only things I heard were the ridiculous sound of a man named Mr. Whisker, and the fact an attorney wanted to see me posthaste. Stuck at the center of a battlefield where humor, shock, sadness, and uncertainty stood with loaded weapons, all aimed at me, I somehow managed to ask, "Why does an *attorney* want to see me?"

I swear I heard her lips purse.

"Well, it really is a matter for Mr. Whisker to—"

"Please, Ms.—I'm sorry, I don't remember your name—just tell me what's going on so I can figure out how to get through the rest of this day."

"Bethany."

"What?"

"My name is Bethany." She sucked in a breath loud enough for me to hear over the phone. "I'm not supposed to . . . Please don't tell Mr. Whisker I told you this, but Mrs. Polk named you as her executor, and she had a fairly sizable estate."

When I didn't respond, she asked, "Were you not aware of any of this?"

"No," I croaked.

My mind raced.

Grammy had never said anything about this—and we talked about everything. At least, I thought we did. I knew she was well-off. Anyone who looked at her home or cars or, hell, her jewelry, would know she was rich, but there were a million other people more qualified to handle her estate. The lawyer calling me was one of them.

Then my perplexity over the executorship surrendered to the reason I even needed to think about it.

Grammy had died.

I squeezed my eyes shut and pinched the bridge of my nose, but the tears still found a way. By the time Bethany spoke again, my cheeks were soaked, and I was choking through sobs.

"Mr. Hawk, why don't you take some time? You can call me back in an hour or two. I'll be here. Alright?"

"Okay. Yeah, that . . . I think . . . yeah. Thanks."

I'd never been so happy to hang up a phone.

I met Mr. Whisker at his office later that evening. It's difficult to say what I expected, but a spherical man whose head barely rose to my shoulders wasn't it. I'd never had a thing about height or heightism or shortness—however it should be said—but between his sharply pointed beak and the black spaghetti noodles waterfalling down his neck to his shoulders, I felt like I was meeting an actor who'd just walked off a set rather than an esteemed counselor.

My lawyer was a doppelgänger for the Penguin from the old *Batman* TV show.

For the first time that day, unless you counted a few self-satisfied grins at Dennis's expense, I laughed.

"Something funny, son?" Mr. Whisker asked as he peered up at me through spectacles with round, thumb-sized metal frames.

"No . . . sir. Sorry. It's just . . . It's been a long day."

Humor evaporated as my host righted his spectacles and began scanning pages in a manila folder that lay open before him. There must've been two inches of paper in that folio, but I didn't care. All I saw was a Polaroid of Grammy stapled to its inside fold. She sat in the same chair I now occupied, smiling brightly as she did.

She was so full of life.

I sat back, desperate to quell the emotions swirling inside my chest before they erupted all over the lawyer's office. He'd probably seen his share of grieving clients, but I didn't want to become yet another. Grammy deserved dignity, not . . .

In an instant, my eyes fled from the image in the photo, but the one in my mind refused to retreat. It replayed, on a loop, the day I'd moved in with Grammy and Pop.

I was ten.

My mom had called her relationship with my dad *complicated*. My preteen brain thought it was fairly straightforward, in the way one human regularly beating another seems crystal clear on the right-versus-wrong scale. Rather than have me witness the countless interventions, arrests, and subsequent counseling, the adults decided it was best if little Cooper went to live with his grandparents.

Grammy and Pop became my world.

We lost Pop when I was fourteen. He and Grammy had been married nearly forty years and still doted on each other like teens in love. Grammy cried at the cemetery, but I can't remember a single time she shed tears in front of me at home. I'd hear her in her bedroom, late at night, when she thought I was asleep, but she never let me see the grief that wrenched her soul.

She was the most amazing, most beautiful woman in the world.

Now she was gone.

". . . list of people Mrs. Polk named in her will to receive various inheritances." Mr. Whisker slid a set of stapled pages across his desk toward me. When they slid off and fluttered to the floor, I woke from my daze.

"Uh, sorry. Could you repeat that last part?"

His lips did a twisting-to-the-side thing I thought might've hurt a little and spoke with deliberate enunciation. "That is the full list of named beneficiaries. Our office will contact as many as you prefer not to."

"Wait. You want *me* to talk to people about whatever Grammy put in her will?"

He blew out a breath, folded his hands, and glared at me over the top of his spectacles. "It's up to you. You can leave that to my people, but there may be some on the list you would prefer to contact. Mrs. Polk specifically requested some receive the news of her passing from a relative, and you are the closest one she had left."

I scanned the pages, flipped once, then twice, then ten times, amazed that Grammy had so much to bequeath to others.

"Holy shit," slipped out when I read the line about a home in the Hamptons valued at more than eight million dollars.

The creak of Mr. Whisker's chair brought my eyes up.

"I would tell you to take your time, but there is a clock on settling estates, and, with one this large, it would be best to get the initial round over with before the contests begin."

"Contests?" I set the pages back on the desk.

He nodded. "Some cousin who thinks he should've received a lottery-winning's worth will probably contest the will, say Mrs. Polk wasn't competent or such. It's nonsense, but we'll have to defend against it. As executor and one of her closest relatives, you will probably get dragged into whatever comes. Please accept my apology in advance."

Grammy died. I'd barely had time to shed my own tears before meeting with her attorney. Now I had to talk to people about stuff I never even knew she owned, and strangers—or worse, family—might come after us—for what? Stuff? Money?

I just wanted Grammy back.

The whole thing made my chest feel like a vice was squeezing my insides. I reached up and gripped a fistful of my shirt, desperate to suck in air.

"Son, are you alright?" Mr. Whisker shot to his feet.

"I'm . . . I just . . . I need a . . . I can't . . . breathe."

"BETHANY!" Mr. Whisker yelled as he waddled around his desk. The door flew open seconds later as Bethany raced into the room. They walked me over to the couch and laid me out. I wasn't sure that was the correct procedure for a breathing issue, but for some mystical reason I'll never understand, it calmed me, and air flowed into my lungs.

"Thanks," I said between deep breaths. "I'm okay."

It took another hour, for which I was sure Mr. Whisker billed Grammy's estate an exorbitant sum, before I'd gathered myself, and we'd completed the arrangements. Mr. Whisker divided the inheritor list, leaving me twelve people to contact, all of whom were relatives or Grammy's closest friends. He'd offered to contact everyone, but I thought those most special to my grandmother should hear the news of her passing—and their inheritance—from me rather than a stranger who looked like a flightless cartoon bird.

By the time I shuffled through my apartment doorway, it was dark outside. I fell onto the couch and sleep wrapped me in her comforting warmth before I could turn on *Survivor*.

My cousins, Jade and Misha, stood to either side of me as Grammy's casket was lowered into the ground. We'd only met once years ago, and I couldn't even recall where either of them lived, but loss has a strange way of uniting people. As tears streamed down my cheeks, the arms of my distant relatives found my shoulders, and we held each other until Grammy completed her journey.

At Mr. Whisker's suggestion, we held a private family funeral, to be followed in a few weeks by a public memorial. Grammy was deeply involved in her community, and he thought more of her friends could attend if we gave them reasonable notice. I really didn't want to go through another service, but Grammy deserved to be surrounded by friends one last time, to know how much she was loved and admired.

My mom and dad were super religious—except for the whole beating-your-wife thing—but I never fully wrapped my head around what happens after we die. I wanted to believe there was more, that we became spirits or went somewhere wonderful. I wanted Grammy to still be . . . something, so she could see how people would respond to her passing.

I really missed her.

A couple days later, as I worked diligently on a pivot table inside a massive Excel spreadsheet, my phone rang.

"This is Cooper Hawk."

"Hi, Mr. Hawk. It's Bethany over at Mr. Whisker's office."

My head drooped.

"Mr. Whisker asked me to call and see how you're doing with your inheritor list."

Well, shit. I'd spent the last two days mourning my grandmother rather than completing the homework assignment Professor Waddles gave me. I mean, I knew it was important, and people would want their money and things, but come on. Can't a guy have a minute to breathe?

"Um, well, I'm working on it."

I heard papers shuffling through the pause.

"So, it looks like you have twelve names on your list. Mr. Whisker has . . . call it sixty."

Out of curiosity, I did a quick Google search while she dug up whatever data she needed.

"Ms. Sands?"

"I'm here. Sorry, just looking for something."

"Can I ask you a question?"

"Found it." The shuffling stopped. "Of course, but if it requires legal advice, you'll need to ask Mr. Whisker."

"I think it's pretty basic," I said. "From what I've read, Tennessee law gives me, as executor, sixty days to compile an inventory for probate, then up to a year to distribute non-probate assets. Those going through probate can take longer."

"Mm-hmm. That sounds right."

"So why are we in this big rush? We just buried my grandmother two days ago."

"Mr. Hawk . . . Cooper . . . I'm so sorry. I know this must feel overwhelming, and when you're coping with such a personal loss . . ." There was another long pause. "The timeline you laid out sounds right, but I believe there's a rule of thumb around *notifying* inheritors that may differ from the other rules regarding probate and settlement. Again, you'd really need to talk with Mr. Whisker about the law. What I know for certain is that Mrs. Polk's—I mean, your grandmother's—estate is significantly larger than most, and with more than seventy individuals and dozens of charities named in her will, this process takes on a whole different level of complexity. She was also very clear in her instructions that certain individuals should be contacted in person by a family member, if possible. Unfortunately, you are the only family member we have. The others she noted all predeceased her."

Predeceased. Such a tidy, clinical term. I tried not to focus on it, but the sound of it echoed in my ears long after Bethany had moved on.

". . . okay with you?"

"What? Sorry, I was thinking . . . Never mind. I'm sorry. Please repeat the question?"

"Of course. How about you tackle two or three names on your list each day? That would have you fully completed in roughly a week. Does that sound reasonable?"

I let my head fall back against the headrest on my desk chair and stared as the ceiling fan spun above me.

"Mr. Hawk?"

"That's fine. I'll . . . I'll get it done."

"That's wonderful. Would you mind emailing me as you complete these so I can coordinate between your list and the one Mr. Whisker is calling?"

Great. I had an accountabilibuddy.

"Sure."

"Excellent. Just making a note . . . and we're done. Was there anything else I could help you with today?" she asked in a sugary tone. Hadn't *she* called *me* to nag about a list? How was that helping me? I bit back the bitterness rising in my throat.

"No, thank you. I need to get back to work. I'll email you."

I didn't wait for her overly pleasant goodbye.

I hung up and watched the fan whirl.

There's an expression the sales guys in our office use all the time: "If you have to eat a frog, do it first thing in the morning. That way, everything else you do that day will seem easy."

I've never been sure who needs to eat frogs in our office, or why they would want to, but the principle rang true as I snatched the phone off its cradle and dialed the first inheritor. If I had to do this thing, I would get it over with.

Damn that frog.

Mrs. Bonnie Willis, a neighbor down the street from my grandmother's house, and a lifelong friend of hers, was to receive five hundred thousand dollars. I waited an interminably long amount of time as she ugly-cried into the phone, an odd maelstrom of sadness coated in elation.

Mr. David Estes was pleased with his lifetime membership to the local country club, one my grandmother used so rarely I thought she'd let it lapse.

Several people received cars. Others more money. One son of a cousin's neighbor's best friend received her beach house in Sarasota. I didn't have ages on my sheet, but the guy sounded younger than me, probably in his early twenties.

While each call forced me to recount the loss of my grandmother, which was a bit like smashing a thumb with a hammer over and over, the "lottery ticket hit" part of the conversations didn't entirely suck. Most were surprised Grammy even thought of them enough to leave something, especially something extravagant.

Perhaps the inheritor I enjoyed the most was a woman I'd never heard of, Eloise Compton. She didn't have a number listed on the sheet, just an address with a zip code I didn't recognize. I followed Waze's voice across town, still missing turns despite the mechanical voice chiding me as it rerouted, and pulled into the driveway of a house, one of a long row of identically disheveled homes, in a neighborhood more akin to those in troubled lands than in the heart of Tennessee's capital.

Life had whittled the woman who descended the rickety stairs, yet there was immeasurable strength in her eyes. She reminded me of formations in a desert, weathered and worn over time beneath intense heat and constant wind, and somewhere in the distant past, powerful water raging over and through them. I doubted she had ever seen a yacht up close or enjoyed fine dining in a club. From the looks of things, she might've struggled to find enough to feed her family most nights.

Despite our differences, the moment I introduced myself as Marjorie Polk's grandson, she wrapped me in a motherly embrace and welcomed me into her home.

"Marjorie told me all about you. My, you're taller than she said, and a lot more handsome."

My face flushed.

"Mrs. Compton—"

"Please, son, call me Eloise."

"Yes, ma'am. I mean, Eloise."

For the first time since I'd started on my list, nerves rattled through my head. This woman was so . . . real, and when she spoke of Grammy, her eyes lit up like . . . well, like mine did when I thought of her.

"How is old Marjorie? She's a card, you know that, right?"

My lips barely twitched. I tried to smile, I really did.

"Grammy—" The words stuck in my throat. "My grandmother . . . she . . . Grammy died."

It took a while to get through the "Grammy died" part. Mrs. Compton was the most distraught of anyone I'd spoken with, including Grammy's best friend and neighbor. I never learned how her daughter had met Grammy. I'd never known that my grandmother visited the prison nearly every week for the past eight years, with Eloise by her side. All Eloise would tell me was how kind and caring Grammy was, things I already knew but savored hearing again.

The stories finally stilled, as each of us lapsed into our own memories. The warmth of her hand on mine roused me from my thoughts.

"Thank you for coming all the way over here to tell me about Marjorie. I'd love to chat longer, but I need to go pick up two of the boys now."

She made to stand, but I put my hand on hers and she settled back in her seat. "There is something else. It's important. According to the papers the attorneys gave me, you have five children, all under the age of ten?"

"That's right. Well, I call them mine. They're my daughter's. She's the one Marjorie and I visited in prison. I do the best I can, but—" Her eyes drifted from a tattered recliner to a rug so worn I could see the floorboards peering through.

"Eloise." I waited until her gaze met mine. "Before she died, my grandmother established a scholarship fund to ensure each of your children—well, your grandchildren—will be able to attend any college or university they choose. They can go to a HSBC or to Harvard without having to worry about tuition, room, board, or any other expense."

Her hand flew to her mouth while her other clamped into a death grip on mine. I could feel her beginning to shake.

"Oh, Jesus. Sweet Jesus."

"There's one more thing."

"Lord. What has Marjorie gone and done?"

"There's also a trust fund in *your* name."

Her head cocked and her brows knitted. "*My* name? But why—?"

"Grammy left you one million dollars, and I quote from her will, 'So she can get rid of that ratty old rug.'"

Eloise's mouth fell open. I felt her hand leave mine, then both of hers flew to her mouth. Her eyes widened, then darted from me to the hole in her rug, then back to me. Her hands flew into the air, a raucous cackle filled her home, and she doubled over and wept so loudly I thought the neighbors might call the police.

It was the most beautiful sound in the world.

The neighbors might not have called the police, but they certainly came to investigate the lanky white guy making Mrs. Compton howl. She insisted I help her tell each one about Grammy paying for the kids' college, but swept her own new fortune under the rug—one without a worn spot.

I untangled myself from her arms an hour later. It was around six o'clock and traffic would be unbearable, so I glanced at my list to see who I might contact next. I'd kept tally by the most scientific method I could dream up: I drew a line through each name as I completed the visit.

There was only one name unstruck.

I was almost done.

Something deep in my gut breathed a sigh of relief at the sight. Aside from Grammy's memorial, this would be the last time I had to have "that conversation" with anyone. I didn't recognize the name or business, but the address was only a few minutes away. So, off I went.

I pulled into the parking space of what looked to be a mechanical repair shop and shut off my car. I'd turned to close my door when a deep, gravelly voice nearly startled me into the next decade.

"Hi. We're about to close up. How can we help?"

I sagged back onto my car and let my pulse slow, then glanced up. Holy shit, Mr. Raspy looked like a muscular biker dude who'd decided to quit the road and, I don't know, go into business or something. I couldn't decide which made him hotter: his thick stubble, the rounded shoulders lifting his slightly-too-tight shirt, or the insanely blue eyes that kept blinking at me.

"I . . . uh. I'm, well, looking . . . Hi. Um, I'm Cooper." Unable to complete a sentence, I stuck out my hand for him to shake. His mouth quirked up at one corner, and his damned eyes glittered as he reached over.

And then I saw it, and the air whooshed out of my balloon.

Well, shit.

A shiny wedding ring glinted in the dying sun before vanishing against my palm.

"Nice to meet you, Cooper. What can we do for you?"

I reluctantly released his hand, then fumbled through my stapled mass of crossed-out names. "I'm looking for . . . Hang on . . . Here . . . I'm looking for Sam Prescott."

Three

COOPER

"I'm Sam," the greased-up hottie said as he hooked a thumb toward his name embroidered onto a patch above his shirt pocket.

I glanced around to find several mechanics and a few customers staring.

"Is there somewhere we can talk in private? This is, um, personal."

Sam cocked a brow. "Sure. Let's go into my office."

My backside had barely hit his poorly padded chair when the door rattled and flew open. Was every car guy in the place a cover model? Holy cow.

"Sam, I'm almost—" the mechanic began. Then his eyes fell on me and darted back to Sam. "Sorry, didn't know you had someone in here."

"Ty, hang on." Sam stopped him from backing out. "Why don't you stay for a minute?"

Then to me, Sam said, "This is Tyler. He's my closest friend and best mechanic. Whatever you need to say, he can hear."

I wasn't sure what to do. This wasn't in Mr. Whisker's script. I glanced back at the guy—Ty, he'd called him—and my eyes decided to take a road trip up and down his body without bothering to file a flight plan with the controller—namely me. It was a most amazing landscape.

Wow. Like really. Wow.

When my eyes finally relinquished control and rose to meet Ty's, amusement filled his emerald orbs.

Heat and crimson flooded my neck, then crab-walked its way across my cheeks.

"Uh, okay, I . . . well . . . I guess—"

"It's fine. Really," Sam said.

Ty smirked, crossed his beefy arms, and leaned against the back of the now closed door. That's when I saw his shiny gold wedding band reflecting the desk lamp accusingly back into my face.

Dammit. They're all smokin' hot but freakin' married.

Then I realized they were both waiting on me because I was still staring at Ty's ring and he was chuckling and Sam was leaning back in his chair with a really wide smile and they exchanged a look and I wanted to puke.

"Marjorie Polk died," I blurted out, unable to control whatever gremlin decided to inhabit my head.

Sam's chair cried as he leaned forward. "Really? Marjorie?"

His face creased and his eyes clouded. I'd delivered this message a dozen times, and the impact of watching someone else grapple with the immediate pain still clawed at my chest. But for some reason, seeing Sam, this burly mechanic, moved by *my* Grammy's passing—that touched me.

"How did you know her? I mean, if you don't mind me—"

"It's okay, Cooper. She was a customer a few years ago, brought in her husband's old Bel Air. God, that was a beautiful car."

Tyler grunted his agreement.

"But, you knew her? I mean, more than just fixing her car. Didn't you?" My voice sounded pleading in my ears. I'd hoped Sam hadn't heard that.

He studied me for a moment, then nodded. "I met her because of the car, but we became friends; a regular odd couple, really. My partner, Miguel, has season tickets to the Sounds. We took her with us to a few games. She loved it, especially when Annie would sing for her." He must've seen the confusion on my face. "Oh, sorry, Annie has the seats in front of Miguel. She used to perform on Broadway. Marjorie and Annie were a lot alike. I'd never seen two old women laugh so much as when we went to games."

The papers that had rested in my lap fluttered noisily to the floor. My brain got stuck on one track and couldn't right itself.

"Grammy liked baseball?"

"She was your *grandmother*? Cooper, I'm so sorry."

Those words were far too familiar now.

I nodded. "She raised me."

The rustle of Ty's arms uncrossing drew my gaze to him. The compassion in his eyes mirrored what I saw in Sam's. Neither of them were anything like what I'd expected as I drove up to the repair shop. I know, I shouldn't make assumptions. Grammy and Pop taught me better. Still . . .

"I'm really sorry about your grandmother," Sam said. "She was a special woman, took care of people in ways nobody knew, in ways that really mattered. There was a light around her wherever she went. You could feel it."

I wanted to wrap myself in his kind words, to savor a stranger appreciating the utter goodness of my foster mother, if for only a moment, but my eyes moistened, and I looked through a window that didn't exist in Sam's office.

"I really appreciate you coming here, telling me." Now his throat caught, and I lost it. Tears fell freely down my face. Before I knew what had happened, my head was buried in Ty's chest as his arms pulled me close. I didn't see Sam cry, but his eyes were soft when Ty released me and I'd finally gathered myself.

"I'm sorry. I've had this same conversation eleven times before you and each time got easier until I came here and you two were so nice and Grammy likes baseball and Broadway and you knew her and that made me happy but also made me really sad so my brain didn't know whether to laugh or cry or just be content that she was happy. Does that make any sense?"

Sam blinked. Ty's mouth hung open.

"Sorry, I kind of ramble sometimes when I'm excited or sad or confused or . . . Sorry, I'm rambling again."

Sam's shoulders rocked as he tried to speak through a rumbling chuckle. "Yeah, a little, but that's okay. You babble all you like. We'll listen."

And he wasn't just being nice. I could tell. People who say things without really meaning it give away their insincerity in little ways, like a twitch of their eye or quirk of their mouth or the next thing they say contradicts the nice thing they just said. I saw all that on an FBI show, oh, and a YouTube video.

"Thanks, Sam, I really appreciate it. You guys . . . You're great."

Ty crossed his arms and resumed his holding-up-the-door lean. "I'm great. That's true. Sam, he's just alright."

Sam rolled his eyes. "Ignore Ty. He was dropped on his head as a baby. There was nothing they could do."

Before I knew it, I was laughing, and the two ridiculously sexy men were chuckling right along.

"I needed that, thanks," I said. "So, there was another reason I needed to come see you."

"Alright." Sam leaned forward, his elbows planted on his metal school-teacher's desk. "Shoot."

"You're in Grammy's will." Sam and Ty exchanged a look; I flipped a few pages. "She left you Pop's Bel Air."

Four

COOPER

Sam's eyes widened. His mouth opened, but nothing came out. I glanced up in time to see Tyler uncross his arms, run a hand through his perfectly silky hair, and meet Sam's dumbfounded gaze.

Something mechanical whirred inside the shop.

A horn sounded on the nearby road.

Still, Sam didn't speak. He clamped his mouth shut and leaned back, eliciting another death cry from his chair.

I lifted the page detailing the car. "Um, the Bel Air is a 1955 convertible. Mr. Whisker and I ran a few searches and estimate its Blue Book value around sixty-seven thousand dollars. If you had it graded and certified, which we believe you could do, it could attract over one hundred thousand dollars at auction. For insurance purposes, Mr. Whisker recommends a policy of one hundred twenty-five thousand dollars."

Tyler whistled. "Fuck me."

My eyes darted to Ty.

"Sorry." He held up both palms and flashed me the most brilliant smile.

Damn, it had been an exclamation rather than a request.

"Who is Mr. Whisker, and why does he sound like a cat wearing a tie on TikTok?" Ty asked.

"He's Grammy's attorney."

"Oh." Ty made a very round letter with his poochy, bitable, likely cherry-flavored lips.

"Why?" Sam's voice pulled my attention back to him. He sounded as if he'd shrunk into a vulnerable little boy version of the rugged man sitting before me. "Marjorie was a sweet lady, and we enjoyed our time together, but . . . to include me in her will? And . . . her husband's Bel Air? She loved that car, said it felt like the only thing she had left of him; at least, the only thing still alive. It's why she said she wanted me to fix it, no matter what it cost."

I didn't know how to answer that. I knew she was amazing and sweet and the kindest person to ever live. I saw that every day growing up. But Grammy had never said a word about Sam or his shop, or going to baseball games with him and his partner, or a Broadway star who'd sing to her. She liked baseball.

Seriously?

Grammy?

She'd never talked about helping a family while the mother of young children served time in prison, or how she'd planned to cover their higher education and ensure the woman who raised them was also cared for. She also never mentioned a half-dozen of the other stories I'd heard while performing my executorial duties.

I was starting to wonder how many secrets she'd kept locked away in her overstuffed handbag of a heart.

The pleading scrutiny in Sam's eyes made all the heartache of the past weeks bubble up in my own chest. I rifled through the papers in my lap, unsure I could even read the now-blurry words, but desperate for something, anything, to save me from—

"I'm sorry, Sam," I choked out. "I was supposed to . . . This is a note Grammy left for you."

I couldn't look up. I couldn't meet his watery gaze.

I couldn't . . . Dammit, I did, and he was close to shaking.

Tyler was now squatted by his side, one arm wrapped around his shoulder. Sam wiped his face and nodded. "It's okay. I'm okay. Go on and read it."

A sealed envelope had been clipped to my list. I unhooked it and reached it across the desk, pausing briefly as I noticed Grammy's flowing script in golden ink that read, *For Sam Prescott.*

"It's sealed. I think you should . . ." I tossed the envelope toward Sam as if it had grown fangs and tried to bite me. He stared for a long moment, then slowly picked it up with the reverence of a priest at mass and pried the flap open. His brows knitted as he read aloud.

My dear Sam,

I could never express how much joy you and Miguel have given me over these last few years. Seeing your love so freely expressed reminds me of the days when my Herbert and I were young. You should've seen us. We teased and laughed, just like you two. He was the light in my world, as I know Miguel is in yours.

It's time I went home to Herbert, but there are a few things I would like to leave you before I go. First, a few words of advice. I know you didn't ask for them, but I'm old, and you'll listen politely, because that's the man you are.

Treasure your time together. Hold him like tomorrow may never come, because it might not. Treasure him, because a day comes to each of us when those we hold dearest fade into the recesses of memory and dreams.

Cherish him, Sam. Tell him how much you love him. Every day. Every hour. Every moment.

Enough of that. Now, to the fun part.

If you're reading this, someone has likely told you about the Bel Air. Don't argue or fuss. Accept it in the spirit of love and admiration with which it is intended. My Herbert loved that car, almost as much as he loved me. I will rest easier knowing it's in the hands of one who will also enjoy and care for it. For that, there is no one better than Sam the Mechanic.

I hope you don't mind; I took the liberty of purchasing something for you and Miguel, a suite at Sounds Stadium. Upon my passing, the Liberty Tire Suite will be renamed "The Marjorie and Herbert Polk Suite." I want you to have it, for you and Miguel—and whomever you choose—to enjoy going to games for as long as you like. The suite will bear our name, but it will belong to you. Think of me when you hear that seventh-inning song. I'll be singing along with Annie.

Oh, I almost forgot. I paid your shop's mortgage, and purchased all of your leased equipment. Everything is in your name, free and clear.

I hope you don't mind.

I do have one favor to ask, because I know I can count on you. My grandson, Cooper, is the son I never had. I love him with every fiber of my being. As any mother would, I worry for him. Would you take Cooper to a game sometime, you and Miguel? I don't think he's ever been to one, and I blame myself for that. I know he would enjoy it, and love both of you. I think meeting you boys would be good for him too.

Thank you, Sam. You have brought joy to an old woman in ways you will never understand. You are a good man, and an even better friend.

I'll watch over you, always.

All my love,

Marjorie

By the time he read the last few words, Sam and I were nearly drowning in tears, and even Ty's head was pressed into Sam's shoulder as his chest heaved.

Five

COOPER

I t was almost time for kickoff, or whatever the baseball equivalent was. Moms and dads herded excited munchkins decked in the red, white, and blue of the Sounds. I felt like Simba in *The Lion King* when he'd escaped from Scar only to get caught clinging to a limb above a stampede of raging wildebeests. Some of those kids definitely qualified as wildebeests.

"Cooper, hey! We're over here."

I followed the voice that somehow carried over the cacophony of eager fans to find Sam standing near the ticket counter, waving a hand high above his head. He wore a Sounds jersey and baseball cap, fully transformed from brawny mechanic to a six-foot-one twelve-year-old who couldn't wait to enter the park.

As I headed his way, Sam turned and said something to a guy standing behind him. Both men turned toward me, and the new guy gave a *sup* head bob, complete with an infectious smile that shone brighter than the neon above his head.

I navigated the current of incoming fans toward the ticket booth. When I got within a couple strides, Sam stepped forward and grabbed my shoulder, pulling me toward them.

"Hey, Coop. Good to see you again. This is my better half, Miguel. He's an asshole cop, so don't take him too seriously."

I could see Miguel's eyes just above and to the right of Sam's head. They rolled faster than a ground ball through the short stop's legs.

"You'll have to excuse Sam. He still doesn't know how to behave at a baseball game, or in public. Come to think of it, I'm not sure there's a place where he does behave."

"Last time I checked, you like it when I misbehave." Sam elbowed Miguel in the gut, earning a grunt, then he noticed the Sounds crimson painted across my cheeks, and his chuckle added to Miguel's amusement.

"Coop, you're going to have to thicken that skin if you're going to survive around us. We're a tough crowd," Miguel said with a glimmer in his eyes.

Sam was hot in a do-you-underneath-the-bleachers sort of way, but Miguel . . . he was *compelling*. That wasn't a word I'd ever used to describe a person, and it probably made more sense about an article or book or something, but that's what he was. There was a no-bullshit set to his jaw, but compassion in his gaze, and his presence drew my eyes into him. His eyes and smile were . . . I don't know, like the last drops of water to a man lost in a desert.

He stepped out from behind Sam and I saw, for the first time, he wore an identical jersey, but in reversed coloring, a team cap, also reversed, and a tatty leather glove that looked like he'd dragged it behind his car down a gravel road.

"Um, I see that." I barely knew Sam and had just met Miguel, yet they acted like we were old chums from the club or school or wherever boys became chummy then drank and hung out and teased each other for a lifetime. Were we chums? I'd never had chums. Wait, isn't chum what you throw in the water—

"You ready?" Sam's grumble washed away the murky water.

"Oh, yeah, sure. Play ball."

Sam glanced at Miguel, and they shared a grin.

Was that the right phrase? Had I just used a tennis thing; maybe soccer? I wasn't a huge sports fan, but I was really smart, most of the time—when calculations were involved, at least. There were stats in baseball, right? I could get good at this.

"Are you a baseball fan, Cooper?" Miguel asked as we turned toward the entry gates.

"I don't know that I'd call myself a fan. The game is interesting. Nashville played one hundred forty-nine games last season and finished second in their league. Five thousand twenty-nine batters stepped up to the plate during that time, scoring over eight hundred nine runs, with a slugging percentage of zero-point-four-three-three. That's interesting because, while they finished second in the league, their slugging percentage was only fifth. When you add the on-base percentage, they rise to second behind Durham, with zero-point-seven-eight-eight."

Miguel and Sam had stopped walking, turned, and were staring at me. Both of their mouths hung open.

"What?" I shrugged. "I like being prepared . . . and spreadsheets. I really like spreadsheets. Stats are fun too. Baseball loves stats, right?"

The guys looked at each other, then back to me.

"Well, okay then." Miguel sounded like a parent whose child had just tried to explain the construction of a cosmic laser using Lego. "Let's go. I'm pretty sure there's beer upstairs. If not, we can come back down and stock up for the game."

Miguel waved tickets and began weaving through the crowd. Sam patted my shoulder, urging me forward, then followed.

Sam handed our tickets to a bored-looking, jersey-clad usher standing beside an unmarked elevator, then nodded back at Miguel. "He's had season tickets for years, but we've never been up top. Mind giving us directions?"

The usher glanced down, then back up at Miguel. "Mr. Nuñez, welcome. I'll show you to your suite."

As the man reached to press the button, Sam asked, "Before we go up, can you tell us if there's beer available upstairs?"

The usher cocked his head, then grinned broadly. "Yes, sir. You'll be just fine up there."

A moment later, we rounded a corner—well, not exactly a corner, as the whole place was round, but a rounded section of wall that would've been a corner had there been any in a round building or stadium or structure. Mr. Usher stopped at a recessed door crowned with golden letters, the fancy metal kind I'd seen in the lobby of Mr. Whisker's office. It read, *The Marjorie & Herbert Polk Suite.*

The usher opened the door and strode in. We froze, like some ancient cavemen gaping up at a spaceship hovering in the sky. I was swallowing down the lump clawing its way up my throat when the usher's voice called from within: "Gentlemen, come on in. I'll give you a quick tour."

The warmth of Sam's palm pressed into my shoulder again, this time accompanied by a gentle squeeze. I glanced over to find understanding eyes and a gentle smile.

"Feels almost like she's here with us, doesn't it? She'd be proud."

I swallowed hard, then nodded as my eyes clouded. Sam pretended not to notice and turned to follow Miguel into the suite.

There was, indeed, beer in the suite—*seven* different brands, in fact—in both fully loaded and lite versions, all blissfully chilled and waiting for us on a bed of ice. In addition, there were three white wines, two reds, and an assortment of hard liquors and mixers. I hadn't eaten since a meager PB&J at lunch, and the spread before us was a welcome sight. Sam hovered, rarely straying more than a few steps away from the food. He razzed Miguel for eating mini quiches at a baseball game, then snuck cranberry and brie puffs onto his plate when he thought we weren't watching. I nearly had a foodgasm when I tasted the Asian sliders for the first time.

"Sure beats bleacher food," Sam said as his eyes rolled back over yet another puff.

I grunted through a mouthful of french fries.

Possibly as important as the food and drinks, the vents in the ceiling blasted arctic air throughout the suite, ensuring we didn't turn into sweaty puddles like the poor folk down below. As strange as it felt to be attending a ballgame in a room named after my grandparents with guys I barely knew, it was an incredibly comfortable, if awkward, experience.

Miguel turned from watching the players warming up. "It's nice, but there's nothing like a hot dog and beer at a game. Or popcorn. You love popcorn, don't you, Sam?"

Sam, with cheeks pooching out like the guiltiest thieving chipmunk, tried to glare menacingly at his partner, only to whirl around when popcorn flew from the doorway and stuck in his tightly cropped hair.

A gray-topped woman wearing a pink Sounds jersey featuring a bedazzled treble clef bowed like she'd just been handed a Tony Award. Sam's face went from angry rodent to brilliant sun in a heartbeat.

"Annie!" Bits of pastry flew out as he greeted the latest arrival.

She giggled and patted her fingertips to her lips. I couldn't remember the last time I'd seen such mischief and mirth in one glance.

"So, this is how the fancy people watch a game?" Her eyes scanned the room appreciatively, then landed on Miguel. "And there's my favorite slab of man meat. Get over here and give mama a kiss."

Sam spit the last of his puff all over the carpet as Miguel lumbered his way past us to scoop up the old woman. Her legs dangled and she wiggled her feet like a small girl being twirled in her father's arms—which Miguel did next. Annie squealed and laughed, then slapped his shoulder.

"Let me down, you brute. I'm a lady, after all."

Miguel didn't need any more encouragement. He buried his mouth into her neck and made farting noises, eliciting another squeal that I thought might shatter the mirror hanging over the buffet. By the time Annie pulled away, tears streamed down her cheeks and she had to brace herself against the wall through bouts of laughter.

"Annie." Miguel gripped her hand and turned toward me. "This is Cooper. Cooper, this is Annie, a dear friend and one of the best Broadway babes you'll ever meet."

My mouth opened, but I couldn't think of anything to say to being introduced to a seventy-something-year-old *babe*, Broadway or otherwise.

Annie cackled and waved a hand. "Oh, Cooper, don't let these boys get to you. Just laugh and roll with it. They might look big and mean, but they're harmless enough."

I started to thank her, to say how nice it was to meet her, that I was honored . . . all that . . . but the door flew open and two more guests joined the pregame party.

"Ty!" Miguel belted, then moved past Annie to wrap the ridiculously beautiful man in a tight embrace. He didn't squeal like Annie had, but he did begin slapping Miguel's meaty shoulders when the giant lifted him off his feet and swung him back and forth.

The guy beside Ty stared intently through eyes obscured by wavy brown hair that flopped across his forehead. Miguel set Ty down and reached behind him to pull Floppy into their hug.

He *did* squeal.

Once everyone's feet were firmly returned to the floor, Ty stepped forward and shook my hand politely. "Cooper, good to see you again. This is my husband, Gabe. He's deaf, but he lipreads, so just face him and talk normally."

For the second time since my last slider, my mouth opened but no sound came out. I nodded like I understood but couldn't stop my brain from stewing on the million or so questions and random thoughts that suddenly screamed for attention. Before I could give voice to any of them, a hand gripped my forearm. Gabe had stepped forward and was gazing into my eyes.

"Hi, Cooper. It's good to meet you." His voice was like marbles in a velvet pouch.

"Uh, hi. You too."

"Alright, everybody, grab some food and a drink. Warm-ups are almost done," Miguel called above the clamor of the joyful reunion.

Sam and I made one last trip to the buffet, then joined Miguel in seats that overlooked the field along the first base line, just beyond the netting that backstopped home plate. I leaned over the railing and squinted, trying to make out the players' faces.

"Great seats, aren't they?"

I turned. Miguel flipped a bottle to his lips and turned it up to drink.

"Yeah, this is great."

"You like baseball?" he asked.

I shrugged. "I guess. Maybe. Honestly, I don't know. I've never been to a game, and I didn't play as a kid. I was more, um, a reader than an athlete."

To his credit, he didn't make fun of that.

"Well, looks like you found your way into a gym at some point." He reached over and gripped my bicep. It was hidden beneath the long-sleeve shirt I was wearing despite summer's heat. Fingers of a totally different fire crept up my arm at his not-so-gentle squeeze and appreciative grunt.

"Yeah, guess I started in college. I was tired of being the beanpole."

He grunted what I think was a laugh. It felt weird talking about working out with a man who looked like he could bench-press a car. I wasn't the toothpick I'd always been, but nobody would call me muscular. I think the online term was *swimmer's build*—and not the hot, beefy swimmers you see on the Olympics, more the lean, toned guys who swam for fun. Yeah, that was me. A fun swim. Fun swimmer. Slim swimmer.

"You know," Miguel's voice stopped my descent down the rabbit hole. "This suite comes with more than just food. We have seats directly behind home plate." He pointed all the way down to a row of puffy blue leather chairs. "We can go down and get a closer look, anytime you like."

"That would be really cool," I said, suddenly eight years old again.

"Finish your food. I'll grab Sam in a few innings, and we'll go take a look. He doesn't even know about those seats yet."

Music blared throughout the stadium and the guitar-shaped scoreboard flashed as one of the Sounds struck out and the third inning came to a close. Sam and I were both moaning over our tightening belts, while the others continued nibbling, drinking, and chatting, completely ignoring how our fully stuffed asses were suffering.

"Alright, you two, time to walk it off." Miguel's head appeared over Sam's shoulder, all teeth and gums. Sam tried to pull away, but Miguel's fingers clamped down on his shoulders as his teeth sank into one of my mechanic friend's earlobes.

"Ow!"

"You love it when we're at home."

"Miguel!" Sam's face now matched the red of his jersey.

Miguel met my eyes, and we both burst out laughing.

"Traitor. I'll remember this," Sam lobbed in my direction.

"Don't blame me if you have marital problems that involve teeth marks." I stood, held up both palms, and scooted my way over to Ty and Gabe toward the exit row. Ty slapped my ass as I passed.

"Hey!"

He shrugged. "Gotta pay the toll. It's the law."

I glanced to Gabe for support, but the deaf guy had gone silent. Imagine that.

Sam finally freed his lobe and ran the same gauntlet, receiving the same slap, followed by the same silent scrutiny from a smirking Gabe.

Miguel, the perpetual sun that shone over this band of misfits, beamed as he skipped the slapping line by climbing over the seats with his long, tarantula-like legs.

He'd nearly made it clear of danger when a loud *whack* sounded, and he stumbled forward. Everyone, including Gabe, doubled over as Annie shook her hand out dramatically and feigned injury from her palm's run-in with Miguel's posterior.

"*Et tu*, Brutus?" Miguel scowled over his shoulder at the aged singer.

She batted her lashes, and waved her fingers. "Call me Cleopatra or nothing, darling."

We could still hear everyone's laughter as we shut the door behind us.

Another usher lurking in the hallway darted over as soon as the door clicked.

"Can I help you with anything, Mr. Nuñez?"

Sam's eyes did that somersault thing again. Miguel simply grinned.

"We were just headed down to our seats behind the plate."

"Seats directly behind home are normally reserved for those with Field Suites, but I believe a row of four seats were purchased as a condition of the Polks' generous contribution to our foundation. This note on your tickets"—he pointed to a series of golden musical notes on the corner of Miguel's ticket—"will get you onto the deck and seating area. I'll take you down our private elevator. This way." He motioned with an open palm, as if we were standing in a five-star hotel with a gilded ceiling rather than a Triple A baseball stadium.

One elevator ride, two glass doors, a seven-stair ascent, then another seven-stair descent, and we arrived at the luxuriest of luxury seats in the front row of the whole stadium. Navy cloth draped over the chair backs was embroidered in gold with *Reserved for Mr. Nuñez & Friends*.

"I could really get used to this," Miguel muttered to Sam as he settled in.

"I was wondering if they'd let us back in after everybody leaves. We could do it in these seats." Sam made a quick show of testing the firmness of the cushions.

I coughed a laugh and leaned forward to scan the field, determined to not meet either of their gazes lest I become caught in their crossfire.

The seats were ridiculous. If I stood and took one step forward, I could touch the netting that protected us from foul balls. The on-deck circle, which was more of a suggestion in the dirt than an actual marked sphere, was close enough for me to hear the player's heavy breaths as he swung the bat. I estimated home plate to be twenty yards away.

It had been one thing to watch the game from the comfort of our suite. From up there, we could see everything and could even hear the *crack* of the bat and *pop* as the ball hit the catcher's mitt, but none of that compared to sitting within arm's reach of the field. I could hear the coach talking to a player, the ump chatting with the catcher and batter, and even the silly banter of the teams in their dugouts. It was like we were part of the game, and I loved it. I wasn't sure I loved baseball as a sport. Other than the stats I'd studied to prepare for this night, I didn't know anything about it, but being this close, sandwiched between the energy of the crowd behind and the intensity of the players only strides in front, gave me an appreciation for the game I hadn't known possible.

My heart beat a little faster as I watched the batter adjust his grip, then dig his toe into the dirt. I could calculate the angle formed by his bat and wrists and knew the power he'd soon unleash on the poor, unsuspecting ball.

Sure enough, number ninety-six blasted a shot over the left field wall, and the crowd erupted as the Sounds took a one-run lead.

I don't remember when I stood, but Sam spun me around for a high-five, then leaned back so Miguel could get his palm slapped. I missed his hand and had to do it again. A woman in the row behind us leaned forward with her palm raised, so I gave her a good *whack* too. My palm stung, but she seemed pleased.

"Next up, from Broomfield, Colorado, number five, Naaaaaaate Stringerrrrrrr," the announcer's voice boomed over the cheers of thousands.

The batter's back was facing me, so I peered across the field at the giant guitar. Nate Stringer's name and stats appeared where strings normally stretched, while a massive image of the player himself appeared in the body of the guitar. He looked cute, with deeply tanned skin, polar white teeth, and several days of black stubble clinging to his chiseled jaw.

Then Miguel yelled, "Give 'em hell, Nate!"

The batter stopped before entering the box, said something to the ump, then kneeled to fiddle with his shoelace. While bent, he glanced back toward where we sat and winked.

"Quit screwin' around and bat, will ya?" Miguel yelled through cupped hands.

The catcher turned and craned his neck around the ump. I could see his grin through his mask.

The batter, Nate, actually laughed, then rose and saluted in our direction with two fingers to the brim of his helmet.

Then, for the briefest moment, his eyes found me. I wanted to look away or down or anywhere else, but he'd frozen me in place with that gaze, and I couldn't move.

He flashed a brilliant smile, then turned and stepped into the box.

Six

COOPER

"**W**ho is that?" I asked no one in particular.

Miguel was focused on his heckling and hadn't noticed my stare-down with the batter.

"That's Nate Stringer. He's their second baseman and a good friend. He played college ball at Vandy. When I didn't go pro, the best way I could stay close to the game was to help with my old program. I'm an unofficial mentor to some of the guys. Nate's only a few years younger than me, but they stuck us together. He's a good kid."

I snorted. "Some kid."

"It's hard for me to think of him any other way. When they put us together, he was a solid player, but really awkward around the team, unsure of himself. He's still pretty reserved, but is more outgoing than he used to be."

"Strike one!" the ump barked as Nate whiffed on a sinker in the dirt.

"Come on, Nate. Don't swing at that crap," Miguel grumbled.

"Wait. You were going pro? As in, professional baseball?"

Miguel nodded as the pitcher threw a fastball wide.

"Was gonna get drafted. Everybody knew it. I had one of the best batting averages in the NCAA."

"Ball," the ump called after another fastball wide.

"Good eye, Nate. Hang in there," the palm-slapper behind us yelled.

"So what happened?"

Miguel's head turned toward me. "What do you mean?"

"Why didn't you go pro?"

His brows furrowed and something—maybe sadness, I wasn't sure—crossed his face, then vanished as he shrugged. "I became a cop."

I was pretty sure that wasn't an explanation. It was barely an answer, but he'd said it with such finality, even turning back toward the field, that I knew it was all I'd get.

"Stiarghhhh!" the ump yelled following a ball down the middle using some ancient dialect of garble I interpreted as "strike."

"That's your pitch, Nate. Stop thinking and swing at the ball!" Miguel's voice was so commanding I noticed a few players in the dugout crane to see who it was coming from.

Nate had to dance back as the next pitch nearly clipped his shoulder.

"He's scared of you, Nate. Use it," Miguel shouted.

I looked past Miguel to find Sam sitting back, snug in his chair, swigging beer and grinning at his husband. The look in his eyes . . . There was an intensity, but it wasn't sexual, though I was sure, by the looks of the two of them, that was a healthy part of their relationship—one I'd love to see on video. No, it was more than that. It was amused and admiring and enthralled. There was hunger and desire mixed with respect and love so deep it hurt. How he put all those things into a single glance . . .

Crack!

Miguel leapt from his seat as I turned and watched Nate's well-struck ball sail over the center fielder's outstretched glove and rebound off the yellow paint of the wall, then careen back toward the first base side. The crowd roared as Nate's foot touched second, and he raised both fists above his head and flashed his pearly whites at the dugout. I found myself standing and high-fiving Miguel, then the woman behind us again.

The other Sounds were bent over the dugout railing, clapping and cheering.

"Nice one, Bean!" one player yelled.

"Bean?" I asked Miguel as we settled back into our seats.

"String Bean. For Stringer, his last name, and because he's a tall, skinny fucker."

I squinted toward second. He was definitely tall, but I couldn't see how skinny he was. Baseball uniforms clung to some places, but fell off others. The only thing I knew for certain was that he had a great ass, and I really wanted to see that again.

The next batter popped out to second, stranding Nate and leaving the Sounds with a one-run lead going into the seventh.

"Everybody up," Miguel said to Sam and me.

I shot Sam a look, but he was already standing without protest.

When I got to my feet, Miguel leaned over. "Time for the baseball national anthem."

'Take Me Out to the Ballgame' blared over the speakers as more than six thousand fans sang along. The Nashville Sound, or whatever the weird mascot thing was called, waved his arms like he was directing a cartoon orchestra. Miguel, as tone-deaf as he was hot, could be heard destroying harmonies over the din of everyone about us. Sam grinned up at him like a puppy gaping at its human.

"We should probably head back up to the suite. Annie and the boys are probably wondering where we are," Sam said, leaning across Miguel. "Besides, I'm hungry again."

My eyes shot across Miguel toward Sam. How could he be hungry after all those puffs?

He caught my glare and winked.

Miguel reached down to grab his empty bottle. "Knowing Ty, Annie hasn't stopped laughing, and poor Gabe might need rescuing."

Sam chuckled. "I'm pretty sure Gabe can handle himself, especially where Ty's concerned. He knows how to tame a lot more than just dogs."

I wasn't sure what that meant, but decided I might need to get to know this Gabe guy.

The stands were jubilant as the last two innings zipped by, with the Sounds holding their opponents to just one more hit. The win put the team atop their league a quarter of the way through the season. Miguel said there were a lot more games to play, but it was great to be ahead of their arch-rival, Durham, this early in the season.

Annie serenaded us with a round of 'We Are the Champions' in a mashup of operatic and Broadway styles. It might've been the strangest rendition I'd ever heard, but the guys laughed and applauded, and Annie blushed and bowed.

As we headed toward the door, Annie wrapped her weathered arms around me. "Cooper, it was nice to meet you. Don't be a stranger, okay? These are good boys."

"We're the best," Ty chirped from behind, earning a terrible chorus of 'Champions' from Miguel, which earned a hearty groan from everyone, including the usher entering as we exited.

Annie's arms fell away and were replaced by Ty's meaty palms on my shoulders. Hot breath laced with Jack Daniels and Asian slider sauce blew past my ear. "She's right. You should hang out with us more often. We're full of shit, but we're good guys. Sam and Miguel are the best."

There was something in the way he said that last bit about Sam and Miguel, something decidedly *not* full of shit. It wasn't the usual Ty bluster I'd already come to recognize. He loved Sam, and I suspected Miguel too, and he meant every word.

I glanced over my shoulder and nodded in Ty's direction, catching a knowing smile on Gabe's face. I'd wanted to spend more time with him, but we'd sat across the suite—or across the stadium—most of the night. Maybe Ty and Annie were right. Maybe I should get to know these guys. It wasn't like I had a line of friends demanding my time.

"Come on, Coop, one last stop before we head to the car." Miguel waved over Annie's head for me to follow him and Sam.

The elevator doors swallowed Ty, Gabe, and Annie as we waved a goofy, unchoreographed goodbye, then Miguel turned to the ever-present usher and said, "We're going all the way down now, to the tunnel."

The man paused a heartbeat, then nodded and pressed a button. When we boarded the lift, he produced a key from his pocket, inserted it beside an unmarked button, and twisted. The button flared to life and down we went.

Seven

COOPER

"Welcome to the tunnel," the usher said as the doors slid open.

Team spirit slammed into our faces from every direction. The mascot grinned down at us, swinging a guitar like it was a bat at a ball adorned with frightened eyes and fearful teeth. Further down the eternal hall, images of current and past players swinging, throwing, pitching, fielding, and standing in every other imaginable pose ushered us toward a destination. The whole thing felt like one of those murder mysteries where I could feel a twist coming, but hadn't quite figured out the wife was really an evil demon-spawn killer—not that I expected one of the players or staff to have horns, spit fire, or spank me with their tail. Though if the batter I'd seen wanted to spank me . . .

"Miguel!" A voice echoed from down the hall where a cluster of two players and three civilian-looking guys stood chatting.

One of the players waved for us to join them. Miguel barreled into the guy's arms, lifting him off the ground as he'd done to, well, pretty much everyone I'd seen him greet lately. I guess it was his thing.

This time, though, it was impressive. Nate, the player getting air-lifted, had to be six one or six two. For Miguel to heft him so *his* feet dangled was, well, nuts. The other player laughed and patted Miguel on the back, but the civilians stepped back to avoid getting kicked.

Nate had changed into a team tee, but he still wore his uniform pants and cleats. Both bled rusty streaks from the infield's red clay.

"It's good to see you again, Smiley. Damn, it's been, what, three years? Maybe four?"

Miguel stepped back and slapped Nate on the shoulder. "I've seen you pretty much every week from the stands, but yeah, it's been that long since we hung out. Guess making a run and having friends was just too much for ya. Eh, Big Time?"

Nate blanched, and his eyes fell.

"Dumbass. I'm giving you shit," Miguel said, wrapping his arm around Nate's neck and pulling his head into him. "Come here. I've got some people I want you to meet."

Nate shot a glance over his shoulder at the others he'd been standing with. "Sorry guys, he's bigger than me. Interviews will have to wait."

"Shit, I'm sorry—"

"Don't be," Nate whispered up at Miguel. "I was trying to escape anyway."

Sam and I were now only a pace or two away, so Miguel did his best Vanna White wave and said, "This is Sam, my far-better-looking other half."

"You got that right." Sam grinned and took Nate's outstretched hand. "Good to meet you, Nate. Nice game."

"Thanks."

"And this," Miguel said, shifting toward me, "is Cooper, a new friend of ours."

Nate turned, and I . . . I . . . I didn't know what to do.

For a split second, I swear something caught or froze or paused. I don't know. It was weird and amazing and crazy all at the same time. My pulse went from resting boredom to canter to gallop in the space of one or two eye blinks.

And he didn't even blink.

His steel gray eyes, with their veil of the faintest blue around the edges, were all I could see. He took a step toward me, and, in my mind, I saw him lean down, wrap me in his arms, and kiss me right there in the tunnel while romantic, baseball-themed music echoed from hidden speakers and someone in the locker room released doves or pigeons or whatever a baseball bird should be.

"Nice to meet you, Cooper," was all I got as Nate extended his hand for me to shake. "Be careful of these two calling you a friend. You wouldn't want to damage your reputation."

Sam and Miguel laughed.

I stood there mute, clutching his hand.

"Hey, Coop," Sam whispered loud enough for everyone to hear. "He's gonna need his glove hand back before the next game."

How long had I stood there gripping his palm?

I yanked my hand back and held it to my chest like Nate had burned it with a lighter or cigarette or match or some other burning device he carried in his pocketless player pants.

"Sorry. I didn't mean to . . . It's just that . . . I mean—"

"He's never met a pro player," Sam offered.

Nate grinned, like he probably did a hundred times a day as fans dogged him for autographs or selfies or the simple pleasure of shaking a player's hand.

"Baseball fan, then?" Nate asked. I hadn't expected a conversation. He was just shaking my hand to be nice. A whole sheep's worth of wool wriggled into my throat, and my brain decided to take its seventh-inning stretch.

"No, not really. I mean, I like the stats. Baseball has some really cool stats. They're all online. I did research before meeting Sam and Miguel tonight, and it's amazing how much data they keep on everything. It's not just team stats. They track every time a player does anything—or doesn't do anything. There's been 22,854 players in the major leagues so far. That's incredible. Oh, you're in the minors. I don't know if they count you guys—not that they shouldn't. You're great, and you're pros and all, but you're not, you know, in the big leagues or majors or whatever you want to call them."

Nate finally blinked.

A faint curl formed at the corner of his mouth where his lips kissed stubble. I couldn't tell if he was amused, irritated, or some combination of the two. The color and heat that had battled on my face earlier shifted to all-out war.

"Sorry, I got a little excited—"

Nate's mouth spread wide in a warm, toothy grin, then he stepped forward, placed a hand on my shoulder, and said, "It's alright. Stats *are* cool."

Eight

Nate

I t was late when Cal and I finally walked into our apartment. We only lived a few blocks from the stadium, but that walk, especially after a game, always felt like an uphill marathon.

"I'm wasted, and we have to be on the bus at six," he said, tossing his backpack against the side of the couch. "I'm gonna pass out. See you way too early, Bean."

Cal was our first baseman and had been my roommate since he'd moved from LA to join the team a couple years ago. He might have his image on baseball cards one day, but it belonged in the dictionary beside the listing for "surfer dude." Everything about him, from his rebellious blond hair to his half-stoned cadence, screamed "beach bum." The guys called him Tutu on account of his overly dramatic ballerina splits he did when fielding a throw from third. I reserved use of that particular nickname for times I really wanted to get under his skin. He hated it.

I'd made the mistake, like a lot of the guys, of assuming he'd be half-assed or whatever, on account of him being a wave-riding, happy-go-lucky Cali guy, but he turned out to be the hardest-working player on the team. He was usually the first to step onto the practice field and the last to leave it. Most days, he ended up in the batting cage after the players had left and only the staff remained to ready the stadium for our next game. In light speed, he'd gone from questionable newbie to an unofficial leader of our motley crew.

He'd also become my best friend.

"Night." I flopped onto the couch and turned on the TV. As tired as I was, my brain wouldn't shut off until it had a good numbing by the boob tube. I flipped past *The Tonight Show* and then three news stations, landing on *Antiques Roadshow*. It caught my eye because Rick was gently turning a guitar over on the display counter, scrutinizing its wood for imprints or imperfections, I couldn't tell which. The patina on the instrument's wood was rich and lustrous, with just the right amount of cherry peeking through its brown tones. A quick glance at my old strings in the corner made me wish I could reach through the television and swap pieces with the seller.

I kicked off my shoes, then padded into the kitchen to grab a drink, half-listening as Rick asked the seller questions about where he acquired the guitar, whether anyone famous had played it, and a dozen other queries aimed at determining its value. By the time I flopped back onto the cushions, a lowball offer was made, rejected, reiterated, then accepted. Rick rarely lost a negotiation.

My phone buzzed as I lifted a glass of iced tea to my lips.

Miguel Nuñez: Hey, bud. Thanks for meeting the guys tonight. It was great seeing you again.

Me: You too, old man. You and Sam seem to be doin' great. I figured you'd end up with an asshole.

Miguel Nuñez: Ha ha. I think he lost that one, getting stuck with a cop.

Me: No shit. Who'd want that? All those handcuffs and stuff?

Miguel Nuñez: I'll have you know he loves my handcuffs—and really loves my other stuff.

Me: TMI (putting my hands over my ears)

Miguel Nuñez: Are all you baseball players dumb? We're chatting. There's nothing to hear. Put your hands over your eyes if you don't want to see how amazing I am.

Me: Why did I ever let you mentor me? Please, baseball gods, explain that to me.

Miguel Nuñez: Those gods and I haven't been on speaking terms in years. You're on your own there, bud. Anyway, I won't keep you up. It's late. Just wanted to say thanks. Let's not wait years before we hang out again.

I started to tell him good night, but then a question popped into my head.

ME: HEY, BEFORE YOU GO. WHO WAS THAT GUY WITH YOU? COOPER? HE WAS KIND OF FUNNY.

MIGUEL NUÑEZ: GOOD GUY. MARJORIE POLK'S GRANDKID.

ME: OH SHIT. SORRY. FRONT OFFICE TOLD US ABOUT HER AND HER DONATION TO THE FOUNDATION. THAT WAS A BIG ONE.

MIGUEL NUÑEZ: YOU HAVE NO IDEA. SHE WAS LOADED. SHE AND SAM HAD ALSO BECOME PRETTY CLOSE. SHE ASKED US TO WATCH OUT FOR COOPER, TAKE HIM TO A GAME, STUFF LIKE THAT.

ME: AWW, LOOK AT YOU TAKING IN BABY BIRDS AND SHIT.

MIGUEL NUÑEZ: FUCK OFF AND GOOD NIGHT, STRING BEAN.

ME: GOD, I HATE THAT NAME.

MIGUEL NUÑEZ: YEP, AND THAT'S EXACTLY WHY IT WILL LIVE FOREVER.

ME: I USED TO LIKE YOU. TELL SAM HI FOR ME.

MIGUEL NUÑEZ: WILL DO. CATCH YA LATER.

I smiled at my phone a moment before tossing it onto the couch beside me and grabbing the remote. Rick was now haggling over a pair of earrings I didn't care about, so he had to go. A few Polaroid flashes later, I settled on a nature show about dolphins . . . or whales . . . I wasn't sure. There was a hot guy swimming around in a wetsuit that showed off every piece of fish bait he had, and that was worth getting sleepy with, regardless of what fish or mammal was being filmed.

A massive shark entering the frame made me question my aquatic crush's choice in careers when my phone buzzed again.

"Jesus, Miguel. It's nearly midnight," I grumbled as I dug between the cushions where my phone had slid. I finally freed it from my couch's evil clutches, held it up to my face to unlock the screen, and flipped the notifications down. There weren't any new text messages, but Instagram had sent me a note.

"Hey, fan mail." The only fans who sent me anything regularly were three old ladies who lived together and spent every waking moment thinking about baseball and food, and not necessarily in that order. There was usually at least one photo of a casserole or roasted beast, along with a detailed recipe and a note telling me how I looked thin and needed to eat more. Outside of my gals, the fans generally flocked to Cal or a few of our flashier players who'd probably finish the season in a major league uniform, leaving the rest of us in the dust, eating casserole.

The shark made an ominous sound, or maybe that was Waldo, the baby whale he was chasing. Either way, I ignored all the fish and punched open the app. There were three messages from Helen, one detailing a tuna dish she made for "her chicks" over the weekend, and two follow-ups asking if I'd tried to make it yet. The only other message was from a handle I didn't recognize: HawkEyeBB.

HawkEyeBB: It was really great meeting you today. Sorry I vomited all over your uniform. You hit really well. I mean, nobody scored off your double

OR ANYTHING, BUT IT WAS A PRETTY SHOT, ALMOST WENT OVER BUT THAT YELLOW PART MADE IT BOUNCE BACK AND THEN THEY STOPPED YOU AT SECOND AND STRUCK OUT THE NEXT GUY SENDING YOU BACK TO THE DUGOUT. IT WAS STILL A GOOD HIT AND YOU HAVE A NICE GRIP. YOUR HANDSHAKE, I MEAN. I DON'T KNOW HOW YOU GRIP OTHER THINGS . . . WITH YOUR HANDS . . . NOT OTHER PARTS. I'M DOING IT AGAIN. SORRY. NICE MEETING YOU.

Vomited all over my uniform? What the hell? I'm pretty sure I would've remembered that, and the only people I saw after the game were two reporters, Sam, Miguel, and that guy, the rich lady's grandkid.

NATESTRINGEROFFICIAL: COOPER?

HAWKEYEBB: OH, HEY. I DIDN'T EXPECT YOU TO BE AWAKE AFTER THE GAME AND WITH YOUR EARLY START TOMORROW. YES, IT'S ME. COOPER. GOOGLE SENT ME TO YOUR TEAM WEBSITE, WHICH SENT ME TO YOUR INSTA PAGE WHERE I MESSAGED YOU. SORRY IF THIS SEEMS CREEPY. I'M REALLY NOT CREEPY.

Promise. We met today in the tunnel after Miguel made your feet dangle.

I actually laughed into my phone. Where had Sam and Miguel found this guy? He'd meant word vomit, not puke vomit. And yes, he had word-vomited all over the tunnel, not just my uniform.

Still, he was cute, with that wavy brown hair with just a hint of ginger that curled at the tips, and those dimples. Jesus. When he smiled, his whole face lit up. And he smiled almost as much as Miguel, which was impressive—and slightly frightening.

Then my heart skipped a beat.

What if he'd clocked me? I'd spent the last five years in the minors without anyone knowing I was gay. Hell, Cal didn't even know. I'd worked so hard and was on the cusp of moving up, of finally getting my shot at the majors. The last thing I needed was a media circus over the new gay guy in the minors. I couldn't let anything get in the way of my dream.

I glanced at my phone, still lit up and waiting, and started to shut it down for the night, but decided to ask one last question.

NateStringerOfficial: It was nice meeting you too. How did you know we have an early start tomorrow?

HawkEyeBB: When I was looking at your Insta, there were pics of some of your teammates, so I clicked on them and went to their Insta and they had posts about how much they hated early morning bus trips but how they looked forward to tomorrow because they would be with all their friends and traveling to a great city.

My head hurt a little reading his Charles Dickens sentences—sans punctuation—but I couldn't help myself. The guy cracked me up.

NateStringerOfficial: So, I've got to ask, what's with the name? Isn't it kind of suggestive?

HawkEyeBB: Huh? Really? My last name is Hawk, so I got called Hawkeye as a kid, and I'm a black belt in tae kwon do. What's suggestive about that?

Well, shit. A black belt. That's pretty bad ass. I hadn't seen that one coming. And thanks to the diver on TV and the impressive harpoon protruding from his rubber suit, I'd assumed it referred to a totally different, more intimate sport where the initials BB most clearly did not involve a belt—unless you were into that sort of thing.

NateStringerOfficial: Oh, that makes sense. Sorry, was just confused. Make sure Miguel brings you down to the tunnel next time you go to a game with him, okay? I'll get you a jersey or something.

There was a long pause before his next message popped up.

HawkEyeBB: That would be really cool. I mean nice. You're nice and handsome and I like your eyes and teeth. You have good teeth.

I actually snorted reading that last bit.

Nine

NATE

Cal and I sleepwalked our way up the bus aisle to two empty seats about midway back. The guys were usually quick-witted and sharp-tongued, but it was five forty-five in the morning. We were barely coherent and moving. I tossed my pack underneath the seat in front of me and rested against the window with my cap pulled down over my face.

Sleep had almost wrapped me in her embrace when Coach Sabro's voice boomed from outside the bus door.

"Where the fuck is Santi?"

I grabbed my phone and flicked it to life. It was six o'clock, on the dot.

Precisely two minutes later, Santiago Abalos, our shortstop and resident trickster-in-chief, lumbered up the stairs. Coach trailed a step behind, practically climbing into his back pocket.

"Get the fuck on this bus, Abalos. When we get to Atlanta, you're leading the team in thirty minutes of slingshots, and if I catch you half-assing, it'll turn into an hour. Don't you ever hold up my bus again."

For once, Santi kept his mouth shut. Nothing good ever came of pissing off Coach Sabro, especially when he was already in a not-so-pleasant mood. The class clown did, however, treat us to a series of ridiculous facial expressions that had several of the guys smothering chuckles. I hid my face again, hoping Coach didn't see the smile that had bloomed on my face. Getting caught mocking him was a sure way to end up doing conditioning drills until game time. Coach didn't care about winning a single game in a season of one hundred seventy contests, not nearly as much as he loved making a point stick.

Once Santi settled into the back, Coach Sabro and his assistants filled in the front few rows, and the bus lurched toward our first stop: Atlanta. Technically, we were going to Gwinnett County to play the Stripers, the Triple A affiliate of the Atlanta Braves. The team wore pinstripes like a fairly well-known major league club up north, and were called the Stripers, but Gwinnett was all Atlanta. Their nickname and stripes actually came from a striped bass and linked the team to the popularity of fishing in the area. To further clarify matters, they stitched a bright green, mouth-agape bass on their logo. He was supposed to look angry, but I always thought he looked constipated.

The roadie's schedule called for us to play the Stripers tonight and tomorrow night, then travel to Jacksonville for two nights against the Jumbo Shrimp (yes, the minors love their seafood), then spin the bus around for one more game in Gwinnett, then trek for six hours to Charlotte to play twice before heading home.

Charlotte had the good grace to call themselves the Knights, ending our streak of hostile seafood opponents. Although, *Knights* didn't make much more sense than naming a team after aquatic creatures. My memory of medieval history pinned armor-wearing warriors to somewhere east of Charlotte . . . and across an ocean . . . a really, enormous ocean.

Seven night games in three cities—four if you counted Gwinnett twice—in seven days. And yes, there was a home stand of four consecutive nights immediately upon our return. There were no days off. Ever. Certainly not during the season.

We were perpetually tired, sore, and hungry.

But none of that mattered.

This was minor league baseball, and we did whatever made kids smile and parents buy more tickets. If that meant wearing poop-challenged fish heads on our caps, bring on the brine.

Life in the minors wasn't the glamorous existence every Little Leaguer dreamed of, and the pay was so meager most of the guys had two or three roommates and lived on fast food and junk food. The poor married guys struggled to keep things afloat, and those with kids . . . I didn't know how they even paid the bills. But we got to play a game we loved. More importantly, we were on the path to becoming major leaguers, and that was very much in all of our childhood—and adult—dreams.

We should've pulled into the parking lot of Coolray Field around ten o'clock, but the perimeter around Atlanta was a twelve-lane parking lot. It wasn't even rush hour when we tried to cut across the city's northern arc, but it sure felt like it. The doors finally opened at eleven fifteen, and Coach was still in the same good mood from his earlier encounter with Santiago.

"Alright, listen up," he said into the intercom. He didn't need it to be heard, I think he just liked using the little walkie-talkie-looking thing. "We have the field from twelve to two."

A chorus of groans welcomed that news. He hadn't told us we would practice today.

"Yeah, yeah. Did you see our game last night? We need the work. I'm sorry Atlanta traffic put us behind and you didn't get to lounge before practice, but life's tough. Get suited up and be on the field at eleven forty-five to stretch and warm-up. Santiago, don't be late."

A few guys sitting near Santi punched him playfully. One tossed a glove at him. We never missed a chance to give each other shit.

"Oh, I forgot," Coach's voice cracked over the speakers again. "We have a guest today."

That got everybody's attention. Injured major leaguers were often sent down to the minors for a game or two after the body part they'd injured had recovered. The league called it rehab. What we really cared about was the tradition that came with a rehabbing player, which dictated they bought dinner for the entire minor league team playing host to their injured ass. The best part was how the major guys bragged about how their meal was the best, creating a competition to spoil us more than the last guy unlucky enough to hurt something.

Most of the players took the easy route and paid for a meal at a local restaurant, but a special few got creative. One guy had Outback cater steaks and bloomin' everything at the ballpark. Another hired a professional sushi chef. We didn't care, as long as it didn't come in a paper wrapper with a side of fries. For a group of guys subsisting on greasy burgers and peanut butter crackers out of vending machines, these meals were cause for celebration.

Coach let the excited murmurs die down before breaking the news. "Tofer Grace will practice and play with us while we're here in Gwinnett. Sorry, Perry, he's on third. Enjoy your nights off."

Tofer was one of the rising stars on the Atlanta Braves. He was young, hungry, and immensely popular. All of which bode well for our hopes of a memorable meal.

"What's for dinner?" someone shouted.

"Yeah, and is he buyin' both nights?" another called out.

"I want mine medium rare," Santi barked, earning a round of grunts and claps.

"You don't even know what's on the menu," Luis, our catcher, said from a few rows in front of Santi.

"Doesn't matter. Medium rare. No burning my shit, please."

Another round of chuckles and chatter.

Coach held up a hand and cracked his first smile of the day. "I'll let Tofer tell you what he's got cooked up. It's a good one. And yes, he's feeding your sorry asses both nights."

A hearty cheer drowned out whatever Coach said next. He shook his head, handed the mic to the driver, and stepped off the bus. Three assistant coaches did their best baby-ducks-following-daddy-duck routine while the rest of us placed bets on what we'd be eating after the game.

The Atlanta midday sun hammered us for the full two-hour practice. Coach was on a mission to eliminate the fielding errors that had plagued us over the last few games. He made Tofer bat for a solid thirty minutes, urging the senior league's top hitter to "knock the infielders off their feet." He nearly succeeded a few times, as he rocketed balls at one baseman, then the next. Our best pitcher struggled to beat him with more than a pitch or two. Even the sound as the bat punished the ball was different, somehow louder and more emphatic.

Then he jogged out to third and showed us what infield was supposed to look like. Perry, our regular guy at third, was a solid player, but Tofer made everything look easy and smooth, and he did it all with a smile on his face. He'd earned the painfully obvious nickname "Tofu" in his first year in the majors, and, watching him play, I thought the guys had missed a more obvious play on his last name, Grace, because that's what I saw. On top of his ridiculous skill, he made a point to encourage our players after nearly every play, shouting a "nice one" toward Luis at short, or a "great stretch" to Cal. I wanted to hate the guy for blowing the talent curve for the rest of us, but couldn't get past his niceness to let jealousy take root. Class and grace, that was Tofer.

Although, in a few hours, he'd be *Chef* Tofer to a bunch of starving guys. That thought made my stomach growl so intensely I fumbled an easy popup and earned a "Fuck, Stringer, what the hell?" from Coach.

"Sorry, got distracted." I raised my glove and squatted into the best ready position I could muster. There was nothing he could yell if I looked like my head was back in the game—or so I hoped.

True to form, Coach signaled the end of practice at precisely two o'clock. Trained to avoid the scathing pain of his ever-present eye, we trotted into the dugout like Little Leaguers eager for the post-game McDonald's run.

The bus drove us to our hotel, a ramshackle dive a few blocks away.

"Holy crap. I think they look for the worst places they can find, just to toughen us up," Cal said as he swiped the keycard and stepped into our room. Faded gold-and-brown floral wallpaper matched the faded brown-and-gold drapery, all of which looked like it belonged on a grandmother's lamp rather than a hotel wall. The beds were covered with a similar, but not quite matching, floral pattern whose colors had long since washed out. Fortunately, I only counted two holes on my comforter.

"As long as the bed doesn't droop and the TV works, I'm good," I said, though I wasn't feeling any better about our accommodations than Cal was.

He grunted and tossed his pack on the floor. He waved a hand in front of his face as dust misted up from where his pack now lay.

"They don't feed us or pay us shit. You'd think they'd at least put us up somewhere nicer than this dump." He flopped down onto his bed. "I can feel the coils. There's wire in my back."

There wasn't anything I could say to make the room better, so I pivoted to a topic that always cheered Cal. "I'm starving. Want to walk around, see what's out there?"

"Good call." He popped up like a jack-in-the-box. "We don't have to buy dinner the next two nights, so let's do something better than fast food for lunch."

I grinned. "Mid-tier slightly-slower-than-fast food coming right up."

A thin, lumpy pillow bounced off my shoulder.

"Bean, you're an idiot. You know that?" His smile had returned. "Lemme hit the bathroom, then we can go find food."

As he vanished into the restroom, it was my turn to test out a mattress. I couldn't quite feel wire stabbing my rear, so I took that as a hopeful sign for a couple of restful nights, even if Cal suffered.

I hadn't checked my phone all day, so I thumbed it to life. There were no emails or text messages waiting, but Messenger displayed a tiny number.

HawkEyeBB: How was the bus? You in Atlanta yet?

His message had arrived at nine twenty-seven. I was a little surprised to hear from Cooper so soon—and so early in the morning—but smiled at his face, grinning up at me in its digital sphere.

NateStringerOfficial: We're here. Just wrapped up practice. Bus trip was long.

The media team regularly drilled us in posting etiquette. They told stories of text messages gone bad—and public—when players failed to exercise good judgment or thought their electronic conversations would remain private. They lectured us on our responsibility to the team and league, and to all of baseball, to be good role models and stay out of headlines for off-field activities. Those messages hit home even harder for us minor leaguers trying to make it. The last thing any of us needed was bad press killing our burgeoning careers. It made conversations like this one with Cooper a bit clinical or distant, but that was just part of the territory.

HawkEyeBB: You probably can't text much. I get it. Media relations and all. Such a burden to be famous.

NateStringerOfficial: Wow. You picked that up fast . . . though, I'm not sure how famous I am.

HawkEyeBB: That's true. Triple A might be the big leagues of the minors, but it's still the minors and with your batting average you don't get much time in the spotlight.

HawkEyeBB: Sorry, that sounded really terrible. You're a great player and look really good in your uniform. I mean, you fill out your jersey well. Crap. I mean your arms tug at your sleeves just right. I wasn't talking about your butt. I wouldn't. I mean, I guess I would. It does look amazing in those pants but I wouldn't say that be-

CAUSE WE BARELY KNOW EACH OTHER AND THAT'S AN AWFULLY FORWARD THING TO SAY ABOUT A BUTT . . . OR A GUY.

I couldn't help myself. This was too good.

NateStringerOfficial: OUCH. SO YOU'RE NOT COMPLIMENTING MY BUTT?

HawkEyeBB: SORRY, YES, I AM. BUT I'M NOT. NO, I'M NOT. I CAN'T, I MEAN, IT'S YOUR BUTT AND IT'S A REALLY NICE ONE, I MEAN HOT, A REALLY HOT ONE. YOU HAVE A HOT ASS, ESPECIALLY IN YOUR UNIFORM PANTS. THEY GRIP IT JUST RIGHT, OR HUG, SHOULD THAT BE HUG? I THINK IT SHOULD, BUT HUG SOUNDS LIKE IT'S GOT TINY ARMS AND I DOUBT YOUR BUTT HAS ARMS. THAT WOULD BE WEIRD.

I was laughing so loud Cal shouted from the bathroom. "What's going on out there?"

"Nothing. Just a friend back home making fun of me."

"At least he's got easy material."

I chuckled. "Thanks a lot. Can you shake it so we can go? I'm starving."

"Jesus, can't a guy pee in peace? Be there in two."

HawkEyeBB: Gotta run. My boss is shouting something. He's an ass, and not the sexy, uniform-gripping kind. Good luck tonight. Hit another double.

NateStringerOfficial: Do my best.

Cooper's status light turned red as the bathroom door opened and Cal stepped out.

"Let's go, precious. I've been waiting on you for hours," he said with mock irritation and a shit-eating grin.

Ten

COOPER

I'd always enjoyed wearing a suit. There was something about the formality of donning crisply starched cotton that made me feel special. It was like when Batman slipped on his tights or leggings or whatever he called his bat suit. Tossing my black tie over my shoulder, then taking the rabbit over, under, and through, raised the stakes from preppy to modern professional. Most guys preferred the tight nub of a half-knot, but I still loved the classic look of a well-formed Windsor. If I didn't fear sideways glances, I'd probably sport a full ascot most days.

Alas, merry ole England we are not.

One last check in the mirror, a tweak of my tie, a flick of a stray hair, a quick pick between two stubborn teeth harboring a last crumb from a power bar that somehow evaded my prewash, toothbrush, water floss, *and* mouthwash, and I was off.

This was Grammy's day.

I would love to say I was looking forward to it, celebrating her life and legacy with those who loved and admired her, but the truth was more complicated and far more emotional. The thought of sitting in front of a hoard of people, some of whom would no doubt cry throughout whatever ceremony Grammy had planned, all while trying to hold myself together with duct tape and paperclips, wasn't something I relished.

The truth was, I missed her, and today was going to hurt.

Thankfully, despite my required involvement in notifying beneficiaries named in her will, I was not involved in the planning or execution of the day's events. She had taken care of all that prior to her passing. She'd spelled out everything, down to picking the invitations and table settings. She'd hired a program manager, catering company, even a small string ensemble for accompaniment—and prepaid each. Each day that passed, I learned more about the woman I thought I knew better than any other. She was deeply involved in her community, most people knew that, even if none of us fully appreciated just how prolific she had been. I was also coming to realize she was as brilliant and organized as she was generous.

And all those years, I'd just known her as Grammy.

Grammy, who made the best pound cake ever baked.

Grammy, whose laugh made my insides tickle until I couldn't hold my own joy back.

Grammy, who held me close when the world turned dark and closed in around me.

Before I realized it, I was standing on the stage of the Ryman Auditorium, staring at a life-sized portrait. She wore a powder blue dress with white lace around her neck and a white belt about her waist. Cottony hair swirled and lay, somehow looking both messy and perfectly neat at the same time. And her smile . . . her smile was sunshine breaking through clouds.

My heart lurched, and I had to turn away.

Standing on that stage, the sacred hardwood where the greats of country music had performed for thirty-four years, a simple sign taped to one of the pews caught my eye:

Reserved for Cooper Hawk, Grandson.

It was the only such sign in the front row.

In fact, aside from the reserved spaces for the media on the balcony, it was the only sign in the entire theater.

For some reason, I couldn't stop staring at it, at the word *grandson*, at the length of empty pew that stretched like a rolling field where nothing grew or flowered. I suddenly felt alone, truly alone, for the first time in my life. Even when my mom and dad went through their battles, they were still there. Sure, they'd passed me off to Grammy and Pop, but then I'd had them. It was never just me.

Until that moment, on that stage, staring at that sign, in front of *her* image.

"Cooper, good, you're early. Mind if I run a few things by you before the guests arrive?"

I turned back toward the curtain to find Janice Monroe, the planner Grammy had hired. Janice had worked in the mayor's office, served as chief of staff to a governor, and currently owned and ran an event planning company she'd founded a few years earlier. If Grammy had been brilliant, Janice was superhuman.

"Uh, sure, but I thought Grammy—"

"She detailed everything." She smiled and nodded while pressing a comforting hand onto my arm. "But there are always details to consider at the last moment. For instance, would you prefer the ushers stand at the top of each aisle once the memorial begins, or step back against the walls and doors? One allows them to be visible for late guests, but puts them into the line of sight for those timely enough to be in their seats. Oh"—she tapped her pad with a pen—"same question with the media. They're set up on the balcony, but one TV station asked to have a roaming camera. I need to give them an answer."

We had ushers? And media? There were television stations covering my grandmother's memorial service? My head was still spinning from seeing Grammy's photo, and realizing I had to spend the next however many hours saying goodbye to her in front of the whole freakin' city. My Windsor suddenly felt like the whole of England's royal family wanted to cut off air to my lungs.

"Uh, well, what do you think?"

"I would have them step back and be invisible. They can always advance if someone needs help. And I would tell the TV people to stay in their cage. We don't need them distracting guests."

I nodded, bewildered, but trying to appear thoughtful. "Fine, let's do that."

I turned, but her voice grabbed me more firmly than her hand had done a moment ago. "A few more things . . ."

The memorial was Grammy: elegant, respectful, perfectly timed, and beautifully presented.

More than two thousand people crammed into the Ryman, with more turned away at the doors. My only participation was to place a wreath on the easel holding her portrait. By that point in the proceedings, I'd thought tears had run their course. I was sorely mistaken. As my fingers released the wreath comprising her favorite pink blooms, I felt myself letting her go, saying goodbye in a way I hadn't done before. I stood and stared, begging her to come back. My hand found its way to her cheek. I needed her warmth but only felt the cold stiffness of canvas.

Someone sniffed through their own tears, and I turned to face the mourning mass.

I was supposed to exit stage right, but I couldn't move, couldn't take my eyes off the thousands who'd come to honor my grandmother, the thousands who stared at me, *into* me, as I stood frozen in the performers' circle.

No one grabbed my arm and hauled me off. In fact, no one spoke, not even Janice. I'd been awed by the skill and precision with which Grammy had planned her own memorial, and here I was destroying that clockwork perfection.

Somehow, it felt right.

My eyes roamed the crowd of mostly unfamiliar faces, landing on a few I'd met over the past weeks. I locked eyes with each, hoping they felt an appreciative embrace, then moved on to the next.

Sam and Miguel were there. Miguel smiled up at me—of course he did—but not in his usual cheeky, over-the-top happy way. This felt more private, intimate, as if he wanted me to know he was there for me, that he would do anything to ease my pain or spark joy into my heart once more. I was caught by that. They barely knew me, yet here they were, standing by my side as I said farewell.

Then again, Sam was saying goodbye too. He'd known Grammy. All of these people had in their own way. She might not have been their world like she'd been for me, but to know her was to know unbridled love and compassion. Of course these people wanted to see her one last time, to feel her presence and goodness, all the things that made her special and unique. Of course they did.

The closest row sat a dozen yards away, yet I felt the guests' love and support as if they stood with their arms wrapped about me.

Those moments were frightening—and liberating. They brought me strength and peace.

I'd never be able to explain it. It still doesn't make sense.

But I needed that time on stage. I needed to see those faces, those thousands of souls, united in admiration for the mother I'd lost and then found again.

When I finally stepped off stage, and the last notes from Belmont's choir faded, I felt Grammy's weathered fingers brush my cheek, as I'd done hers on stage. A hint of rose tickled my nostrils, her favorite scent still in bottles of cream at her home. I squeezed my eyes shut and willed her eyes into my mind as I listened to her voice, her laughter, tinkling like the merriest of bells on a distant breeze.

And then she was gone.

The reception that followed was held in the Omni Hotel's ballroom. Servers in blindingly white shirts and black bow ties served every flavor of booze and cocktail weenie ever created. I couldn't stop the ringing of my mental cash register as I watched bartenders draining one bottle after the next, almost as quickly as they uncorked them. Then I remembered Grammy's bank balance, and I told that register's bell to stuff it.

My job at this post-mourning morning party was to be the physical representation of Grammy's family, offering comfort and thanks to each guest who needed a good handshake or hug. It was annoying. I was the one who'd lost his grandmother, yet here I was, being pimped out as a super-greeter for an indeterminate number of hours.

I blew out a sigh, sucked down a Jack and Coke, then took my place near one of the food stations Janice had designated "the receiving line." Was I a bride? A royal? Why did I need to receive anyone? I tried not to think about it as an elderly man with wisps of hair clinging to his head like a rookie climber to a mountainside reached for my hand.

An hour later, Prince Cooper was still fulfilling his royal obligation. The first dozen stories about his grandmother had been heartwarming. The hundreds that followed faded into background noise. I learned to nod politely, smile, make eye contact without really seeing the person, then do it all over again. I would never make a good politician. What masochist enjoyed this torture?

"Can I get a hug instead of a shake?" a pleasantly familiar motorcycle engine purred.

Ignoring the occasion or propriety or the fact Janice was standing nearby monitoring my every movement, I leapt into Sam's arms and squeezed him with every ounce of strength I had left.

"God, I needed you here. Thank you so much for coming."

"Can't . . . breathe. Cooper—"

I dropped back. "Sorry, I'm just really glad to see you guys."

Miguel stepped forward and pulled me into his chest. Damn, his pecs were hard. Had I noticed that before? I didn't think I had. And they're huge. And hard. Did I say hard? I wanted to reach up—

"You okay down there?"

"Oh, uh, yeah, sorry. It's been a really long day. My mind is kind of wandering on its own, like when you take a dog on a walk in the woods and let it off the leash but it runs away and goes wherever the path is, or isn't, because they sometimes like going in the open woods where there isn't a path."

Miguel blinked.

Sam chuckled.

"Well, okay." Miguel blinked a few more times. "We know you're busy here, but wanted to invite you over to our house after this is over. We'll just be grilling out and—"

"Yes."

Miguel cocked his head and blinked again.

"I'd like that. Please. Really. I need it, to be around friends and just hang out and not think about any of this or these people. Or anything. Please and yes."

"Alright, then. We'll text you our address. Come whenever you can break free."

"I'll text when I'm done." They started to turn, but I grabbed Miguel and hugged him again. "Thank you, Miguel. Thank you so much."

For the first time that day, surrounded by thousands, I didn't feel so alone.

Eleven

Cooper

"Hope you like Asian flavors. Ever since our day at the park, Sam's been all about grilling his version of those sliders." Miguel ignored my outstretched hand, pulling me through the doorway and manhandling me into a hug.

I didn't usually get too close to people—or maybe they didn't get close to me. I was never great at making friends in school. Books made better companions than people anyway.

So, what was the deal with Sam and Miguel? Why were they so nice to me? I had a pretty good sense about people, when they said one thing but meant another, and there was nothing in either of the guys that set off even a hint of an alarm. Grammy might've put them up to spending time with me, but I could tell they genuinely enjoyed my company. They wanted me around. That was . . . something. Something I'd have to get used to.

"Sounds great. I'm starving."

He led me through their house, pointing out pieces of art scattered about on tables and shelves, keepsakes from their journeys together over the past five years. We halted before a wall of framed photos artistically arranged in a way that spoke of a pattern but without appearing to have any order at all. I never understood how people did that—decorated. I must've skipped that day of Gay School.

"This was a weekend trip to Key West. We flew down to Tampa, then rented a car and drove to Fort Myers, where we boarded the Key West Express."

"That's a boat?" I asked.

"It's so much fun. There's tables and booths for eating or games, but we spent most of our time on the upper deck. Sam's hair is too buzzed to blow in the wind, but he still claims he had a *Titanic* moment on that boat. If he brings it up, just humor him. It's not worth the fight."

His eyes twinkled in the sweetest way when he said Sam's name.

"When was this?" I pointed to a photo of Miguel receiving an award from Nashville's mayor. He was striking in his sharp navy-colored uniform.

"Last year, maybe the year before. Time goes so fast these days. That was actually for the case that brought Sam and me together. I'll let him tell you about that though. He loves that story."

He scanned the photos, then pointed excitedly. "Oh, and here we are in the North Georgia mountains. We rented a cabin Sam found; more of a house really. We spent a long weekend doing nothing. Tyler and Gabe joined us with their dogs."

We'd only spent a few minutes shaking hands and passing popcorn at the game, and I had a hundred questions about Tyler and Gabe. How had they met? How had Sam met Tyler? I knew they worked together in Sam's garage, but watching the two interact felt more like watching brothers banter than coworkers. How did Gabe and Tyler communicate? I saw how well Gabe lipread, but still, that had to be a challenge. Unless you were facing him, he had no idea you were speaking.

I was curious by nature, and their relationship dogged my mind, so to speak. I wanted to asked everything all at once, but what came out was, "They have dogs?"

"Dom and Audie. You'll love them. Great pups."

He pointed out a few more photos before Sam's voice interrupted our tour of the past.

"Hey, babe, can you help me with something?"

Miguel gave me a wry smile. "Duty calls. Come on. He's probably about done with the burgers."

As we stepped through the sliding glass door onto the patio, Sam glanced over his shoulder and waved with a long metal spatula. "Hey, Coop. Grab a beer. If you'd rather have wine, it's in the kitchen. Help yourself." He pressed the spatula to a patty and leaned in to inspect it. "Dinner'll be done in three minutes. Babe, can you grab the tots from the kitchen? They're in a bowl on the counter covered by a towel."

Miguel had snuck up behind Sam while he was checking the burgers. When he wrapped his arms around Sam's waist and playfully bit his neck, Sam nearly flipped a burger onto the ground.

"You—go! Tots—now!" he barked, wielding his spatula like Excalibur of old, but there was nothing but amusement in his voice and a curling at the corners of his mouth. I looked from Sam to Miguel and saw the same unrestrained, absolute love in his eyes. It was such a simple moment, yet an amazingly beautiful one.

When Miguel turned to retrieve our missing tots, I must've been staring like that wide-eyed cat from *Puss in Boots* because his grin spread as he quipped, "Yeah, we're pretty sappy when you get me out of uniform and him out of his greasy bowling shirt."

"It's a mechanic's smock, not a bowling shirt, asshole," Sam chirped without turning.

Miguel leaned over and whispered, "Because *smock* sounds so much manlier, right? Like a fabulously gay painter or something."

I coughed a laugh, torn between defending Sam's honor and agreeing with Miguel. He was right, after all. I couldn't stop images of burly, beefy Sam wearing a neon rainbow frock with pink feathered trim around his neck and wrists dancing through my mind. Thick black hair covering his legs and arms contrasted with the delicate colors of the feathers, while a forest of fur tried to claw its way out of his neckline. He'd also grown translucent wings that twitched each time fairy dust flew out a magical wrench held high above his head.

He was the Fairy Gaymother.

That made me laugh harder.

Sam turned and shooed us with his wrench . . . I mean spatula.

"We'd better obey or, well, never mind. He'll do that to me later anyway." He winked again, then pressed his palm into my back to get me moving.

Burgers cooked, tots and beer retrieved, the three of us settled into cushioned chairs around a patio table shaded by a melon-colored umbrella. The sun had begun to set, but the Nashville summer still simmered, and sweat was soaking through all of our shirts.

It had felt so comfortable, Miguel greeting me at the door, then ushering me through their home. The guys had an easy way of making someone feel welcome; but for some reason, as we sat munching on the first few bites, an awkward silence draped itself about us like some looming specter in a horror movie. Every time I glanced up—or even thought about speaking—the creepy fucker glared down and bared ravenous fangs. The tots were a tasty distraction. I focused on them.

Miguel and Sam shared a look, then Sam nodded, as if urging Miguel to break the spell.

"So," Miguel said through a mouthful of Asian dreaminess. "How do you feel?"

That wasn't what I'd expected.

"Uh, good?" I asked more than answered. "What am I feeling about?"

Miguel's chuckle was more of a grimace laced with a grunt.

"I bet today was a long day," he said in a near-whisper.

I started to respond, to tell him I was fine, that it was just another in a series of eternal days. I wanted to play it off, to be tough, to be strong like these two. I wanted to pretend I didn't hurt still, that Grammy's absence hadn't left a gaping hole where my happiness once nested. I wanted to tell them I wasn't scared for the future, a future without her, without her guidance and compassion, without her shoulder for my tears or arms for my weakness. I wanted to say so many things.

"I'm . . ." My eyes fell to the tot I hadn't realized I'd crushed into bits, then dropped it onto my plate and covered my eyes with my palms. Sam sat at the head of the table, next to me. In a flash, he was out of his chair and pulling me into his comforting warmth. I felt Miguel's presence a moment later as my shoulder began quaking for the hundredth time in only a few weeks.

Neither of them spoke. They just held me. Their grip was so different from that of Grammy's spindly arms—like being wrapped in bands of steel—and yet, somehow, the comfort that flowed from their hearts felt startlingly similar, as if her spirit somehow flowed through them and into me, lifting me up, encouraging me, letting me know everything would be alright—and that she would always be there for me.

I don't know how long we sat huddled there together. A minute, a dozen, probably longer. When I finally pulled back,

Sam gripped the sides of my head and pressed his forehead into mine in a gesture so intimate it stole my breath.

"We're here with you, Coop. You're not alone, okay?"

I stared into his eyes. There wasn't anything sexual or wanton in his gaze. He wasn't asking for or expecting anything. There wasn't even the slightest hesitation or wavering—or anything other than strength and kindness.

Miguel's hand pressed into my back. "What he said."

Sam grinned. "He's good with words."

For some idiotic reason, that made me grin.

Miguel's three simple words had shattered the melancholy of the moment, and I felt a weight ease. It hadn't fully lifted from my shoulders—that would take a lot more than a nice hug and a few words—but I felt better, somehow lighter.

And I knew these two had become something more, would become important in ways I'd yet to fully comprehend.

And, for the first time in weeks, I wasn't afraid of what the future might hold.

"I'm okay," I said, pressing my hands into Sam's chest and becoming completely distracted by how his pecs might actually be harder than Miguel's. The guys were becoming good friends, but some things about the pair just weren't fair to the rest of us mere mortals. "Thanks. I mean, really. I can't tell you how much I appreciate all your support."

They stood and returned to their seats. "We're glad you're in our lives now. Good friends are rare."

I nodded and took a long pull on my beer.

"Sam," Miguel said right as Sam tossed a cold tot in his mouth. "Coop was asking about how we met."

"Oh, I love this story," he half-chewed, half-mumbled, then swallowed and finished his beer to wash it down.

"I'll grab us another." Miguel snatched both our empty bottles and disappeared into the house.

"So," Sam began. "There was this missing woman . . ." He detailed the case of Emily Shale, the woman who'd gone missing, sending the whole city into a massive search. "The case was upgraded to a murder investigation when her car was found with the back seat splattered with blood. The police department's bays were full, so they sent the car to a local garage. Only, they made a mistake and sent it to my shop instead. I was trying to leave for the day when a tow truck showed up, followed by a police cruiser. Miguel was one of the cops handling that case."

"And Sam was all over me the moment I stepped into his shop. It was embarrassing, really." Two *thunks* heralded the arrival of our fresh bottles.

"Very funny. You practically licked me with your eyes."

"As I recall, you liked my eyes."

Sam smirked as the bottle reached his lips. "Maybe. A little. I liked how your ass was swallowing your uniform even more."

Miguel spat beer across the table.

"Sorry, Coop." He tossed me his napkin.

"Hey, I've been wanting to ask you something since you visited me at my shop," Sam said.

"Shoot."

"It's okay if you don't want to talk about this, but curiosity's about to kill me. Marjorie—I mean, your grandmother—was, um, really generous. Like, crazy generous."

I nodded slowly, not sure where he was headed. The way he struggled asking whatever had tickled his interest made me leery of the question to come.

"You said you'd already talked to several people about their inheritance from her will, and the attorney's office handled another batch. Just how rich was she?"

"Sam!" Miguel's voice felt like a nun's ruler on a wrist—and it wasn't even aimed at my wrist.

"It's alright. A lot's been reported in the paper already," I said.

"Really?" Miguel shifted from annoyed to keenly focused.

"She left TPAC two million dollars, the Coleman Foundation five million, enough for Baptist Hospital to name a ward after her—oh, and the Sounds Foundation a million—and another seventy or so people varying sums or items."

"Like the Bel Air?" Sam said more than asked.

"Exactly. She didn't have many relatives, but she had more friends than most people deserve. Those who were especially close to her ended up with a beach house or boat or piece of art they'd once admired but long since forgotten. Grammy never forgot anything."

"That's a lot of millions."

My eyes slipped to the table.

"And you? You were like a son to her. She told me that herself, many times."

"Really?" My eyes drifted up to his.

"Coop." Sam gave me that *you're shitting me, right* head tilt. "You *had* to know that. She wasn't shy when it came to sharing her emotions or affection. Hell, I could barely pry her arms from around my neck every time I dropped her off at home after a game or dinner."

My chuckle was wry, wistful. "Yeah, that sounds like her."

The neighbor's sprinklers kicked on. The whirring of their heads and splashing of water against the fence filled the silence.

"What about you?" Sam asked.

"What about me?"

Miguel's hand reached up and gripped his on the table. Their eyes locked briefly, then he turned to me with a lighter tone in his voice. "No boyfriend or other love interest?"

The change of topic was a relief, but I still squirmed in my seat before struggling to meet his gaze. The new topic wasn't *that* much better.

"Um, well, no, not exactly. I've tried to date, but it's hard. You have to meet people to date, and people are sometimes really weird. I mean, I like weird . . . sometimes. Not kinky weird, although kinda depends on the definition, I guess, because one person's normal might be another's kinky, or vice versa. I'm pretty vanilla, even by modest standards, but I haven't done much so maybe I'm secretly wild and just don't know it. Maybe I should buy some leather or whips or something. Oh, Miguel, you have handcuffs, right? I could try those sometime, lock myself to a bedpost . . . but then I'd need someone to unlock me and now we're back to meeting people."

I sucked in a breath, then blew out another stream.

"I do like to get physical; I mean, *be* physical, like doing tae kwon do or running, but that really doesn't count on the kinky scale, does it? Unless you're into slapping each other. Then maybe that counts. Although I don't know if getting slapped with a foot is a turn-on. Some people are into feet. I read that, or saw it—maybe in a movie, but not a dirty movie or porno, not that there's anything wrong with them. I wank off like anyone. Shit, did I just say that? How did we get there? Oh, right, martial arts and being physical or kinky—martial arts would be good training because you learn control and I guess you'd really want control if you're slapping certain body parts . . . because they get sensitive in places . . . and stuff."

"Truer words," Sam purred, and saluted Miguel with his bottle and a wink.

"Hey! I'm the one with a hungry ass, remember? Let's leave *my* sensitive parts out of this." His smirk fell as he looked up and noticed the crimson blooming in my cheeks. "Oh, Coop, I'm sorry. I didn't mean . . . I mean, I did . . . but that was really—"

I laughed. "Miguel, Sam's right about your ass. It's world class. I can't really attest to how hungry it might be because I never really thought about asses getting hungry. They're more of an outie than an innie anatomically, though now you've made me wonder about their ability to eat. Based on what I saw earlier when you led me through the den, yours is ravenous because your pants didn't look like they stood much of a chance."

Miguel's mouth fell open.

Sam nearly doubled over, wheezing through breathless laughter, "Oh lord, help us. The cub's got teeth. I love it."

And as silly as it sounds, I beamed at his praise.

"Okay, let's give Miguel's ass a break—*for the moment*." Sam snickered as he gathered himself, causing Miguel's color to deepen. "No boyfriend. Got it. You mentioned tae kwon do. Was that random or—"

"Oh no." I leaned forward, suddenly excited to talk about something I knew really well that didn't involve dating or meeting people or money or asses—unless you counted those I kicked, then we were definitely talking about asses.

"I'm a black belt."

"No shit," Miguel said.

"Yes shit." That didn't sound right, but I barreled forward anyway. "I started when I was eleven, maybe twelve. I didn't really fit in at school, so Grammy found me a place where everybody was judged on their effort and skill and where *respect* was demanded, not an optional benefit that came with being popular."

Miguel perked up. "Wow, that's awesome. A few of our instructors in the department are black belts in one discipline or another. They're amazing. Do you still practice, or whatever you call it?"

I nodded. "Yeah. I go to the dojang three times a week for sparring and form work."

"What's a dojang? Wait, you still work *forms*? After, what, ten years?"

"How old do you think I am?" I blurted. His math made me twenty-two years old. "I'll be twenty-eight in a couple months. That means I've been doing tae kwon do for, what, seventeen years or so? A dojang is where we practice, like a dojo for other disciplines. And yes, I still do forms. Everyone does. Masters spend hours on them virtually every day."

"How old were you when you got your black belt?" Sam asked.

"My belt ceremony was held on the fourth anniversary of my first lesson. I remember that because Grand Master Change made a big deal out of it, insisting we move heaven and earth to hold the ceremony on that date. He took the symbolism behind dates very seriously, and an anniversary like that was special, especially for someone receiving a black belt so quickly."

Miguel's eyes widened. "Wait, *four* years?"

"It's pretty quick, but not unheard of. Most take five or six years to earn the black, but I kind of threw myself into it. I'd moved in with Grammy and Pop a year before starting lessons, which meant a new school and totally new group of kids. I was pretty far into my shell at that point, and they didn't exactly welcome me with open arms. I guess the dojang became my safe space. I went there every day after school and stayed until after dark. Grammy had to drag me out most days."

"Still, that's really impressive. What degree of black belt do you hold?" Miguel asked.

"Fourth. I got my last stripe a couple years ago. My goal's to earn my fifth by the time I'm thirty. It'll be tough, but I think I can make it happen. The levels are a little like the Richter scale—they get exponentially harder as you go up."

Miguel whistled.

I shrugged, lifted the bottle to my lips, and resisted the urge to shift in my seat.

Miguel blew out a sigh. "I'm sweating my balls off. Why don't we go inside? We've got some of Ty's homemade ice cream in the freezer."

"God, I think I just . . . Shit . . ." Sam's eyes pleaded for Miguel to save him.

"So good you almost *jizzed* thinking about it?" I finished his thought.

Miguel coughed out another mouthful of beer, as Sam sputtered a startled laugh.

"Did you forget the cub's teeth already?" I stood and winked at Sam, then walked into the house like I owned it.

"Guess he found a little confidence after all," Sam muttered, a little too loudly.

"You have no idea," I called out from the kitchen, earning another round of guffaws.

Twelve

Nate

T he ride home was eternal. They always are, especially after a week-long trip. The bus jerked to a halt in the stadium lot around two o'clock. Cal and I stumbled into our apartment around three.

"I can't believe we have to be back in two hours." I dropped my pack and flopped onto the couch, wanting nothing more than to close my eyes and dream of anything but baseball. For a guy whose dream revolved around baseball, that was a tall order.

Cal groaned from his room. "I'm with ya, brother. I could sleep for days."

I'd already fallen asleep. Somewhere in the back of my mind, I'd heard him and agreed, but my waking mind didn't care enough to stir. The couch was a massive marshmallow, clinging to my arms and legs, pulling me in with its sticky, squishy goodness, wrapping me in a warm, sugary embrace. I could taste the sweetness.

Deep breaths drew in air from an unseen confectioner's oven, twisting my lips and filling my chest with childlike glee until—

My phone buzzed and that damn waking mind yanked me out of a really pleasant, if weird and diabetically challenged, dream.

It took three *whacks* of my hand against the hard wood of the coffee table for my fingers to finally brush the screen. I could've just turned, but that would've required opening my eyes and exerting effort. I just wanted the buzzing to stop and the dream, now likely lost to the depths of my demented subconscious, to return.

I'd barely drifted off when the stupid thing buzzed again.

"Fuck, what?" I groaned as I reached over, grabbed it off the table, and flicked it to life. "Jessica?"

There was a text from Jessica Braun.

Jess was the first person I'd met outside of baseball when I moved to Nashville. I was a wide-eyed recent college grad who'd been drafted directly into Triple A ball, and while I was feeling pretty proud of myself, I was also terrified of falling flat on my face. She was a friendly smile and willing ear, probably open to more than I could ever offer, but also kindhearted enough not to walk away when she saw me clearly. She was the only person, aside from my sister, Jenna, to know everything about me.

Jess was a student at Belmont, a singer hoping higher education might give her a leg up in a town filled with talent—though I'm not sure it gave her much more than student loans to repay.

Music bonded us almost immediately. My guitar had always been a welcome escape from the grind of being a three-sport athlete in high school. Some of the guys thought it was weird, but shrugged it off when they saw how the girls ate it up. I hadn't fully understood my sexuality back then, and my reluctance to woo every girl who swooned at my songs somehow added to my musical mystique and made me more desirable. I never understood why women always seem to want what's unattainable. Why put yourself through that?

But every burgeoning gay needs a good cover, and, in that moment, I was too drowsy to think, so I let those questions drift away unanswered.

Getting a break in Nashville was next to impossible. Every student, bartender, and server in the city was also a musician hoping their demo track would impress the right producer. They rarely did. The petri dish of music that was Nashville did, however, offer the rest of us an abundance of live music listening opportunities. Even the most humble of restaurants featured live performers most nights, hoping melodic tones would drift into the streets, mingling with the scents of their freshly cooked delicacies, drawing in passing tourists and locals.

It usually worked; and so the shows went on.

Hey, String Bean. I grimaced. I'm playing the Bluebird tonight! Can you believe it? Only took me, what, five years? I have a seat for you. Please come.

My head fell back against the sofa cushion as I let out another groan. The last thing I wanted was to leave the stadium at whatever-the-fuck o'clock when we got done and head to a bar for another two hours.

Another text arrived: Pretty please, puddin' cakes. I need you.

"Ow." I banged my head back, expecting fluffy softness but feeling the sharp pain of our couch's threadbare armrest. "Yep. That's how I feel."

I stared at my phone a moment before texting back: I'd never leave my baby doll on stage alone. See you when Coach sets us free.

My phone bounced off the coffee table onto the floor as my eyes closed and imaginary marshmallows stole me away.

A bus painted deep navy with a cartoonish bison stepping through a swing at the plate sat running near the player entrance when Cal and I arrived for the game. Most of the Buffalo Bisons (yes, they used the incorrect plural of bison) had already de-bused and were dressing or warming up.

"They're pretty solid this year," Cal said as we entered the tunnel.

"Halfway through and they're fifth in the league. I'd say that's pretty good. Hope Fritzy is feelin' the mound tonight."

Walter Fritz was our resident ace and one of the top starting pitchers in the league. Most of us were surprised he hadn't already been called up to the majors. Personally, I was glad to keep him on our mound as long as possible. He made the rest of us look good.

We passed a trainer and a few ground crew. Cal called each by name and tossed them a toothy grin. I gave each a combo *sup* chin raise followed by a half bow, like some awkward knight of the diamond-shaped table who couldn't speak and refused to smile.

"Feelin' your ass tonight?" Cal asked quietly.

"Huh? No. Why?"

He shook his head like I didn't get it.

I didn't.

A dozen yards from the locker room door, we could already hear the guys. Most were laughing hysterically, but a few raged, hurling every curse in my vocabulary—and a few I'd never heard.

"Oh shit," I muttered.

"Sounds like Santi's up to no good again."

Santiago had been a Sound for three years. He was a damn fine shortstop, with quick hands and incredible field awareness. His easy smile and laid-back attitude made him hard to dislike—which was precisely why he usually got away with whatever devilry he inflicted on teammates without paying a painfully steep price in swift retaliation. Players both loved and feared him; at least, they feared his next prank would be worse than anything they could do in return.

Ronald Reagan might've coined the phrase, "Strength through superior firepower," but Santi perfected its application.

"Fucking motherfucker asshole bitch!" Nick railed as he shook what looked like shaving cream out of his cleats.

A quick glance down confirmed he'd tried to lace them up because foam coated both of his socks, and a trail led from the bench in front of his locker to where he stood, waving one shoe like it was burning, in front of an entirely-too-sunny Santi.

Most of Santi's pranks were harmless, good-natured fun, like the time he sewed an underwire bra inside one of the guys' jerseys, a player he happened to know was running late and wouldn't arrive in time to fix it before walking on field. Coach has always been brutal about punctuality. No one stepped on field late before a game—bra or no bra.

Our team's reaction wasn't nearly as funny as that of the visiting players, as a discordant rendition of Kelis's 'Milkshake' echoed from their dugout and was quickly picked up by the thousands in the stands. Coach, born with his own evil streak, made the poor guy field groundies for five minutes before letting him run back inside and de-boob himself. To cement his legacy in the baseball prank hall of fame, Santi talked the booth guys into playing 'Milkshake' every time that sad soul stepped up to the plate. How he'd arranged musical accompaniment after we'd taken the field was a mystery that sparked both awe and fear.

Everyone wondered when and where Santi would strike next.

"I'm gonna squish all night," Nick shouted, as though invoking that indignity would rally the rest of us to his defense.

We were all laughing too hard to defend anything.

"Isn't it usually your ass squishing?"

The laughter tittered out, as an uneasy hush fell over the locker room. Cal and I edged our way around to the bench in front of our lockers, avoiding eye contact with Santi and Nick.

"Hey, Nick, I'm sorry. I was just giving you shit. I didn't mean—"

"The fuck you didn't." Nick wheeled and hurled his cleat into his locker, startling a half-dozen guys to duck and cover their heads.

Rumors about Nick being gay had swirled around the clubhouse all season. Until that moment, none of the players had raised it, even in jest, as if the topic might soil—or burn—anyone who came too close. Coach was old school, and our owner was even more so. Our beloved major team and organization stood proudly with the local LGBT community, but Nashville's club had yet to get the memo. Knowing Coach, he'd gotten it, but tore it into tiny bits before burning the scraps.

There wasn't even any proof about Nick. No photos of him kissing or holding hands or even standing side by side with a man. The guys gossiped about it—of course they did, they gossiped about everything. "He doesn't act gay," was the most common thought, whatever the hell that meant, as if all gay guys walked around holding their dicks in public or something. The whole thing pissed me off, but I couldn't afford to be too vocal. It all hit far too close to home.

Still, I felt bad for Nick. He was a really good guy and a decent player. He'd never be a major league standout, but he would probably make a roster and enjoy an average career. That's what his batting average and outfield error count predicted, and that was a respectable future for any player.

The rumors threatened all that, and that pissed me off too. I could sort of understand other players being uncomfortable in the locker room, wondering if the gay guy was checking them out all the time, but even that was stupid. Who cares? If it happened, take it as a compliment and move on. Besides, contrary to popular belief among the thick-headed herd, gay guys have standards and don't lust over any two-legged being with a cock.

Okay, maybe if they're hot and the cock is—

No. We have standards.

And there was the rub. I'd used the word "we."

This wasn't just Nick's fight. It was our fight. I was in this thing too, even if the rumor mill hadn't picked up on it yet. Hell, for all I knew, this wasn't Nick's fight at all. It was all mine.

And here I sat, on the sidelines, letting him take the punches.

My gut twisted as I watched him slink back to his bench and begin wiping out his cleats.

"Who pissed in all your Wheaties?" Coach's voice jolted everyone out of whatever collective thought-funk we'd been experiencing.

When no one answered, Coach shook his head, then lifted his clipboard to read out the starting lineup and give his pregame pep talk. We all knew who was starting and where. It was posted online and emailed to each of us prior to every game, but this was a tradition, and Coach loved his traditions.

"Damn, Fritzy, you tryin' to impress a scout or somethin'?" Santi elbowed Fritz as a trail of dusty, sweaty men tromped back into the locker room. Clay scattered from our cleats, forming a trail remarkably similar to the Oscars red carpet. "One effin' hit! That's awesome, dude."

A chorus of "Dude," with the longest *u* sound ever uttered, flowed from every player.

Fritzy, blushing like a recently deflowered virgin, tossed his glove in his locker, stripped down, and practically ran into the shower to avoid the team's adulation. Given his performance that night—and most any night he took the mound—he'd better get used to receiving praise. The applause only got louder as you moved up the ranks.

Buffalo was a solid team well within striking distance for the league championship, and we hadn't just beaten them, we'd picked them apart. With fourteen hits, two of which were mine—both doubles, thank you very much—we'd shut them out eight to nothing, and Fritzy's performance on the mound was a masterclass. And our fielding . . . damn, that was a thing of beauty. Between Sant at short, Tutu splitting his nuts at first, and me spinning like a top at second, we'd turned five double plays, tying the team's single-game record.

The locker room buzzed. Even Nick looked like he'd forgotten his pregame entanglement with Santi and was grinning from ear to ear. A single and a homer will do that for a guy. The team's exuberance was something akin to a sugar high, all adrenaliny and testosteroney, sure to wear off as soon as the weariness of the week's roadie kicked back in. But for the moment, we were on top of the world.

"Hey, Bean, Cal, group of us are headed over to Von's. You guys in?" our catcher, Luis Martinez, leaned across to ask. At thirty-four, Luis was the oldest guy on the team and played the role of mentor to most of us. He'd taken me under his wing the week of rookie training before I'd even stepped onto the field. He probably wouldn't ever get a shot at the bigs as a player, but he'd make an incredible coach one day.

Cal perked up. "You bet. Haven't been there in months. Best pulled pork in town."

"Please don't let Cal eat the baked beans. I had to sleep in my car last time."

Cal cracked me with his towel. Luis chuckled.

"Sorry, Luis, I can't tonight," I said. Cal's head snapped around, and I shrugged. "I promised Jess I'd go hear her perform. She's playing the Bluebird."

"Shit, good for her. That's supposed to be a prime gig," Luis said.

"Yeah." I nodded. "That's what they say. I'm not sure how many really get picked up, but producers are supposed to go there all the time. She's pretty excited."

"Alright, free pass on that one," Cal said. "You blow us off again, though, and I'll sick Santi on you."

I winced. The memory of Nick's awkward retreat was still too fresh to joke about, at least in my mind.

Luis cocked his head, and Cal's eyes narrowed.

"You okay?" Luis asked.

"Fine," I said, glancing around the locker room, relieved no one appeared to be listening. "Things just got weird earlier, you know, with Nick. I hope Santi lays off for a while, lets everything settle before he pulls anything new."

Cal grunted and bent to untie his laces.

Luis scrunched his brows in the way he did when he was considering something. He would've made a terrible poker player. "Probably a good idea. Maybe I'll talk to him, get him to lay off a bit."

Fifteen minutes later, I'd showered and pulled on jeans and my best sky blue, pearl button, country bar shirt. Jess didn't sing country, per se, but this was Nashville. Country attire was *always* in fashion.

"Don't wait up, sweetheart," I called over my shoulder at Cal as I entered the tunnel, immediately feeling self-conscious, then feeling stupid about feeling self-conscious because we gave each other shit in front of the team all the time. As I climbed into my Uber, I couldn't help wondering if the dustup between Santi and Nick hadn't bothered me more than I'd realized.

The Bluebird Café opened in 1982 and boasted more than seventy thousand diners each year. It's nondescript glass storefront and faded canopy I thought used to be teal or navy—or some other shade of blue—was nestled in the midst of an unassuming strip mall in the heart of Green Hills, one of the more affluent areas of the city. If I hadn't had the address scrawled in Sharpie on the back of my hand, I would've never found the place. From the outside, it looked more like a small-town drug store than a world-famous club featured in vaunted publications such as *National Geographic Traveler* and *The New York Times*. Everyone from Supreme Court justices to actors and musicians of every stripe had dined or played there. For whatever reason, the owners had never thought to replace the tattered tarp above their door.

More traditions, I supposed.

The postage-stamp-sized parking lot was overflowing, so I was glad I'd Ubered and didn't have to deal with parking or paying the valet the outrageous twenty bucks they charged. The clatter of plates, chatter of diners, and a guitar player tuning his instrument hit me like a rush of winter wind as I opened the door. The sweetness of maple-coated bacon drifted on that wind too, and my stomach added its rumble to the jovial sounds pouring out of the club.

"Hi. Welcome to the Bluebird. What name is your reservation under?" A perky hostess whose hairline barely reached my chest grinned up at me, all teeth and painted-on cheerfulness.

"I'm a guest of one of the performers, Jessica—"

"Oh!" The hostess's face somehow brightened further, in a way that looked painful rather than pleasant. "You're the baseball player." Her voice dipped into a baritone growl as she said the last bit, and I was suddenly very aware I'd left too many of my pearly buttons unsnapped.

"Uh, yeah. That's me. I'm Nate."

"Sugar, it's so good to meet you." I was sure syrup would ooze out of her pores at any moment. She stepped around and hooked her hand over my arm, squeezing my bicep for good measure. "Let me take you to Jessica's table."

We strode past every table toward the front of the club, right up next to the stage where a singer's spittle might flavor my beer if they got to belting too hard. I could feel a wave of stares follow me as we passed. I was a confident, athletic, somewhat successful guy who was used to performing in front of thousands every night without the slightest stage fright or whatever the baseball equivalent might be, but for reasons I still don't understand, this crowd's goggling, in the intimacy of the club, made my skin wriggle and itch.

As I pulled my chair back from the table, readying to sit, the hostess squeezed my bicep one last time, then stroked my arm like it was some fluffy Persian cat. "If you need anything, *anything at all*, you ask for Ruby, alright now?"

"Uh, okay, thanks, Ruby," I said, snatching up a menu and clutching it like it was a life preserver.

A server appeared, and I ordered a beer and some pot stickers. I'd barely set the menu down when slender fingers crept around my head and covered my eyes.

"Please be Jess," I said.

The fingers flew off my face and one hand slapped my shoulder. "And who else would it be, Mr. Popular Baseball Player?"

I turned, a broad grin parting my lips, just as Jess's arms wrapped around my neck.

"Need . . . air. Can't . . . breathe."

She snorted. "You're so dramatic. I can't stay out here, but I saw you walk in and had to say hi. Thank you for coming."

"Jessie, you know I wouldn't miss it. I'm excited for you."

She finger-clapped and emitted a barely contained squeal. "Me too. Oh . . . my . . . god. I'm so excited. Oh, sorry, they're waving at me. I've gotta go. Wish me luck."

My table was suddenly silent in the wake of the Jessica drive-by. I shook my head, but the grin she'd planted wouldn't smooth. She had that effect on pretty much everyone. It's one of the million reasons I loved her.

My beer and appetizer arrived, and damn, if it didn't smell like heaven on earth. The first bite was halfway to my mouth when meaty fingers, decidedly not Jess's, assumed the position over my eyes. A husky voice, also not Jess's, said, "Guess who, sugar pie."

I knew that voice, but it had been a really long week, and I still hadn't had a bite of my heaven-on-earth pot stickers.

"Uh, I—"

"Nobody loves a bean like a String Bean," the owner of the hands singsonged into my ear, and my grin returned.

I nearly laughed. "I hate fuckin' cops."

And just like before, the fingers vanished and my shoulder got slapped.

I hopped up from my chair to find Miguel waiting with outstretched arms. We bro-hugged for the crowd, then Sam stepped up. "Mechanics need love too."

Miguel rolled his eyes. "You just want to feel his pecs."

"Guys!" I half whispered, grabbing Sam and pulling him into his own closed-fisted-on-the-back, one hundred percent straight, not-affectionate-or-loving-at-all hug.

As my head rested briefly on Sam's shoulder in the least guy-loving-another-guy way possible, I noticed the third in their party who'd apparently been skulking behind a woman with a silver beehive and sequined miniskirt, only to be revealed when said bedazzled woman finally sat.

My mouth suddenly went dry.

"Oh, hey, Coop."

Thirteen

Nate

"What are you guys doing here?" sputtered out of my mouth.

Miguel's eyes narrowed, but his broad smile remained firmly in place. "We just finished dinner. The last singer is one of Sam's favorites, and we decided to invite Cooper to join us. What are you doing out so late? Didn't you have a game tonight? And a roadie all week?"

"Have a seat guys." I blew out a breath and fell back into my chair. "I'm so tired I can barely stay upright, but my best friend is playing the next set, and she needed moral support."

"Playing the Bird is a pretty big deal," Sam said.

I nodded. "Huge. She's been flirting with producers for a year now. I think she might have a shot at breaking through . . . or out . . . whatever they call it. Anyway, she reserved this table for me, so here I am. It was starting to feel a little like being on stage up here by myself. I'm glad you showed up."

"Don't get too comfortable," Miguel said. "I got handed another big case today, and I'll need to be up early in the morning. We were leaving when Coop spotted the hostess groping you on the way to your table."

I snorted. "Tennis balls get fewer strokes than I did tonight."

"Great, thanks for that mental image." Sam rubbed his eyes like I'd thrown acid.

Miguel and Sam stood. "Sorry to bail, but we really do need to leave. Let us know when you have a free night. We'll grill or something."

"Fine. Leave me here alone. I see how you two are."

Cooper cleared his throat. "I could stay, you know, so you're not alone up here, not really on stage, but sort of in the spotlight in front of all those people who just want to eat and listen to music and probably won't even see you or realize you're a professional baseball player because that could get uncomfortable and they might want autographs or stuff. You do carry a Sharpie, don't you?"

The three of us gaped at Cooper. Was I supposed to answer a question or respond to one of his ten points, or just sit there and notice how blue his eyes were in the dim club lighting? No, definitely not that last one. His eyes were not on the menu—I mean, not something I was supposed to talk about or respond to or even notice.

Shit. Now he had *me* babbling.

"Uh, sure. That'd be great," came out of my mouth, but I was sure one of the guys must've said it and thrown their voice. I glanced up. Sam and Miguel had the same stunned expression I wore.

"Okay, that's settled. See you guys later," Miguel said.

They turned and made the long, meandering trek to the front of the restaurant. Ruby craned her neck to better appraise their asses as they pressed through the glass double doors.

My eyes fell to my now-cold pot stickers, then rose to find Cooper sitting quietly, blinking loudly, staring blankly. There *had* to be a million things running through his head—mine was sure spinning—but he looked as though he was asleep with his eyes open. His hair flowed back neatly with just enough wave to be the perfect amount of messy. He'd trimmed his beard down to a scruffy, rusty shadow. The black T-shirt he wore reminded me of those ads on the internet for shirts that hug muscles in all the right places. I hadn't remembered his arms stretching fabric when I'd seen him at the ballpark, but they did then.

And then he smiled, and I thought they might've flipped the stage lights on.

I fumbled for my fork, knocking my knife to the floor, ignored it, then stabbed a pot sticker and stuffed it into my mouth so I wouldn't say anything stupid.

Coop's grin widened.

"So, come here often? I mean, have you been here before? I wasn't trying to pick you up. That would be silly because we're already sitting together and there would be no need to pick you up. Besides, you look heavy."

I'd forgotten to chew. The silence reminded me, and my mouth began working again.

I'd never met anyone who could baffle and intrigue me all in one elongated, unpunctuated sentence.

I swallowed.

"This is my second time. Jess and I came here a while back to hear one of the girls in her songwriting group."

"Oh, that's nice. How do you know Jess? She's the next singer, right?"

I nodded and stabbed at another pot sticker, then remembered how full my mouth had been and decided to cut it in half before shoving it in.

"I've known Jess forever. She's amazing, and not just her singing. She's sweet and really pretty, beautiful—a beautiful soul too."

Cooper scratched at his scruff like he was pondering something deep and meaningful.

"You love her?"

The piece of pot sticker fell off my fork and rolled off the plate onto the table. We both stared at it like we expected tiny legs to pop out as it made a break for freedom.

"I guess I do, now that you mention it. Nobody's ever asked me that."

"Not even her?"

God, this was a strange conversation.

"Uh, no. I mean, she says she loves me like all best friends, but . . . wait . . . that's not what you're asking, is it?"

He reached across, grabbed my water glass, and took a long sip. For the second time in as many minutes, I blinked, unable to translate Cooper into English, but this time his actions, not his words.

The club lights flashed twice, saving me from whatever that was. I ended the pot sticker's hope of escape, but only got it halfway to my mouth before Jess's arms wrapped around me from behind again. The darn dumpling leapt off my fork again and this time fled to the safety of the floor.

"Two minutes. Wish me luck. Love you lots." Jess squeezed me, then gave me a peck on the cheek. I couldn't see her face, but Cooper's expression shifted, and I was sure they'd made eye contact. She gave me another peck, then vanished back stage.

Coop cocked a brow.

"Best friends. Promise," I said.

The server reappeared for her last visit before the show, and, since the last one was so successful, I ordered another round of pot stickers. Coop got a beer. That was cool. I'd pegged him for a wine guy.

The lights flashed one last time, then spotlights flooded the stage where Jess sat alone on a wooden stool, a guitar cradled in her arms like a precious baby or family pet. Knowing Jess, it would've been a twenty-pound cat, a tabby that should've been five pounds but was fed table scraps since birth by its overindulgent mother.

The moment she opened her mouth, she owned the place.

I'd heard Jess sing a million times, but I'd never heard her *perform* like that. A woman at the table next to us dabbed her eyes midway through the second song. By the time Jess sang her really achy-heartbreaky stuff, the woman was blubbering uncontrollably. It sounds weird to say out loud, but I could feel the mood of the room bend like a reed in the wind; first this way, then that, as she gave voice to the full spectrum of emotions.

Coop sat riveted, his lips parted in an easy smile that remained until the last notes drifted from the stage. A couple times I caught Coop watching me out the sides of his eyes. It was too dark to see him blush, but as soon as our eyes met, his fell and he shifted in his chair. I swear, the corner of his mouth twitched. I might've stared a moment or two after he turned away.

"Wow. You weren't kidding. She really is great," Coop said as our eyes struggled to adjust to the suddenly bright restaurant lights.

"Yeah. I hope she gets a break soon."

There was one last pot sticker staring up from the plate. I made the universal *would you like that?* gesture, and Coop politely declined with a silent open palm like he'd been eating for hours and couldn't possibly handle one more bite. I scarfed that sucker down.

"Did you always want to play baseball?" Coop yanked me from my dumplingasm.

I nodded through the last chews. "Yeah. I played basketball and ran track in high school, but the multi-sport thing isn't really an option in college, especially at a school like Vandy. I had to pick, so baseball won."

"But . . . you always wanted to play pro sports, not anything else?"

"I'm not sure what else I'd do. Baseball's what I'm good at."

He considered that a moment, and something in the way his lips squished together made me think that answer hadn't satisfied him.

"Your high school team was good?" he asked.

"Oh yeah. Top twenty in the country. That really set me up for scouting season."

"What's it like?"

"What?"

"Playing pro ball?" He crossed his arms and pressed his elbows onto the table, leaning forward.

I hesitated. We got this question all the time, usually from twelve-year-old boys dreaming of their future in a major league uniform. I could recite the answer we gave kids in my sleep. But Coop wasn't a kid, and I didn't want to give him some scripted answer. I wanted to open up to him, to share with him. That thought was both thrilling and terrifying.

"Well, getting drafted is a rush. I mean, you spend your whole childhood and college years working and sweating—and dreaming—and then you finally get that tap on the shoulder. It's not just a reward or trophy, it's real validation that you're on the right track, that there's a future in the game for you. It's also a beginning, the start of something new and unknown. I still remember every detail of that day, and it's been almost five years."

He took a sip of his beer. "And now?"

"Now it's my job." A sardonic laugh tumbled out. "Don't get me wrong, I love it, more than anything. Playing on a team is like having a whole roster of brothers. There's all the shenanigans and shit that comes with brothers, but they also have your back in a way I'm not sure most people ever experience. We've all been through the grinder—are still going through it, still hoping to take that next step. We get each other. Hell, we *need* each other if we're going to make it.

"But it's a lot of work, the pay is crap, and the travel sucks. Roadies are usually five or six nights in a row, and they put us up in some real fleabag hotels. A lot of people think we live some glamorous life because we're professional players, but we don't."

"Really? They don't pay you guys well?" he blurted. "Sorry, that's personal. I shouldn't—"

"It's okay." I wasn't sure why I wanted to tell him all this stuff. We barely knew each other. The league was clear on keeping a lid on anything that could reflect poorly on the game or team, but my gut said I could trust this guy—and I wanted to. "It ranges, but there are lots of guys making less than thirty grand a year."

"Seriously?" I hid a grin at the edge in Coop's voice. He was passionate about everything.

I nodded. "There are guys with families, with kids. I don't know how they make it."

"I had no idea."

"Most people don't. But hey, I'm chasing my dream, and this is the dues-paying part of it. There aren't many people who get to play a game for a living."

"Yeah, I guess."

I decided I'd danced on the league's boundary line long enough. "What about you? You look pretty athletic. You play anything?"

"Tae kwon do."

"Huh? The martial art?"

He nodded. "Yeah. Started as a kid. Competed all through high school and college. Even tried out for the Olympic team."

"No shit." I leaned forward, mirroring the elbows-on-the-table thing he'd done earlier.

"Yeah. Got knocked out in trials. The talent at that level is like moving to another planet."

"I bet. That's what majors feels like to me, but to get that close to the Olympics—"

The server appeared. "Sorry to do this to you boys, but we're about to lock up. This is for you, sir."

My check was in her outstretched hand. I reached for it, but Coop, with the reflexes of an angry adder, snatched it before I could budge.

The server chuckled as she glided to her next table.

"You let me crash your table. I've got this."

"Aw, Coop, come on. You don't have to—"

He leaned over, gave me the *come here* crook of his index finger, so I leaned in. He whispered, "Grammy took care of me. Let me buy your dinner."

I wasn't entirely sure what that meant. I knew who his grandmother was and that she was a well-off supporter. All the Sounds knew that. I hadn't paid much attention to the news after her passing, and Miguel and I hadn't talked in a couple weeks. Based on his conspiratorial tone, I was dying to ask just how rich she was and how she'd taken care of him, but propriety thumped the back of my head, and I let it drop.

"Well, thanks. I'll return the favor, okay."

"I'll hold you to that." Coop caught the server on her way past, handed her the check and cash, and told her to keep the change. "I believe, based on my research, you have a night off after this home stand."

"Uh, yeah, I think so."

I knew I should've been uncomfortable; first, because he'd looked up my schedule, which fell into the gray area between fan and stalker, and second, because he'd just asked me out.

Holy shit. He'd just asked me out.

"I'll cash in my raincheck then." He must've seen the battle raging behind my eyes. "Just as two friends having dinner, no different from you and a teammate eating out."

I nodded, swallowing back the glob of nerves that had shot up my throat a moment earlier.

There was nothing in having dinner with Cooper that felt like eating out with one of my teammates—and I was darn sure we both knew it.

Fourteen

COOPER

Nate and I sat on the curb, waiting for our Ubers and watching the last few diners leave the Bird. A car drove by, then a truck.

"I really had fun tonight. Thanks for letting me steal a seat up front with you."

Nate didn't turn, but I could tell by how his cheek lifted he was smiling. "It was fun. Thanks for . . . not letting me sit there alone. Oh, and thanks again for dinner. You really didn't have to do that."

I shrugged like it was nothing—because it *was* nothing, given what Granny had left me.

"I just outmaneuvered you into having dinner with me. There was nothing selfless in that act. You might be pretty, but you're still a dumb jock."

"Hey!" He turned, saw my shit-eating grin, then broke out into one himself. "You think I'm pretty? Should I wear pink lace next time?"

I cocked a brow. "With your dark skin, that would look amazing. Maybe toss in some purple? You'd be the hottest chick in town."

"Please don't ever let Miguel hear your choices in wardrobe for me. I'll never hear the end of it, and every holiday will be another reason for him to add to my closet, probably something frilly and sequined."

I steepled my fingers. "That sounds like another bargaining chip. I'm not above blackmail, not by a long shot."

"Great. First Miguel, now I have you?"

I know he didn't mean . . . *that* . . . but my heart fluttered at the idea. I mean, it had come out of his mouth. Did that mean he was thinking about it? Or that he wanted it to be true? Or was that a slip of the tongue? Oooh, I definitely wanted a slip of his tongue.

"Uh, Coop?"

I startled out of my spit-swapping daydream.

"I think that's your Uber." He pointed to a black Honda pulling into the lot.

I checked the app and nodded. "Yep. Plate matches."

I stood and brushed off the back of my jeans, catching his eyes dart to my ass then dart back to the pavement near his feet. I felt a scissor-kick from my heart and fought the urge to kiss Nate right there in front of the Bird, the Uber driver, and the massive moon glaring down at us.

"Talk to you later," I said, unsure how else to end the evening with this not-date-but-wanting-to-swap-spit, checked-out-my-butt guy.

"You bet," he said as he bro-punched my arm.

Great, a bro-punch. At least he touched me.

I climbed into the back of the Uber and waved through the window as we drove away.

My phone was out and AJ's number punched in before we'd fully turned onto Hillsboro Pike. It rang five times before a bleary, slightly annoyed voice said, "Cooper?"

AJ and I had been friends for years. He was a fellow black belt and had also tried—and failed—to make the Olympic team. We'd wallowed together, then picked our collective asses off the mat and moved ahead together. It sucked that he lived in San Diego, but we talked a few times each week, and that kept us close and in each other's lives.

AJ was just the right amount of off-kilter to get me, and everyone needs a friend who truly understands them, even if you're utterly un-understandable. His infuriating straightness was barely over-matched by his unshakable loyalty and love for those close to him. Lord help whoever threatened his friends. He was a tiger with claws . . . and big, pointy teeth.

"I know it's late. I'm sorry to wake you, but I'm *not* sorry because I had to call and tell you about tonight. Oh my god. It was the best night ever and I didn't even know it was going to be great until we got there and all of a sudden he was there and they left and we were alone—well, not alone, there were about a hundred other people—but we were up front, just us, and the singer, she was there, and it was romantic and beautiful and he smiled and bro-punched me."

The silence that crackled through the phone was deafening.

"Are you drunk?"

Hadn't I just said I was great? Was he not listening? And drunk? When had I ever been drunk?

"I'm amazing. Only had two beers all night. Didn't you hear about the bro-punch?"

There was another pause. "Well, yes, but I don't know what that is. Did someone hit you?"

I chuckled. He was so out of touch.

"A friendly hit, like a fist-bump but on the shoulder."

"Oh," he said without even a hint of enthusiasm. How could he not be positively giddy for me?

"AJ, I think this guy's . . . I don't know . . . *something*. I mean, we haven't known each other long, and I don't know much about him other than what I've read online and in the sports pages, but he's so nice and has an amazing smile and pretty teeth. You would love his teeth. Oh, and his biceps are like little bowling balls, all hard and round, but smaller because bowling ball arms would look funny, but they're still huge. They make you want to squeeze them just to see if they'll give at all."

"Cooper, I'm happy for you, but I really need to—"

"I know. I'm sorry, but I'm really excited. This guy could be . . . I can't say that. The last thing I want to do is jinx this, and everybody knows saying something out loud is the best way to jinx a thing, like saying I was going to win a tournament or something before ever stepping onto the mat would be a terrible jinx and—"

"Good night, Coop. I'm hanging up now."

"Uh, oh, okay. Night. Love you."

I sat, staring at my phone, trying to decide whether or not to be upset he'd nearly hung up on me mid-sentence. Then I caught Ben, the Uber driver, staring at me through the rearview mirror. Unsure how to respond to his amused glare, I waved, like I was standing on a cruise ship saying goodbye to my poor landlocked friends as the ship's horn bellowed and the dock drifted slowly away. His eyes curled into a grin, and he waved back, with only his fingertips wiggling in the mirror.

I shrank back in my seat and tried to avoid eye contact.

Then my fingers grew tiny minds of their own and began punching into my phone. They couldn't know if Nate was paying attention to his Insta, but they pecked out a message anyway.

HawkEyeBB: My Uber driver is scary.

NateStringerOfficial: Are you okay? Do you feel unsafe?

OMG! He's worried about me. If Creepy Cruiser hadn't been keeping tabs on me, I would've happy-danced all over his back seat.

HawkEyeBB: Nah, I'm fine. Black belt, remember? I could kick his ass in three directions, all at the same time, without ever breaking a sweat.

NateStringerOfficial: Really?

HawkEyeBB: No, but that's a lot cooler sounding than, "I can jump out the door when he slows down if things get crazy."

NateStringerOfficial: Now my Uber driver is staring back at me. Thanks for making me laugh like a maniac or some kind of nut.

HawkEyeBB: It's all my pleasure, Nutty Nate.

NateStringerOfficial: Oh no. No, no, no. I already have enough nicknames. You can't give Miguel any more ammo. And the guys on the team . . . I don't even want to think about the torture *they'd* inflict.

HawkEyeBB: Wow. Again, it appears I have blackmail material. Leverage, that's called in the business world. Very interesting.

NateStringerOfficial: You're a sneaky little thing, aren't you

HawkEyeBB: Who said I'm little?

Oh shit. Fingers, what were you thinking? Did you really just type that? Where's the stupid unsend? Crap, he's typing. Maybe I should jump out of the car now.

NateStringerOfficial: You might not want to compare, um, the size of our bats. I am a professional, after all.

I blew out the breath I'd been holding since sending my last DM, relieved he'd taken it in jest and snarked back with his own retort.

HawkEyeBB: Why do I get the impression you're competitive at everything?

NateStringerOfficial: Because you're afraid of losing to me at everything? Possibly? Maybe? Perhaps?

HawkEyeBB: Oh, it's on now. You didn't know competitive until you met me. Brush with Olympic glory, remember? I will crush you like a bug.

NateStringerOfficial: Big talker. I'm still competing and climbing the ladder. You'd better bring a big swatter.

HawkEyeBB: Squish, squish. See? Bug guts. All over my Uber. Now I'll have to pay a cleaning fee.

NateStringerOfficial: Great. Now my driver thinks I'm drunk. LOL you're insane.

HawkEyeBB: Good insane? The kind of crazy that makes you smile and want more? Or bad insane that makes you run for a tranquilizer and white suit with the sleeves tied on the back?

NateStringerOfficial: I'm pretty sure a tranquilizer would do you some

GOOD, BUT YES, THE GOOD INSANE. YOU'RE
FUNNY.

I wanted to scream and squeal and giggle and . . . all of that . .
. all at the same time . . . in the back seat of my Uber. I couldn't
tear my eyes from the screen, dying to know what he'd say next,
if he'd compliment my hair or shirt or arms. He had to like my
arms. I worked really hard on them. Then again, his were world
class. Damn, guns of steel. Or was that buns of steel? Who cares,
it was before I was born. His arms were amazing, but, more
importantly, he thought I was funny.

NateStringerOfficial: PULLING INTO
MY APARTMENT. THANKS FOR A FUN NIGHT.
TALK TO YOU LATER. SLEEP WELL.

HawkEyeBB: OKAY. YOU TOO. AND SAME
HERE . . . I MEAN . . . ABOUT THE FUN NIGHT.
I'M NOT HOME YET OR PULLING INTO YOUR
APARTMENT, BUT TONIGHT WAS FUN. AND
SLEEP WELL YOU TOO. I MEAN, YOU SLEEP
WELL TOO. SHIT. I'M LOGGING OFF NOW.

Fifteen

Cooper

As I filled my mug for the first time the next morning, I couldn't help smiling as the night with Nate replayed on a loop in my mind. Of all the memorable moments in the few hours we sat together, the moment he peered over Sam's shoulder and saw me that first time, when his eyes widened and he looked like something huge had lodged in his throat, that moment had made everything worth it. I'd never mastered the art of the flirt, and dating was like speaking a foreign language, but I could tell when someone's radar flicked on—and Nate's was pinging so hard I half expected him to yell, "You sank my battleship!"

Okay, maybe that would've been a little out of his wheelhouse, but he looked like he'd just won the lottery, and I was the ticket with his magic numbers.

Again, probably too dramatic for a pretty chill dude, but I was in a grand ole mood and nothing was going to bring me down.

"What's with the stupid grin?" Dennis asked through curled lips like some frothing Doberman. Marge trailed in behind him, taking up her spot to his right like a backup singer waiting for the band to start.

I stepped away from the coffee machine and made a grand gesture, welcoming them to its use. "I'm in a fantastic mood this morning, and nothing, not even your petty jibes, is going to ruin it."

His snarl somehow widened. "Raj wants to see you."

My smile nearly slipped. Nearly.

"Great. I like Raj. He's a good guy."

Marge's eyes widened. I wasn't sure the three of us had ever said a kind word about our boss. I was careful to avoid anything negative Dennis might repeat out of spite, but I hadn't exactly been a Raj banner man. Marge muttered about him all the time, and Dennis, he was outright insubordinate. Then again, he rebelled against anyone who, well, wasn't him. He was just a grumpy old man at the ripe ole age of twenty-six. One day, if he kept working hard at it, he would be a truly miserable, actually old man. I didn't plan to stick around for that bit of his show.

"He sounded really pissed. Good luck," Dennis said without turning as he shoved his mug under the coffee maker's spout. Marge averted her gaze and gave me a pathetic half-grin as I strode by.

Indeed, Raj was pissy. Royally pissy. Beyond royal, more god-like pissiness, if gods got pissy. I wasn't sure of the theological soundness of that, but it sounded right.

There were errors in our sales reports; not the ones I'd produced, but the ones from three others in our department, including Dennis. Raj had presented all our data to senior management, and the CFO had used it as the basis for his quarterly report to investors, the stock exchange, and our regulators. The legal filings were a pain, but the loss in confidence from the investor community was unforgivable, especially since we'd had such a strong quarter. All the positive press we'd received would be drowned out by talk of our team's competence, or lack thereof, which meant senior management would be carrying scoopers and poop bags for months.

"You need to clean this shit up," Raj bellowed, loud enough for the whole cubicle nation to hear him. "Now!"

I flipped through the disheveled pages he'd handed me, pausing on one, then stopping on another.

"Raj, these were done by—"

"I know whose work that was," he spat through gritted teeth. "I'm not blaming you. In fact, you're the only one I trust to fix it. Take that as a compliment and get it done before this week ends."

I wanted to ask how this got past him, the gatekeeper between the bigwigs and his lowly team of spreadsheet grunts. Had he even checked the work? He was ultimately responsible, so I expected it was actually his head on the block. Senior management probably didn't know who any of us were. But questioning the Great Raj when he was in a mood, especially after what had to be an ego-crushing, career-wounding morning, wasn't wise.

"That's three days? It took the whole team weeks to produce these reports."

He crossed his arms, his eyes shifting between the stack of papers in my hands and the door. "You're going to fix it this week or all our asses will be in the sling . . . more than they already are. The CFO is talking about hiring an outside firm to handle all our work, outsourcing everything we do. You know what *that* would mean for all the people sitting around you?"

I nodded, numb.

On any day, there were a dozen accounting firms and consultancies falling over themselves to wheedle their way in. With blood in the water, they'd be circling faster than ever.

"Go. Save our butts, Cooper. The spotlight's on you—and it's never been brighter."

"What do you mean? Why is there a spotlight on me? The CFO doesn't even know I exist."

Raj coughed through what I assumed was a laugh. "Oh, he knows who you are. The entire board does. I told them you were the one I trusted to get this right. I expect they'll be asking for daily updates, so you'd better get started."

He turned, edged around his desk, and sat in his overstuffed chair. I stood, gaping stupidly, as he grabbed a pen and began writing in a leather folio. In a clear sign of passive-aggressive dismissal, his eyes remained fixed on what I was sure were mindless doodles. I wheeled about and closed his door behind me, a tad bit harder than was technically necessary, but I wanted to bang something, and his door was within arm's reach.

When I finally settled into my chair, the heads of Dennis, Marge, and two other members of the team appeared like nosy neighbors staring over a fence.

"What did he want?" Dennis asked.

"Why was he so pissed? He was pissed, right?" Marge chimed in.

"How bad is it? Did he fire you? Are you cleaning out your desk?"

I scowled up at Dennis. He was such an ass.

"He wants me to work on something; yes, he's pissed, more than I've ever seen; and no, I wasn't fired, although you might want to start checking the classifieds." For the slightest moment, I felt a twinge of guilt as the shock registered on Dennis's face. Then the greeting end of the dog returned, and my guilt evaporated.

"Very funny. Fine, don't tell us. We'll find out eventually." His head descended beneath the carpeted wall. One by one, the others vanished, leaving me a moment's peace.

I wiggled my mouse and my screen flared to life. Eight emails from Raj had arrived since I'd left his office. Eight. He hadn't sent me eight emails in five years. Each one contained no less than three attachments, which I assumed were the aforementioned shoddy work I was to repair, the electronic versions of the printouts now blanketing my desk. I moved the cursor to open the first email, but my phone vibrated before I could click, and I glanced down.

DANDELION: HEY. SORRY I WAS SO SHORT ON THE PHONE LAST NIGHT. I HAVEN'T BEEN SLEEPING WELL LATELY, AND YOUR CALL STARTLED ME AWAKE.

Despite my brilliantly happy night, then suddenly shitty morning, I smiled. AJ did that—found a way to warm my heart when all around me lay frozen. Was that a best friend thing? Whatever it was, he'd figured out how to make me feel better in almost any situation. Hence, his name on my phone had morphed into a flower. AJ Dandillo was just too easy to pass up turning into Dandelion, especially when I knew it drove him crazy.

ME: IT'S OKAY. SORRY I WOKE YOU. WHY AREN'T YOU SLEEPING?

DANDELION: OH, I DON'T KNOW. I'M GETTING OLD. IT JUST HAPPENS.

ME: OLD. HA. YOU'RE A YEAR YOUNGER THAN ME.

DANDELION: I GUESS. MY KNEES FEEL LIKE THEY'VE LIVED A FEW LIFETIMES, ESPECIALLY IN THE MORNING.

Besides his remarkable ability to make me smile through the darkest times, AJ also possessed a freakish level of telepathy.

DANDELION: WHY DO I GET THE FEELING YOU'RE NOT AS GIDDY RIGHT NOW AS YOU WERE LAST NIGHT? DID THAT APE BREAK YOUR HEART ALREADY? DOES HIS NAME NEED TO GO ON THE LIST? WHAT HAPPENED? YOU WERE IN SUCH A GOOD MOOD LAST NIGHT. YOU MET A MAN? DID I GET THE GIST? IS HE NICE? DOES HE HAVE A JOB? HE NEEDS A JOB, SON. YOU KNOW THAT, RIGHT? I'M GUESSING YOUR BAD DAY DOESN'T HAVE ANYTHING TO DO WITH THIS NEW BOYFRIEND? I HOPE IT DOESN'T. HE SOUNDS NICE, NICER IF HE'S EM-PLOYED.

'The list' was a mental catalog of all the men I'd dated who stopped dating me for whatever reason, which was all of them, but only numbered, like, three. I wasn't even sure three men, or things or items, comprised a full list, more like a few bullets on a page—not that I wanted him to use bullets. They were nice guys, just not a match or not into me like I wanted or they wanted or whatever.

Me: No. We haven't talked since 1 a.m. And yes, he has a job. I'm just having a really bad day. Talking to you makes it better.

Dandelion: Are you sure this has nothing to do with him? You have that pouty tone. I can see your bottom lip pooching out, and we're texting!

Me: Ha ha. No pooching. My lips are perfectly in place, if a bit chapped.

Me: No, today has nothing to do with him. His name is Nate, he is employed,

AND HE'S NOT MY BOYFRIEND. FOR ALL I
KNOW, HE'S STRAIGHT, ALTHOUGH WE DID
HAVE A GREAT TIME LAST NIGHT AND WE
HAVE DINNER PLANNED FOR LATER THIS
WEEK AND HE'S REALLY HANDSOME AND I'M
SUPER EXCITED TO GET TO KNOW HIM AND
SEE WHERE THIS MIGHT LEAD BECAUSE HE'S
NICE AND HOT AND HAS GREAT TEETH.

DANDELION: WELL, THAT'S NICE, DEAR.
ORAL HYGIENE IS IMPORTANT. IT SAYS A
LOT ABOUT A MAN'S CHARACTER. AND HIS
BREATH.

What does one say to that? It was rare when words failed to form, but I was genuinely stumped by a motherism from my bestie.

DANDELION: OKAY, SO THE BAD DAY ISN'T
ABOUT NATE, THE GAINFULLY EMPLOYED
FLOSSER WE'RE DATING THIS WEEK. WHAT
THEN? DID SOMETHING HAPPEN AT WORK?
WHAT HAS RAJ DONE NOW? I KNOW IT'S HIM.
A MOTHER ALWAYS KNOWS.

Damn, he *did* always know. Maybe he was a mother after all. Again, I was torn between being creeped out and flabbergastingly impressed.

ME: YOU'RE GOOD, YOU KNOW THAT, RIGHT? YES, IT'S RAJ. WELL, NOT SO MUCH HIM AS THE CRAP THE TEAM DUMPED ON HIM. SORRY FOR SAYING CRAP. I KNOW, IT'S RUDE. HE SAID MY WORK WAS GREAT, BUT THE REST OF THE TEAM SCREWED UP STUFF THE BOARD SUBMITTED TO INVESTORS AND NOW EVERYONE WITH ANY FLAVOR OF VICE PRESIDENT TITLE IS PISSED. SORRY FOR SAYING SCREWED UP AND PISSED TOO.

DANDELION: HE DOESN'T BLAME YOU, DOES HE? AND THANK YOU FOR RECOGNIZING HOW FOUL YOUR MOUTH IS. YOUR REAL MOTHER WOULD BE AGHAST. YOU'RE EXCUSED BECAUSE THIS IS A STRESSFUL DAY, BUT I EXPECT BETTER IN THE FUTURE.

ME: YES, MA'AM. AND NO, HE DOESN'T BLAME ME. HE EXPECTS ME TO PULL A MIRACLE OUT

OF MY ASS AND FIX ALL THE SHODDY WORK THE TEAM SUBMITTED . . . BY THE END OF THE WEEK. THAT'S A MONTH'S WORTH OF WORK BY A WHOLE TEAM THAT I HAVE TO UNTANGLE IN JUST A FEW DAYS. IT'S CRAZY.

ME: OH, SORRY FOR SAYING ASS, BUT THAT WAS AN ANATOMICAL REFERENCE RATHER THAN A CURSE. I'M FAIRLY CERTAIN IT DOESN'T COUNT. DOES SHODDY COUNT AS A CURSE? IF SO, I'M SORRY AND WILL DO BETTER.

DANDELION: :) SHODDY IS PERFECTLY IN BOUNDS AND APPROPRIATE. NO APOLOGY NECESSARY. AND IF ANYONE CAN UNTANGLE A MESS OF NUMBERS CREATED BY A BUNCH OF FUCKING IDIOTS WHO DON'T KNOW THEIR ASSES FROM THEIR GODDAMNED CALCULATORS, IT'S MY MOTHERFUCKING BRILLIANT BEST FRIEND.

Again, I was speechless, though we were texting, so that should probably be wordless. Yes, I was wordless.

Utterly wordless.

ME: MOM, UM, YOU CURSED. I MEAN, LIKE A SAILOR . . . OR A WHOLE BOAT FULL OF SAILORS, ALTHOUGH THEY WOULD BE MAD AT ME CALLING THEIR SHIP A BOAT. THEY'RE TOUCHY ABOUT SUCH THINGS. YOU HAVE A POTTY MOUTH!

DANDELION: OH, HONEY, I WAS RAISED BY HIPPIES. EVERYONE SMOKED POT AND CURSED. I'M ALLOWED. IN FACT, WHEN I GO HOME, IT'S REQUIRED. BESIDES, HOW ELSE WILL I BECOME A CRUSTY OLD MAN WHO DOESN'T CARE WHAT PEOPLE THINK? IT'S A NATURAL PART OF AGING. NOW, GET OFF THIS PHONE AND GO KICK SOME MOTHER-FUCKING ASS.

ME: WOW. JUST WOW.

DANDELION: LOVE YOU, SWEETIE. TOODLES.

Sixteen

Nate

Coach called another practice on the day of a game. He announced this last-minute schedule change via text message three hours before the one o'clock *be there or you will regret it* start time. It wasn't uncommon for us to practice on game days when we were traveling. There wasn't much else to do, other than sit in our hotel rooms and annoy each other, but to call a practice on a home game day was . . . well . . . this was the only time he'd done it all season. I briefly wondered what he would do if some of the guys missed the message or failed to attend because they had other plans. Only a quarter of our players were married, and fewer had kids, but still.

"This sucks," Cal said as he pulled on his practice pants, which required more effort from the gentle giant than one might expect.

At six foot five, the only thing easy for Cal was reaching cans on the top shelf in the kitchen. Everything else required bending down or ducking so he didn't end up on the DL with a concussion and a host of new nicknames the guys would never let die. It took even more effort on my part not to laugh as he pretzeled himself, got his foot stuck in a pant leg, then hopped across the locker room before tripping and landing on his butt, pants falling legless before him. Thankfully, we were the first to arrive and none of our less respectful brothers were there to razz him about his dance moves.

"M'lord, doth thou needest thy chamber maid?" I said in a horrendous mock English accent, complete with a lisp that didn't make sense but was entirely appropriate and funny. To cap off my performance, I dropped to a knee and bowed my head, as if waiting to be knighted or something. Cal had clearly missed all the movies where kings did the shoulder-tapping thing with their swords because all I got was a tossed towel at my respectfully bowed head.

"My liege!"

"Fuck off, you miserable peasant serf pig farmer." His grin mirrored my own when I tossed off the towel and raised my head.

"Equine sherpa. Please use the correct term, m'lord."

"Equine porker is more like it."

He couldn't fall when sprawled out on the floor, so he wriggled into his pants, then stood and buttoned them up. How players made something as simple as putting on pants a humorous ordeal was beyond me. I guessed being crammed into a locker room or bus for a hundred sixty games would do that to any group of people, especially twelve-year-old boys pretending to be adult professionals.

The others filed in and assumed their spots on benches next to their lockers. We'd had a moment of levity, but they had yet to crack the sour shell encasing their moods. There was none of the usual banter, no name calling or teasing, no towel snaps, no wise cracks, not even any small talk. As if by some prearranged code, each man entered, assumed his seat, and began changing with barely a glance at the rest of us.

Coach's eleventh-hour practice had been received about as well as a screaming baby on a plane, sitting one seat back with a bulging diaper and refluxing over the headrest. That was the look on their faces: upset, disgusted, frustrated, and unable to find an escape.

Baby poop, puke, and noise.

Plain and simple.

I'd finally bent to lace up my cleats when Coach Sabro graced us with his presence and began an uplifting pre-practice rant. It felt a little like that scene in every fantasy movie where a human gets stuck standing before a bellowing dragon or behemoth, or other really big, really angry monster, all teeth, tongue, and spittle—and a thunderously, horrifically, eardrum-shatteringly loud voice.

Yeah, we were the tiny humans.

"The errors stop today. Do you understand me? Every man in this locker room hopes to feel the MLB's tap on their shoulder one day, but it won't happen for a single one of you if you keep dropping the fucking ball. We're going to drill until you can't hold your gloves. Tomorrow, we'll drill another hour for every fuck-up lighting the scoreboard with an E in tonight's game. If that means we practice for five hours, walk off to change, then walk back on to play, so be it. You will not shit on my field again. Got it?"

"Yes, Coach," we muttered in halfhearted unison.

"That wasn't encouraging. DO YOU UNDERSTAND ME?"

"YES, COACH."

He glared around the room, locking his eyes on each player before moving to the next. When he settled on mine, he lingered through his next statement.

"Good. You'd better. My fingers itch every time I pick up our lineup."

The coach's pen was a not-so-subtle, not-so-veiled threat, a reference to being traded to another team or cut from the league altogether. It warmed my heart that he decided to stare *me* down as he painted such an inspirational image.

"Nothing like getting screwed without the lube, right, Nick?" Santi growled as soon as Coach was out of earshot. If the room had been tense before, it was now like watching a pride of starving, angry lions leer at each other. Nick had flushed to full crimson, and those of us close to him glared at Santi. A few of his usual cadre laughed uncomfortably at his needling.

"Dude, not cool," one of the guys a few lockers down said.

Another chimed in. "Give the guy a break. It's not funny anymore."

Santi, never one to back down from anything, plastered on his brightest smile, puffed out his chest, and said, "Come on, ladies, Coach just shoved a bat up all our asses—metaphorically speaking, of course. I was only asking our resident expert how it feels for real. You don't mind, do ya, Nick? It's all in good fun."

I'd hoped the asshole's friends on the team would grow a pair and pull him back, at least tell him to knock it off. He might be a dick at times, but they were generally good guys just trying to make it in the league without any sort of controversy. In that moment, when everyone's fur was standing on end and poor Nick was gritting his teeth, all they did was laugh. I supposed it was somewhat reassuring that they looked about as uncomfortable as a rabbit that'd wandered into that lion's den, but that consolation was brittle at best.

Then Nick's eyes found mine, and I wanted to crawl into my locker and never come out. Why was he looking at me? And why hadn't I said anything, stood up for him, told Santi where he could fuck off to? Where had my backbone gone when one of my family was being mocked?

Was I afraid of standing up for a guy we all knew was gay, like that would cast an eye of suspicion onto me? I wanted this career, this lottery-ticket opportunity, more than anything. It had been my childhood dream since my earliest memories. But my parents raised me to stand up for what's right, to defend those who couldn't protect themselves, to never turn away from a fight—not when it was a fight between good and so clearly evil. Thinking whatever about gay people or being gay was one thing, making fun of someone for it, making them miserable, especially in front of their teammates, their family, that was way out of bounds.

And my fear, my lack of conviction or strength or whatever, that was out of bounds too. I knew it. In my heart, I felt it. So why didn't I stand up? Or speak up? Or do anything but sit there silently and avoid Santi's scornful gaze?

Then something else caused a spike of panic and fear. Why was Nick staring at me? I mean, we were friends, but not particularly close ones. Did he suspect I might be gay too? Nobody knew. They couldn't know. This level, this team, didn't keep guys like—

Nick turned back toward Santi when my eyes fell to the dingy carpet.

Two of the players sitting near him rose, their eyes ablaze, but Nick gripped each of their wrists and held them back. "Don't. We have practice, and all this shit will just make things worse with Coach. Come on, let's hit the field."

Practice sucked. Coach was an ass. Santi was an ass. Basically, there were a lot of asses on the grasses.

And shit, now my brain was rhyming about asses.

This was bad.

My moral compass apparently came with a pendulum that swung between regret and guilt, like a metronome stuck on the widest possible setting so it took forever to click. Every time it did, I felt another stab of guilt or frustration or anger. From how everyone else looked on the field, they were feeling it too. Even Santi and his flock stank up their positions—and no one could hit the damn ball. If I hadn't known better, I might've thought Coach replaced the baseball with a marble, or a BB. Thanks to one locker room run-in, the ball was now invisible and impossible to strike. Well, that's not true. There were plenty of strikes, just none of the good kind.

Coach kept us out there, roasting in the summer sun's peak, for three hours. Practice didn't end as much as he gave up trying to make it better. He could get pissy, but in the years I'd been on the team, I'd never seen him throw or break anything; but, as he stormed off the field toward the dugout door, his clipboard shattered against the masonry wall, sending papers, pens, and bits of wood in all directions. To punctuate an already well-hammered point, he grabbed a batting helmet and flung it back onto the field, then slammed the door behind him, as if to say, "Don't fucking come inside, ever. I'm done."

Of course, we eventually went inside—slowly, quietly, with our heads cowed and feet shuffling—a safe fifteen minutes after he'd left us gawking at Cal's helmet as it rolled to a stop near the mound.

That had been one hell of a throw.

I trotted over and retrieved the helmet, dusted it off, then turned toward the dugout where the rest of the team was filing through the door. Apparently, the fates hadn't finished toying with me, because Santi and I were the last in line to exit the grass.

"That was brutal," he said, oblivious to the lingering animosity he'd created earlier.

A few strides later, we'd reached the wall where the remnants of Coach's notes fluttered about. As I stooped to gather them up, Santi quipped, "Look at the good little Boy Scout, helping Coachie with his things."

I knew he was teasing. I knew he didn't mean anything by it, and that he was trying to lighten the mood. That was Santi, and most of the time, his tactics worked and were good for team morale, but on that day, he'd said more than enough.

My backbone snapped back into place as I rose and squared with him. "Santi, you need to ease up. The thing with Nick was over the line. If Coach hadn't just reamed us out, that shit would've turned into a fight none of us can afford. Scouts and coaches, and especially front office types, want players, not guys who cause controversy."

He held up both palms. "Easy, dude. I was just playin'—"

"No, you weren't. You were hurting a member of our team, our family. That's gotta stop."

His palms moved from surrender to planted defensively on his hips. "Who died and made you captain? Last I checked, nobody listens to you anyway, least of all the majors."

Now he was hitting below *my* belt. My fists balled, and my jaw clenched. I'm not sure what would've happened next if Cal hadn't appeared in the doorway.

"Nate, you coming? We've got just enough time to clean up, change, and grab food before the game, but we need to move."

With my eyes firmly locked onto Santi's, I nodded and mumbled, "Yeah, I'm done here anyway."

We won that night. There were no errors. Our batters delivered, though I landed a hat-trick with three strikeouts, not exactly the accolade a player hopes for in the morning papers. Winning fixes most things: momentum, confidence, and team morale.

Then we won again the next night, and the next.

Coach didn't strut around the locker room beaming or anything, but his frown no longer inflicted mortal wounds.

Unfortunately, winning couldn't fix unmasked prejudice or homophobia. While Santiago kept his jokes directed *playfully* at his close friends on the team, razzing them about their "dance move catches" or slides into bases that stopped just short of the actual base, I caught more than a few of the guys glancing at him with furrowed brows. Each night was a repeat of the last. We left the field on a high, greeted each other with slaps and high-fives in the locker room, then settled into our post-game routine. That's when the mood shifted, when we had time to think . . . and to remember.

Something else new happened after each game of that home stand. Nick slipped out before most of us had finished showering and changing, before anyone had time to react. My heart lurched after him, saddened to see a quality guy no longer feeling welcome in his own home.

"You ready? I need food," Cal said as he stuffed the last of his toiletries into his locker and slammed it shut.

"Yeah, almost. Kinda late to eat, isn't it?"

"It's just ten."

Cal could eat twenty-four seven and never gain a pound. If I looked at a cupcake after the sun had set, my love handles would threaten to pop out. If I wasn't a professional athlete who worked out for hours each day, my waistline would probably need to be measured in feet rather than inches.

"Can we just grab it and head home? I'm beat."

"Old man." He grabbed a nearby bat and hobbled around, using it as a cane to mock me, a toothy grin betraying his sarcastic tone.

"Respect your elders, young man," I retorted.

"Yes, dad," he said as he replaced the bat in the bin and grabbed his pack. "Let's get out of here before you-know-who can show his ass."

Great, now *we* were fleeing our home, and we hadn't even been in Santi's crosshairs.

On the way down the tunnel that led to the parking lot, Micha Eddelston, our batting coach, yelled from behind, his voice bouncing off the walls like a foul ball.

"Hey, Bean. Wait up a sec."

Cal groaned, then his stomach grumbled. I looked up with a grin and shrugged.

"What's up, Edds?" I asked when he huffed to a stop before us.

"Coach wants you in the cage tomorrow. Ten o'clock."

"Aw, come on, Edds. Tomorrow's our first real day off in weeks."

He shook his head and lowered his voice. "Don't fight this, Bean, please. Hat-trick two nights ago, oh-for-two last night, oh-for-four tonight?"

"Everybody has bad games. I'm just tired, need a day off," I said, a little too acerbically.

"Don't do this, Nathaniel." He spoke my name like a frustrated parent wanting to leave for school as I fumbled around for my lost shoe. "There's some solid talent in the Dubs, and they're nipping at your heels. You need the work. Let me help you."

Coach Eddelston was one of the nicest guys on staff. He never had a harsh word to say about anyone. If he got serious, we were idiots if we blew him off.

I sighed. "Alright, Edds. I appreciate the help. See you in the morning."

He gave me one nod, as if he'd just checked off the last box on his to-do list, then turned and jogged back up the tunnel.

Cal's hand on my shoulder pulled me out of a dread-laced daze. "Get your reps in. You'll be fine."

God, I hoped he was right.

Batting practice lasted two hours, despite Edds trying to wrap things up after one. Neither of us had seen Coach Sabro and a front-office-looking guy I didn't recognize sitting halfway up the stands along the first base line, at least not until the one-hour mark when we made to leave and Sabro barked from his seat.

"Stringer, go to the plate. Live pitch."

I glanced through the cage's netting to see one of our bullpen guys trotting out to the mound. For a brief, hopeful moment, I thought Coach might be testing him rather than me.

"Sorry, looks like the boss wants to see more. Let's show him your best, alright?" Edds said.

My bubble burst.

Clearly, I *was* in the spotlight, and Coach had planned this little stage appearance, probably in concert with the suit sitting beside him. The only thing I didn't know was if this was a positive review or a trade-deadline decision process. The last thing I wanted was to get shoved back into the lower levels or sent to another city—not five years in.

Despite the churning in my gut, I jogged from the cage to the batter's box, shadowing a few swings before the show began. I took pride in working hard. There was a lot that players couldn't control, but we could always control our effort and hustle—and nobody was going to out-work me. Looking back, that's probably what won me a spot in Triple A more than anything. I had talent, but there were plenty of players with more. What they didn't have that I displayed every waking moment was a passion and drive to win every play, hit every pitch, to give every ounce of sweat for as long as I wore a jersey. That kind of dedication couldn't be taught.

So, of course I'd jogged across the whole length of the vacant field, while Edds trudged after me in an old man's hobble.

I'd been focused on my form when our backup catcher snuck up and squatted behind the plate. Jermaine Hobbs was a nice enough guy who we all expected to be wearing an MLB jersey by this time next year. He smacked his fist into his mitt a few times, then glanced up at me.

"Don't fuck this up, Bean. They dragged us out here on our day off just for you."

Shit, this *was* all about me. Worse, the guys knew it. The whole locker room would soon buzz about the headsman sharpening his axe, or some other version of *Nate's in trouble*.

"Do my best, Hobby," was all I could think to say.

Coach Eddelston finally made it to stand in the on-deck circle behind me. He clapped a few times and called out, "Alright, Bean, show 'em how it's done. Keep your elbow—"

Fastball down the middle.

Pop.

The ball hitting the catcher's mitt sounded like a rifle firing.

"Shit, I didn't know he was starting," I muttered to no one as I crouched into my ready position.

Hobbs held up a hand to hold the next pitch, then whispered, "Bean, he's gonna give you all fastballs at first. Use 'em to get into a rhythm before Coach makes him throw the shit."

My eyes fixed on the pitcher. "Thanks, Hobby."

Crack.

I launched the next pitch over the left field wall.

Crack.

The next one rebounded off the Chick-fil-A logo at left center.

Crack.

A homer to dead center, all the way to the moon.

"Shit, Bean, this is more like it," Hobbs said.

I grinned—on the inside. On the outside, I was all business, laser focused on the enemy on the mound, the guy trying to bury me and my brothers in a sea of Ks.

Not today, Satan. Not today.

By the time the pitcher had exhausted his bucket of balls, Edds was already trotting toward me.

"Fuck, Bean, where you been hiding all season?" His wide smile was nearly as warm as his praise. "That was big league stuff, and Scotus was puttin' some real stink on the ball."

Suddenly, I was an eight-year-old in a Little League uniform after his first base hit. I danced on my feet, and grinned like a drunk laden with beads at Mardi Gras.

"Thanks, Edds. That was awesome. So awesome."

He laughed and shook his head. "Yeah, it was. Go on, get outta here. I'll go talk with Coach."

"Thanks, Edds. See you tomorrow."

I didn't jog off the field. Jogging was for losers who struck out. I sprinted my ass into the dugout, slapping the *Winners' Walk* sign above the door as I hooted my way into the locker room.

God, I loved this game.

Seventeen

COOPER

I barely noticed when five o'clock rolled around and everyone rose from their cubes for the daily exodus. The past three days felt like years, while simultaneously flying by entirely too fast. I counted six hours of sleep, twelve cups of coffee, one Red Bull, and two apple fritters over the past forty-eight hours.

I only reference the fritters because I am usually very picky about what I eat, never touching processed sugars or carb-heavy foods, but I'd needed fuel and fritters were the most substantive item on the menu in our vending machine. That lemon twist of irony likely said more about the healthy options available to the workers of one of the world's largest healthcare companies than anything, but that's a story for another day.

The board's reports were complete. All that remained were the final cross-checks and validations, and I could drop the national-budget-sized stack of papers on Raj's desk and free myself from his tyranny . . . at least, that particular portion of tyranny. He was creative. There would be more.

At ten after five, the cube farm stood empty. The only sounds were the ticks of our '80s high-school-style clock and the pecking of my keys and mouse as I clicked through the report. Then my phone added its buzz to the silence. I finished the row I was checking, then tapped the screen.

NateStringerOfficial: Yo!

Yo? First I get a bro-punch, now I'm greeted with an incomplete yodel? How does one even respond to a *Yo?* Was that friend-zone stuff or just how Nate talked to other guys? He was a ballplayer, and I supposed it fit with locker room chatter he was used to. I hadn't been stupidly insecure like this since my first dates in college.

For whatever reason, this guy scrambled my eggs.

HawkEyeBB: Yo Yo.

NateStringerOfficial: You bobbin' up and down?

HawkEyeBB: Huh?

NateStringerOfficial: Like a yoyo. You must be fried to miss my lame jokes.

HawkEyeBB: Yeah. It's been a long week. Hey, I know you owe me dinner, and I fully intend to hold you to it, but I still have another hour or two before I'm done here. Would it be too late to meet at 8?

NateStringerOfficial: Nah. Not too late at all. We don't have practice tomorrow, so I don't report to the field until four.

HawkEyeBB: Oh, nice. Um, where should we eat? I don't even know what kind of food you like, other than pot stickers, which you're not very good at eating and should probably be avoided unless there's a dog in the restaurant who will eat them off the floor.

NateStringerOfficial: Ouch! Not letting me forget that, are you?

HawkEyeBB: Not a chance.

NateStringerOfficial: I would say I eat healthy, but we're on the road so much, fast food keeps me alive.

HawkEyeBB: Um, no. How about we meet in the middle for comfort food. Ever been to Swett's? It's over on Clifton.

NateStringerOfficial: Oh yeah. Old-fashioned, deep-fried Southern goodness. I'm down.

HawkEyeBB: Like your pot stickers?

NateStringerOfficial: Wow, you're cranky when you're tired.

HawkEyeBB: Don't cut yourself on my wit. Let me put the phone down and finish these reports. See you at 8.

I set my phone aside and wiggled my mouse to wake the PC. "This is a date, isn't it?" I asked myself. "I mean, we talked all week on Insta. That's not like phone conversations, but it still counts. Now, we're doing dinner. That's not a friend thing, is it?"

I tried to focus, but the numbers couldn't win out against my racing mind.

Sam and Miguel hadn't said anything about Nate being gay, but they hadn't said he wasn't. He didn't act gay or give off any rainbow vibes, although, with the advent of metrosexuals, it was hard to tell what *acting* gay looked like anymore. Then I realized how insulting that whole phrase was, the whole concept. Nobody acted anything. They just were. And they were beautiful and good being themselves. So there.

Cell B1278's calculation had an extra colon.

Why was I moralizing about people acting or not acting gay? The question was whether or not a certain baseball player batted for the home team. The more I thought about it, the less sure

I was. Had I misread his intentions? Was he actually a straight guy who didn't have many friends and was grasping for human contact outside of his world of pro sports? That would've been a shame. He was Grade A beef, and I really liked his teeth.

On a whim, I snatched up my phone and dialed Miguel.

"Hey, Coop. How ya doin', buddy?" I could *hear* him smiling through the phone.

"Hi, um, Miguel. Good. I'm good."

There was a pause.

"Were you . . . calling for something?"

I slapped my palm over my face. "Oh, sorry, I was trying to . . . I wanted to . . . Shit. How do I ask—"

His laughter rang with the clarity of a church bell—a really low-pitched one that might be a tad cracked.

"Just ask whatever it is. I'm a big boy."

"Oh? Really? Um, that wasn't the question, but, well, thanks, I think."

I was pretty sure he'd held the phone away from his face because his laugh somehow sounded distant even though it managed to grow louder.

"So, what's up?"

I sucked in a breath, then blurted, "Is Nate gay?"

This pause felt different, somehow sharper, less expectant, and more wary.

"Why would you think that?"

"I don't know. We hung out after you guys left, at the Blue-bird, I mean, for a couple hours. Then we talked on the step and DMed all week and are having dinner later tonight. I just ask because, um—"

"You don't want to get your hopes up if he's straight. I get it." His voice was filled with fatherly concern. "Coop, I can't help you here. In all the years I've known Nate, he's never dated or even mentioned a date to me. I tried to bring it up early on, but he danced away from the topic with excuses about being married to baseball. That's pretty typical of a minor leaguer, by the way."

"Oh," was all I could think to say.

He blew out a sigh. "Buddy, he's a tough guy to read in general, doesn't really wear his heart on his sleeve or anything. Either way, he's a great guy and an even better friend."

There was that word again: *friend*.

I didn't want another friend. I had AJ. Friends were like shoes. Why did I need more than one? I only had two feet. How many pairs of tennis shoes did I really need? Maybe one extra pair in case I blew out my old ones, but certainly not a closet full. And for dudes, we didn't have all the outfits and styles and colors women had. We needed to match black and brown. Period. Why have more?

One pair. One friend. Nate should be gay.

"Was there anything else?"

Shit, I'd forgotten Miguel was on the other end of the line.

"No, sorry, I got lost thinking about shoes."

His chuckle returned.

"Have fun with that. You coming to the house this weekend? I think Sam wants to do some kind of stuffed pork loin he read about somewhere. He's getting pretty good around the kitchen. I think Gabe and Ty are coming too."

"Sounds good. Ask Sam if he needs anything. Shoot me a text, okay?"

"You got it. Have a good night with your . . . shoes."

His laughter echoed in my cube long after I hit the end button.

Eighteen

Nate

I walked across a fairly empty parking lot to stand before a nondescript building nestled in the middle of ramshackle houses and modernistic condos trying too hard to be the cool kids in a class of band geeks.

"Hey, you." I followed the voice to find Cooper standing at the building's corner, his right hand half raised in a wave.

Two things happened when our eyes met: his hand fell to his side, where he stuffed fingers into his jeans pocket down to the knuckles, and he flipped on his high-beam smile that somehow brightened the overcast sky. My heart decided to thump faster than Bugs Bunny fleeing Wile E. Coyote.

"Hey, Coop," I said, coming within arm's distance. I began reaching my hand out to shake his, but that felt weird. Were we supposed to hug? We'd never kissed, and we weren't in Europe, so lips were out. I'd never been particularly sharp when it came to gay protocol, and, having not dated since the dawn of time, I was even more clueless when it came to dating rituals.

So, I did the only thing a dumb baseball player knows to do in such situations.

I stuck out my fist for a bump.

His eyes drifted down, then his head cocked, then one brow raised and the other struggled to decide where to land. Tentatively, he unpocketed his fingers, balled them up, and tapped knuckles.

"Hungry?" I asked, desperate to free us both of the mental molasses I'd poured over us.

He nodded. "I've had an apple fritter, coffee, and a cherry Danish today. I could eat my car tire right now."

I reached across and pulled the door open. "In that case, after you."

The smell of baroque smoked meats and roasted vegetables slammed into me as I followed Coop into the restaurant. Saliva threatened to dribble down my chin as my stomach rumbled louder than the biker who passed by outside. Coop glanced back with an amused twinkle, but held his tongue.

We each grabbed a tray, then slid down the metal counter to ogle a buffet that would make any cafeteria envious. Coop insisted I go first since I'd held the door for him walking in. It was cute, in an I-will-out-Southern-gentleman-you-all-day sort of way.

"Oh, they have mac and cheese . . . and fried okra." I could almost feel Coop vibrating with excitement. "And carrot cake.

We have to get carrot cake. I don't care if you play in the World Series tomorrow, that cake is worth it."

I grinned. "You tryin' to make me fat or something?"

His eyes left a searing trail down my chest. "I think you're doing just fine. One night of warm blanket food won't kill you."

God, the way he looked at me with that lopsided grin and—

"What'll ya have?" a portly woman wrapped in a blue apron asked.

I shook myself free of his gaze and scanned the bar. "How are the ribs?"

She cocked her head, as if examining a bug crawling across her windshield. "You been here before? This is Swett's. We are ribs. They're our thing. You take one bite, and if you don't wanna slap your mama, you bring 'em back up here and I'll get ya somethin' else, alright?"

She said that last word with no consonants so it sounded more like "ahhight."

"Deal. Rack 'em up."

She cackled. "Oh, now you done gone and challenged me to pool. You're pretty, but I'll whoop that tight little ass at the pool table."

I felt Cooper's grin as crimson heat clawed its way up my neck to perch on my cheeks. My widened eyes only encouraged the woman, and her cackles filled the place. She didn't ask what veggies I wanted, just filled my plate and handed it over the glass.

"Trust me, hon. You'll like all that." She turned to Coop. "What about you, Peaches?"

I nearly dropped my tray.

When I turned back, Coop was nearly as red as the Swett's sign hanging overhead, and the woman was dabbing her eyes with a cloth she'd had slung over her shoulder.

"I, uh . . . well . . . I would like the . . . uh . . ."

"Spit it out, shugah. Food won't jump over the glass."

That one got me, and I laughed all the way to the pay counter, leaving Coop alone with his torturer, but close enough to hear if she dropped any other pearls I might use later.

"How about mac and cheese, fried okra, and baked beans?"

I peeked out the corner of an eye to watch the woman slop veggies onto his plate, set the metal spoon down, then plant both fists on her hips. "You best not tell me you're one of them vegetarians. I think I ate one of them for lunch today."

The cashier and I both lost it then. Warm wetness trailed down my cheek. The kid handling the register, who was laughing nearly as hard as I was, handed me a napkin and motioned to the tears. He then glanced at my plate and tossed a few towelettes and another stack of napkins onto the corner of my tray.

"You'll need those for the ribs," he said.

Behind me, I heard Coop finally order. "Fried catfish with extra tartar, please."

A moment later, he joined me at the register. I reached back for my wallet, but he grabbed my wrist and shook his head.

"My invite, my bill."

A jolt streaked up my arm at his firm grip.

"Aw, Coop, you don't have to—"

"Please, I want to. You can get the next one."

I was suddenly torn between admiring the boldness in his assumption we'd have a next dinner, and terrified by how thrilled I was that he wanted to see me again. I knew Coop was gay. Miguel had told me as much. I had no idea what he thought about me. I'd stayed so deep in the closet for so long, I doubted many of my closest teammates suspected I might like guys. They seemed to buy the "I'm married to baseball" line because most of them felt the same way, even if they still dated or messed around. Baseball was not a sport of saints.

Getting to know Cooper felt like treading on some unseen line that either started or ended something, and I couldn't tell what that something was. I'd made a promise to myself not to date until I wore a major league jersey. Only after I reached that mountaintop would I give my personal life room to breathe and grow. I wasn't usually one to overthink, but this dinner felt more like a date than two guys hanging out, and I wasn't sure how I felt about that—or if I was ready to . . .

As the kid handed him back his change, the serving woman's voice drifted over the glass. "Smooth, Peaches. Real smooth."

I had to hustle behind as Coop did an Olympic fast-walk into the dining room.

"You alright? You look a little rosy in the cheeks . . . Peaches." I tried to look innocent and concerned. It took a second for his glare to shift into amusement.

"I seem to recall you not wanting certain nicknames to make it back to your teammates."

I nodded and grinned. "Sounds like we've got a little *mutually assured destruction* going on here. Makes us both safer."

"Alright, Mr. Reagan."

"Hey, that's Mr. President, thank you very much."

"So." His tone shifted to pensive. "You know a little history?"

"Think I was just a hunky piece of baseball meat?"

That earned a laugh. "You're a piece of something, that's for sure."

I liked this side of Coop: playful and teasing. He was freakin' sharp as they came and wasn't afraid to throw an elbow—but I could tell it was just playful banter.

His eyes closed, and he groaned as the first spoonful of mac and cheese vanished into his mouth. "Oh god, that's better than I remembered."

Without thinking, I reached my fork across the table and snatched a bite. His eyes widened as they trailed my fork up and into my mouth.

"Holy crap, that really is good," I said.

He looked down at his plate, then back up at me. "Did you just—"

"Family style, my friend. What's yours is mine, at least if it's on the table. Those are team rules."

"Team rules? Did you just make that up?"

I plastered on my most innocent, puppy-in-a-store-window face. "I would never."

He punctuated his smirk with an overly dramatic eye roll, but all I could see were the dimples nuzzling into his cheeks. They were the most adorable things ever to grace a guy's face, and I wanted to pinch—no, I wanted to kiss them.

Damn, I wanted to kiss Coop.

An army of centipedes wearing tiny tap shoes on each of their hundred feet clickety-clacked from my neck, down my chest, to camp out in the forest of curly—

"So." Coop made all the little critters still and turn toward him. "You sound a lot better today."

"What do you mean?"

"The other day, you said you were having a really bad one. I don't know, in the DMs, it sounded like you were pretty miserable about something."

I grabbed the ribs, failing to keep barbecue sauce from coating my fingers. My face echoed Coop's mac and cheese ecstasy, complete with an eye squeeze and groan.

"Oh, man, you've gotta try these," I said, holding the remains of my half-eaten rib across the table.

His gaze followed the rib, then his brow furrowed, and he looked up.

"You're not shy about sharing, are you?"

"Nope." I swallowed the last bit of meat. "I'm around hot, sweaty messes all day. There really aren't many barriers inside a team. Guess I'm used to somebody grabbing food out of my hand to take a bite."

"Like a big family of brothers?"

I nodded. "Exactly like that. Most days, we get along great, but sometimes I want to strangle them. Just like brothers."

We ate in silence a moment, save for the moans each time Coop took another bite of his cheesy goodness. Watching him made me smile. He took such pleasure in the simplest things without letting adulthood complicate or burden his joy.

"What about you? Get everything done today? Sounded like you were really up against it."

He nodded. "Yeah. This was a pretty big deal. I guess I should be flattered that Raj—he's my boss—knew he could count on me, but the whole thing was a mess. I mean, literally, it was a mess I had to clean up—and he was *such* an ass about it. All he had to do was ask and I would've helped, but he had to blow up at me, like I was the one who'd screwed up."

As he spoke, his shoulders slumped, and the light that shone so brightly in his eyes dimmed. This was only the third time I'd seen Coop in person, but each time, and in our Insta conversations, he'd been a bundle of excitement and innocent vibrance. There was a delicate strength to him, an odd dichotomy, beautiful and endearing.

An overwhelming desire to wrap my arms around him, to protect and shield him from anyone who might hurt him or steal his light, flooded through me. I was suddenly furious at this Raj guy—and I didn't even know him. Hell, I barely knew Cooper.

"So why stay?"

His head cocked. "Huh?"

"If Raj is such an ass, why keep working for him? You're a sharp guy. I bet you're really good at your work. There have to be other places where you'll be appreciated and treated with respect."

He blinked once, then again, then blushed, and his eyes fell to his plate.

"Thanks," he muttered. "Sorry, guess I'm not great at compliments."

And just like that, the furry tap routine returned to my chest. I didn't fully understand it, but Coop's unassuming nature and humility drew me toward him, made me crave his smile, that blush, those dimples. His hand rested on the table, and I wanted to reach across and smother it, to soothe his pain, to feel his warmth and offer him mine.

Then the woman behind us coughed, and one of the kids to the right dropped a fork to the floor, and I remembered we sat in the center of a public place, surrounded by people with eyes and cameras and social media accounts, the latter being the most problematic for a well-closeted pro athlete, and I shifted in my seat.

Coop's stare intensified. "You okay?"

"Oh, yeah, good. Anyway, what were you saying?"

He eyed me a second longer, then picked up his fork. "Raj is okay, and I really like our company. It was just a rough week, I guess."

"What do you like about it? Your company, I mean. I've never worked in an office."

"Huh. Guess you haven't. I hadn't thought of that." He grinned through a bite of beans. "The company's huge, but feels like a small family most of the time, and our primary mission is better healthcare, which makes me feel good about what we do. I'm nowhere near the actual care or patients, but somebody has to run the numbers."

"Feel like you're helping patients in your own way?"

"Yeah, something like that. We get a bad rap because some people just hate big companies, no matter what they do. I try not to let them get to me. The good definitely outweighs the corporate greed."

His fork hovered over the beans, then shifted to scoop mac and cheese. I couldn't suppress a grin at the inner battle that must've been playing out in his head, complete with a rambling monologue.

"What about you? Why baseball?"

"Why would I ever want to do anything else?" I grinned and crossed my arms. "I love it, always have. There's something about walking out onto a freshly dragged field, smelling the cut grass, stepping over the crisp lines. It just feels . . . like home. It's where I belong."

He kept shoveling, which gave me a moment to daydream.

"And there's the team. There's nothing like being bound to a group of guys through a shared goal. In our case, it's a shared dream of making it to the majors, and our best chance of that is to play well together, as a unit. Standouts will always make it, but for most of us, we have to show we can mesh well, be good partners to eight other guys, pull our weight. There's a brotherhood forged when you practice together, play together, travel, eat, and everything else together—and we do that seven or eight months out of the year. Hell, most of us hang out in the off-season too."

"I don't know what having a family is like."

His voice was an echo of unspoken memories.

I wasn't sure how to respond, so I waited and watched.

His eyes grew distant as he set his fork down. He was no longer looking at me, but past me, into a time and place far removed from the restaurant, or even Nashville.

"I thought we were a family. Mom said we were. It wasn't always easy, not with their lifestyle and all, but we were together . . . until they passed me off."

He kept staring over my shoulder into the darkness of the corner, seeing nothing, yet everything.

"Do you still see your parents?" I ventured.

His head shook ever so slowly. "No. I haven't talked to either of them since I was fifteen. Mom called me on my birthday, said she was coming to see my next tournament."

I watched as the memories in his mind darkened the features of his face.

"She never came. I remember walking out onto the mats, scanning the crowd. Grammy and Pop were there, but the seats next to them were empty." His eyes finally fell to the table. "She never called again. Grammy said she tried, but . . . I guess she was over having a son."

It felt like I was intruding on the most sacred of ground, the deepest, most intimate memories. It felt wrong to press forward, but my heart ached to know more. "What about your dad?"

He chuckled wryly, and his eyes rolled. "He called once, when I was twelve, I think. Out of the blue."

His voice drifted again. "I was outside, playing with some neighbor kids, soccer or something with a ball. I wasn't very good, but didn't have many friends . . . Grammy called out. I can still hear her shouting across the yard that my dad was on the phone. It felt like the whole world just froze. I couldn't think. I remember her hand landing on my shoulder, but never saw her walk toward us."

"Did you talk to him?"

He shook his head again. "No. I begged her to tell him she couldn't find me."

"Wow, Coop, I'm sorry."

He shrugged and glanced up, the light dancing off the moisture clinging to his ocean-like eyes. "Grammy and Pop became my family, and they were amazing."

He eyed my plate. "You still have work to do."

I'd been starving when we arrived but still had a healthy hunk of rib left when I tossed my napkin onto my plate in surrender. Coop was practically licking his plate clean.

"Where do you put it all?" I shook my head in wonder, allowing him to lead us away from such delicate topics.

He leaned back and patted his stomach. "Gotta keep a growin' boy . . . um . . . growin'?"

His face flushed at the flub of whatever joke he was trying to tell, and I swear his dimples deepened.

Without a word, he shoved his dinner plate aside and slid the carrot cake into its place. Dessert fork in hand, he sliced off a piece, then raised it slowly to his lips, peeking up to make sure I was watching. His tongue teased around the edges, lapping up cream cheese. A little stuck to his upper lip.

I leaned in and rasped, "Are you trying to seduce me? Right here in the middle of Swett's?"

His fork slipped. He tried to save it, but only managed to shove cream cheese all over his mouth as the fork clanked off his plate and the remaining cake disappeared into his lap. I wasn't sure whether it was the wounded look on his face, the thought of him picking cake out of his crotch, or the Groucho Marx-like smear of a cream cheese mustache that cracked me up more.

"Smooth, Casanova. Real smooth."

"I . . . I don't know what you're talking about. I was just eating my cake because you didn't want any, but I wanted to make sure so I went slow to give you time to change your mind, but then the cake fell and I dropped my fork and . . . what?"

I pointed to my lips and tried—poorly—to stop laughing. "You have a cream cheese 'stache still."

His fingers flew to his mouth only to be coated by sugary sweetness. He stared down in horror for a second, frozen, so I pressed my advantage.

"Want me to lick it off?"

His eyes bulged, then darted from his fingers to me, then back to his fingers. I could feel his pulse racing from across the table. It sounded like drums booming over the mountain as Barbarian hoards readied a charge.

I couldn't torture the poor guy anymore, so I stood and said, "I need to use the bathroom before we go. Be right back."

Halfway across the dining room, I glanced back to find him still staring after me, white-coated fingers still held before his face, mustache smear intact.

Nineteen

COOPER

It's pretty common knowledge that I don't hold back well. When something pops into my head, it inevitably tumbles out, sometimes in a jumble of words that threaten to drown anyone nearby. I'm sure there's a fancy technical term for it, but no one's ever told me what it is. AJ calls it "spewing," and that sums it up fairly well.

What I've never done well, or often, is share highly personal experiences, thoughts, or—heaven forbid—feelings. (I had to suppress a shudder just then.)

As I watched Nate cross the dining room, enjoying each step as his butt shifted in his jeans, I realized I'd just blown verbal chunks all over the hottie I was, well, hot for.

And that wasn't even the strangest part of our date (or whatever it was—I still hadn't figured that out).

For once in my life, I was having a normal conversation with an awesome guy without prattling on like a DVR whose fast-forward button got stuck, and then, out of the blue, my inner psycho decided to rear his head and spill the most painful, darkest memories I had of my parents as they walked out the door and stomped on my ideas of what family should be.

What the hell? Who does that?

What's worse, I realized in a blinding moment of post-mac-and-cheese clarity, I'd *wanted* to share with him. He'd been so sincere, so empathetic, so . . . not a jerky jock—not that he'd ever acted like that toward me. He hadn't, but I'd never expected him to go all Mr. Sensitive on me and open his shoulder for all my tears.

Why was I such an emotional sap?

I ran my fingers through my hair, wondering if I'd just blown it with the first guy in years to make me hope . . . Who was I kidding? For all I knew, the guy wasn't even gay, just a good man who saw a friend crumbling before him.

"Ouch," I said. Apparently, my fingers-in-hair thing had turned violent. Now my scalp hurt almost as much as my chest.

"You okay?"

My knees banged the table as I jumped at Nate's voice.

"Whoa," he said through a chuckle. "Didn't mean to startle ya."

I settled back into my chair and tried to calm what was left of my highly frayed nerves.

"It's okay. I was just thinking and when that happens sometimes I get lost in a deep place and don't really see or hear anything around me and that's when someone, like you, could come up and scare the ever-loving shit out of me because I was thinking about something else that definitely wasn't you."

One blink. Then another.

"I just did it again, didn't I?"

I prayed silently, *God, please stop my mouth from moving—ever again. Put a holy sock in it, or something equally silencing and theologically appropriate to stop a rambling idiot.*

Nate smiled. "Wanna get out of here?"

"Yes, please."

The sun had set while we'd eaten. The humidity still felt like walking through Elmer's Glue, but it was a moderately warm glue, rather than the blazing hot kind we'd felt earlier in the day.

"How do you play in this? I'm already drenched," I said.

He shrugged. "I'd say we get used to it, but that'd be a lie. I guess, when I'm on the field, I kind of zone out everything that isn't baseball. Does that make any sense?"

"Yeah. Kind of like tae kwon do, especially at the black belt sparring levels. Let your concentration slip for a second and a foot slams into you."

Nate glanced at his phone. "It's nine. I don't have to be up early, but you probably have to be at work at some crazy hour."

"Nope. I got my reports done, printed, bound, and emailed. I already told Raj I was taking the morning off."

Nate's face brightened. "Does that mean I can take you some-where else now?"

We'd reached our cars, so I turned and leaned against mine, eyeing him. He actually looked like he wanted to spend more time together.

"Uh, sure. What did you have in mind?"

"Can I surprise you?"

"Um, okay. Does this involve throwing icy Gatorade on my head?"

He barked a laugh. "No. Why would I want to do that?"

"Isn't that what you pros do to each other?"

His eyes grinned. "We've been known to douse a teammate or coach, but that's usually saved for celebrations. I try not to douse civilians, especially cute ones I like spending time with."

Oh shit. Shit, shit, shit, shit, shit.

He just said—

"Are you okay with that? I mean, I've had a nice time tonight." His brows knitted, then he said, "I know it couldn't have been easy or comfortable, but I respect you for telling me about your parents, about your family."

My mouth went completely dry, and I forgot to breathe, then my eyes fell to my shoes.

"Come on. I'll drive. This place is on the way back, so we can get your car then."

I was numb, unsure whether to follow or object or pass out, because this freakin' hot man just said he was glad I'd dumped all my shit on him. He *respected* me for it.

Of all the words . . . of all the things he could've said . . . to *respect* me? For what? For being honest? For sharing things that hurt me so deeply, I was afraid to face them alone, much less share them with anyone else?

I didn't know why I told him all those things. I hadn't talked about them in years, not with Grammy or Pop, not with AJ, not with anyone. I'd relived those conversations a thousand times in my dreams. They always ended the same, with tears and an aching cavity left by the loss of parents who didn't find me worthy.

I hated giving them so much power, so much control over my heart. I was a grown-ass man. I should be able to control my emotions, my feelings, my goddamn pain. I should be able to heal and move on without unloading on other people. I shouldn't have to share. Hell, I'd promised myself I would never share any of that—with anyone.

But I'd shared them with him.

With Nate.

And he *respected* me for that.

"You coming?" he asked from the driver's side of his car.

"Oh, yeah, sorry."

Nate made me cover my eyes halfway through our ten-minute drive.

"No cheating." The playful tone in his usually stoic voice made my heart flutter more than it had at any point in the evening. He was really enjoying this—whatever *this* was.

He slowed, then rolled forward a bit, then pulled to a stop, and shut off the engine.

"Okay, we're here, but don't peek. We've got to go inside and down a couple hallways before we get where we're going. Do you need a blindfold?"

I snorted. "I think I can manage keeping my eyes shut, but you'll have to make sure I don't walk off any cliffs."

"I won't let you do that. It would ruin the surprise when I push you off."

He was teasing, and I knew it, but that still sent a jolt of nerves through my chest.

The warm rumble of his laughter settled them quickly.

"Hey, Billy," I heard him say without slowing our pace.

Billy, I assumed, mumbled back, "Late night?"

Nate whispered something I couldn't make out, and I thought Billy laughed or coughed. I wasn't sure which, and I wasn't sure which was more disconcerting.

Our footfalls echoed as we trekked down a long hallway. The brightness of street lights and whatever had lit the parking lot no longer seeped through the edges of my hands, cloaking my vision in near darkness beneath my palms. One of Nate's hands gripped my arm, while the other was wrapped around my shoulder, hugging me into him. It might've been dark wherever we walked, but the light filling my mind was blinding. I could've died happy in that moment, with his arm around me, clutching me, guiding me, holding me close.

I stumbled.

"I've got you." He held me tighter, and the balminess of his breath tickled my ear. My knees went a little weak at that sensation.

We walked another twenty or so steps before stopping. The comfort of his arm vanished, and I heard him step in front of me.

"Stay there. I need to open a couple doors for us. Be right back."

Before I could protest, a door opened and closed, leaving me standing alone in darkness with my hands over my eyes. I suddenly felt silly, a grown-ass man playing peek-a-boo or whatever. Then my mind raced with possibilities of what Nate's surprise was. Where had he taken me? There weren't any smells to trigger a memory. When we'd entered, it felt underground, but we hadn't descended as we'd traversed the hall. I listened carefully, hoping to pick up something, anything, but I was surrounded by a silence as complete as my blindness.

I was so tempted to peek. God, I wanted to, but tae kwon do had taught me respect and discipline. Nate had given me respect earlier, so I would return it, along with a healthy dose of discipline in the face of excruciating curiosity.

The door groaned again.

"Alright, the coast is clear. Two more doors and we're there."

Strong hands found their homes again, and I resisted the urge to melt right there.

The funny thing was, I still didn't even know if he was gay, or if this was a date, or if he was just a really cool friend who liked to surprise his other friends. That sounded weird when I thought it out loud—well, out loud in my head, which really wasn't out loud, but it sounded that way when I thought it because it's more of a voice talking than me thinking, which made it sound out loud.

Jesus, I was babbling in my brain.

Click.

The second of the two doors shut behind us, and the summer night's air filled my lungs again—along with the smell of . . . something familiar—freshly cut grass?

"Have you brought me somewhere to cow tip?"

I felt his chest heave with laughter and he nearly let go of me.

"Cow tipping? Of all the things I could surprise you with, *that's* your first guess?"

His arm-wrap released as he pressed a hand into the small of my back, urging me forward. Grass crunched under my tennis shoes.

One step, two, then ten, then twenty. *Crunch, crunch, crunch* . . .

Thud.

The change in sound and feel beneath my feet was disconcerting, and lasted for a whopping three strides.

"Okay, stop. Now turn around." His hands wheeled me about, then I felt him release me and step a few feet to one side. "Now, open your eyes."

I did as he commanded, dropping my hands and raising my chin to peer around . . . at ten thousand empty chairs staring back at me. The ballpark was dimly lit around the edges, with only the light of the nearly full moon smiling on the grass and dirt. Nate had positioned me just in front of the rubber on the pitcher's mound, and I stared at home plate, the luxury box, the rows and rows of blue seats riveted into concrete.

The stadium hadn't felt particularly large when seen from a spectator's position, but here, where professionals played, it felt like a world unto itself.

My head turned, taking in first base, the dugout, the on-deck circle, then scanning back to where pitchers warmed up. They called that the bullpen, I think. Baseball had been a distant thing, a game played by others that barely interested me, but then, standing on that mound, it felt real and strangely personal. Add the moonlight, evening air, and presence of my favorite Sound, and First Horizon Park was simply magical.

"Well?" Nate sang his first tentative note of the evening.

"It's beautiful."

I turned to see Nate's smile light up the night.

"I love it here at night, when no one else is around. On a night off like this, the groundies get most of their work done early, so the place is empty except for a few guards and late crew."

It was like watching twelve-year-old Nate stepping onto a field. The wonder in his eyes and the joy in his voice was infectious, and I found my own smile nearly matching his.

"Come here." He grabbed my arm and pulled me off the mound toward the gap between first and second base. "This is where I work. This is my office."

He assumed his ready position and patted the palm of an imaginary glove, then tipped the imaginary bill of his imaginary cap.

The whole thing made my heart do an Irish jig.

"You really love it, don't you?"

"More than anything." He straightened. "I don't know how to explain it. When I'm out here, nothing else matters. There's no news barking or people fighting; the whole world fades away, and it's just me, my team, and that ball. Our opponents don't really even matter, only the ball. There's a lot to be said about focusing on something so simple."

"I get that. Tae kwon do gives me those moments of peace and clarity, of singular focus."

"Yes! That's it. Singular focus. I really like that."

I beamed at his praise like a golden retriever about to receive a treat, at once feeling stupid and silly—and overwhelmingly happy.

"Can I give you the tour?"

"There's more than this?" I waved a hand around the field.

He chuckled. "Well, nothing compares to the garden, but there are some other cool secrets in this castle."

"I feel like we're off to slay a dragon and rescue a princess."

He clapped me on the back. "Come, Frodo. Mordor awaits."

"Uh, Nate, there are no dragons, or princesses for that matter, in *Lord of the Rings*."

"Oh, my dear Cooper, how wrong you are. There were multiple kings, several with daughters, which, by definition, made them princesses. One might even argue the princess of the horse kingdom needed rescuing, since her father was under the spell of an evil wizard for a time. As for dragons, there were the giant eagles at the ending, and Tolkienologists might argue that Nazgul shared distant relations with beasts not unlike dragons. Though you are correct, there were no traditional dragons in the Great Work."

"The Great Work?" I was trying really hard not to laugh at his extraordinarily serious, scholarly tone that suddenly morphed into horrified offense.

"How else could one refer to JRR Tolkien's masterpieces?"

At a loss for any intelligible reply, I said, "You surprise me, Mr. Stringer."

"There is so much more to this pickle than just a cucumber."

I lost all resistance and spit-laughed all over his shoulder.

"Great, now I'll be thinking about your cucumber . . . or pickle . . . all night."

Then I realized I might've just come on really hard to a straight guy. Heat flooded my face, and I braved a peek in his direction as we descended the steps by the players' bench. His smile hadn't fallen. In fact, there was a twinkle in his eyes I hadn't noticed before.

"This is the dugout," he said, doing his best game show helper wave. "Fans know this as the place where we watch our team bat, or sit while we're not playing."

"Why do I get the feeling there's more?" I couldn't wipe the grin from my face.

"This," he said, stepping toward me, "is where we play the best pranks on each other."

"Oh." My mouth actually made an O and froze—because he'd taken another step toward me, so close I could feel his breath on my face.

"Um, are you going to prank me?" I asked, unsure why he had consumed the last inch of my personal bubble. I made to step back, but the cold cement wall fixed me in place. He was only a few inches taller, but it felt like he towered over me, then one of his hands reached up and planted itself on the wall beside my head, hemming me in.

"No," he rasped, as his face inched closer. "I'm not pranking you at all."

And then his lips pressed into mine.

Keys jingled as the dugout door handle rattled. Nate leapt back faster than a base runner checked by a pitcher. By the time the uniformed security guard's head poked through, Nate had already yanked a bat from a nearby bin and was mid-swing, as if showing me how to hit the perfect line drive.

"Oh, hey, Bean," the guard said. Tufts of wiry gray poked out the sides of his blue police-style cap.

Nate stopped his swing and turned toward him. "Hey, Mr. Parker. Doing your rounds?"

"Yeah. Thought I heard voices out here."

"Just us. This is a friend of mine." He motioned toward me with the bat. "Giving Cooper the grand tour."

The guard chuckled and tipped his cap toward me. "Not sure how grand it is, but welcome."

"Thanks," I said, still a bit out of breath and flustered from Nate's surprise lip-lock.

Nate tossed the bat back into the bin and motioned for me to follow him. "We're going to walk through the locker room, then head back out the tunnel. See you tomorrow."

"Yes, sir. You ready for the Mangoes?"

An odd laugh tumbled out of Nate. "I'm not sure anyone's ever really ready for that bunch, but it should be fun."

The guard's face lit up. "Fun is right. I'm actually bringing the grandkids to see the show. The missus wouldn't forgive me if we didn't."

"Doubt the kids'll care much for us boring players when the Mangoes are in town, but bring 'em down if they want some signatures. I'll get the boys to gather round."

"That'd be great. Thanks, Bean."

"Come on, Coop. Let's hit the locker room and leave the yard to Mr. Parker."

Nate clapped the guard on the shoulder as we passed. I smiled and scooted by, unsure of the protocol when passing an armed man in a dugout. We only walked a dozen paces before entering one half of a set of wide double doors with red and blue paint that formed a stylized letter *N* interlocking a massive treble clef.

"This is our locker room." Nate waved his hand around at benches and lockers that could've been found in any gym in America. The only distinguishing features were the players' last names stenciled above each alcove and the interlocking *N* and treble clef painted on the shiny cement floor. The room even held the characteristic smell of game-worn socks and sweaty underarms. Nate grinned when he saw my nose wrinkle.

"You should smell this place after a practice."

"Uh, I'm good, although the mental image of all the players . . ."

He chuckled. "Yeah, the view's nice. Can't argue with that."

"Here." He stepped over to a locker with *Stringer* stenciled across the top. "This is my spot. That's Cal's." He pointed to the seat next to him.

"Cal?"

"He's our first baseman. Also happens to be my roommate, best friend, extended family . . . all that."

"Ah." I scanned Cal's locker to find a word painted in blue script.

"Tutu?"

Nate laughed. "Yeah, that's Cal's nickname. He stretches like a ballerina, so they call him Tutu. It's pretty funny when you know him. He's this six-five beefy guy with legs that stretch for days, nothing about him frilly—except his nickname."

I grinned. "And you're Bean?"

He nodded. "Like a string bean, because I'm long and lanky."

"Sounds like you got away with that one. I could come up with much better—"

"Don't even think about it." His voice was filled with child-like glee belying the words of warning. "These guys don't need any help torturing each other."

"What's a Mango?" I asked.

"It's a tropical fruit, about this big—" Nate was making a mango shape with his hands when I hit him with a nearby towel.

"With reflexes like that, you might fit in around here." He chuckled again as he tossed the towel aside. "The Memphis Mangoes are an exhibition team, kind of like the Harlem Globetrotters but for minor league baseball. They do all sorts of stunts and tricks on field, dance during plays, pull crazy skits, that sort of thing. Even the umps are in on their acts. They're actually a lot of fun. The kids eat 'em up."

"Are they part of the league?"

"No. Think of them like a show. Most of the time, they put on exhibition games in Memphis, playing against their own team in different-colored uniforms. I'm not sure how much they travel, but we play them every other year or so."

"Huh." I tried to picture whatever shenanigans a team like the Mangoes might pull off to make the crowd laugh, but was struggling to grasp the concept.

"You could come. I think Ty and Gabe are bringing Ben, Gabe's honorary younger brother. We have a three-game roadie starting tomorrow, then play the Ms here at home."

That actually sounded fun. I'd hoped to get to know Tyler and Gabe better, but hadn't had the chance.

"Yeah, sounds fun. I'll call the guys and see if they mind a tagalong."

"If not, I know somebody who can get you a ticket," he said with a wink.

I started to make a smart remark, but my thought was rudely interrupted by Nate's lips again. He'd crossed the painted *N* and clasped my face with both hands, planting his mouth on mine so fast I'd barely had time to suck in a breath—not that I cared much about breathing in that moment. A heartbeat later, he pulled back, but continued to hold my face in his hands.

"Sorry I had to dance away in the dugout. Some of the coaches are pretty old school, so I'm still deep in the closet."

A dozen questions swirled through my head, but all that escaped was, "Oh, okay."

"Can you keep all this—I mean, everything—between us?" The confident pro baller I was coming to know vanished, and an utterly terrified little boy shuffled his feet before me. "I should've told you. I mean, I never date. I promised myself I wouldn't until I made it, but you came along, and I just . . . I wanted to get to know you. Coop, I'm sorry. I should've told you. If any of this got out—"

I pressed a hand to his chest. "It's okay. I get it. I won't say anything to anyone."

He blew out a breath and sagged against my palm. There was something—sadness—in his eyes. Of all the things he could feel in that moment, sadness wasn't what I expected and certainly not what I hoped for, but I supposed it made a strange sort of sense, given the world he lived in and how much he had to hide—and lose.

"You ready to go? I've kept you out pretty late on a school night."

He turned, then paused before a locker bearing a stenciled name that appeared to have been recently covered. He reached up and ran his fingers over the blacked-out paint. For the second time in only a handful of minutes, his brows pinched together and a frown darkened his features.

"What's wrong?" I asked.

"I'm not sure."

Twenty

Nate

The drive from Nashville to Memphis isn't long, only around three hours, but it felt eternal. There's very little to see beyond hills and fields of tobacco or other crops that roll like oceans in every direction. Despite the short trip, Coach made us board the bus at 6 a.m., so most of the guys slept.

I stared out the window. Endless fields of corn made me think of Coop's wavy brown hair. I could still feel the heat of his cheeks against my palms, the softness of his lips as I pressed into them. That had surprised me. Mine were always chapped thanks to endless hours practicing beneath the Nashville sun, but his were supple and smooth, and they tasted sweet, like a berry I couldn't quite place.

There was something oddly addictive about Cooper Hawk. He was smart, but not quite nerdy, odd to the point of quirky, and handsome in ways usually reserved for athletes. Though, with his background in martial arts, I supposed he qualified as an athlete. Crap, he could probably kick my ass in three directions without breaking a sweat. I chuckled. That would be worth seeing—or being on the receiving end of—if he'd kiss it and make it feel better afterward.

That thought made something stir downstairs and I had to shift in my seat.

And the guy made me smile more than anyone I'd met in a long time, even when he babbled—*especially* when he babbled. He seemed to get nervous at the silliest things, and that turned normal conversation into an epic event. My cheeks pinched just thinking about his prattle. It was adorable and hilarious, and a dozen other things all rolled into one long, punctuationless sentence—and I loved every minute of it.

I hadn't been looking to meet anyone. In fact, dating was a distraction I'd removed from the menu until I'd made it into the majors. The last thing I needed was to pine over some guy while trying to hit a ninety-miles-per-hour fastball. Add our team's attitude toward the whole gay thing, and dating was a terrible idea.

But here I sat, mooning over a guy with wavy hair and sparkly eyes.

Cal's tongue stuck in his throat as he snored, jarring him awake and shaking me free of Cooper's gaze.

"Sorry," he mumbled, then settled back against the seat, unable to get his giraffe-like frame comfortable in cushions made for average-sized humans.

My eyes drifted across his prone form to rest on the empty seat across the aisle. Nick hadn't boarded with the team, and Coach hadn't called out his name or stomped his usual angry routine when one of us was late. In fact, no one had said anything about Nick, which was more unsettling than if they'd announced he was sick or on the DL and not traveling, the two primary reasons players missed roadies. He could've been traded, but the coaching staff usually gave us a heads-up when that sort of thing happened. Plus, it would've made the local news, and there was nothing on the blogs.

I grabbed my phone and rechecked. Still nothing.

My mind couldn't help but replay the run-ins with Santiago and a few of the others over the past weeks. Good-natured jibes came with the uniform, but they'd been ruthless, almost sounding like they wanted to run him away. Maybe they had. I hadn't pegged Nick for a quitter, but he did look pretty miserable last time I'd seen him. How long could a guy slink in and out before it became too much? Hell, we didn't just work together, we lived, ate, and traveled together too. We did everything as a team.

It would've been a miserable existence for him.

My heart sank as I remembered the look in his eyes. There wasn't simply sadness, but betrayal and grief. It was as if the guys were stealing something from him.

Then it hit me. They *were* stealing something—something precious.

His dream.

Every guy in the locker room had dreamed of the day he would one day play in the majors, Nick included. Here he was, standing on the doorstep of achieving that life's ambition, and homophobic assholes were guarding the entrance, daring him to cross the threshold.

Nick and I weren't particularly close, but he was a good guy, and we shared that dream. I knew what it felt like to want something so badly, to want it more than anything. I knew what it tasted like to be so close, yet feel a million miles away. I knew what it felt like to hide part of yourself as a sacrifice on the altar of that dream.

Maybe I knew Nick better than I'd thought.

"I know that look. You're thinking again." Cal rubbed his eyes and shifted to face me. "Nothing good comes of you using that pea-brain of yours."

I gave him my best eye roll, then smirked.

"Go on, out with it. I can see it's serious." He was now fully awake. There was no escaping once his lasers locked onto their target.

I sucked in a breath, then whispered, "Nick's not on the bus, and Coach didn't wig out."

Cal's voice lowered to barely a breath. "You haven't heard?"

I quirked my brow.

"They traded him. Last night. Got a draft pick or something in return, so we're not adding to the roster right now."

"Traded? Why? He was doing great. Hell, his batting average was—"

"He got caught with a dude."

"What?"

"Some reporter snapped pics of him making out with a guy."

"Shit. Where?"

"I haven't seen them, but the guys said they were at Nick's apartment complex, in the parking lot."

"Wait." I leaned back against the window. "Somebody snaps a pic of him kissing a guy at his own apartment and we drop him? Just like that?"

Cal shrugged. "Sucks, I know, but you know Coach. Worse, the GM was all over it, and he's more old school than Sabro. Even if that's the reason, they'd never admit it. You know how the PR teams are these days, all sunshine and rainbows on the outside. They'll say they needed the draft pick for next season, for team building or whatever. Nobody will care if it was for *the other* reason, not in this town." He was quiet a moment, then said, "Maybe he ended up on a better team, you know—better for him. These guys were real assholes to him."

"Yeah, maybe," I said. "Shit."

I sank back into my seat and stared out the window again. What else was there to say?

Memphis was our perpetual arch-rival. We were in the same league, in the same state, and played each other more than any other team on our schedule. Add to that, their guys were jacked-up bullies who baited us from the moment we stepped onto the field. Even our mascots tussled, and not the good-natured antics one might expect from massive furry friends. The last time Memphis visited Nashville, those two went at it so bad the security guards nearby had to break them up. Kids in the front row were either cheering or crying as the giant redbird (since they were the farm team for the Cardinals) and Booster the Rooster, our mascot, traded winged jabs. Booster won that bout, knocking the cartoon head right off the cardinal before the guards broke things up.

I'd hoped for an uneventful road trip in which our team got its mojo back, but three pitches into the first inning—two of which nearly struck Cal's shoulder—told me this was going to be a long three days. By the time our third batter stepped up to the plate, Coach was already yelling at the ump to toss the Memphis pitcher for intentionally hitting Santi's leg with a fastball. Every Sound in the dugout leaned over the wall, ready to launch themselves onto the field, and the crowd, most of whom wore Cardinal crimson, screamed for their pitcher to "take out another one."

In the midst of this madness, we were still expected to perform. I stuck a tentative foot into the batter's box, dug my toe into the dirt, and ignored the "watch your heel" from the catcher, as he tried to amp up my nerves over the series of not-so-wild pitches that had either hit or nearly hit our guys.

I fouled off the first pitch, let the next two pass for balls, fouled the next into the third base stands, then whiffed on a nasty curve in the dirt to strike out, ending the inning. Our pitcher retired his side without incident, though he did brush one of their guys back to send the message we weren't afraid to play their game if they kept it up.

By the fourth inning, the scoreboard was filled with zeros. This had turned into a pitchers' duel, which put even more pressure on each at-bat to produce. While my first trip to the plate had been fruitless, I'd at least made contact a few times. The only contact I made on my second bout with the pitcher was when I tapped my bat against home plate. Three pitches, three swings, three strikes. Well, they were all actually balls, I just made them strikes by swinging at the air where I hoped the ball would be. Some nights, the ball was a watermelon I could see from the pitcher's hand all the way to my bat. That night, it was a pea I could barely see even after it was safely in the catcher's mitt. Coach turned away from me as I dropped my bat back into the bin and grabbed my glove.

As the bottom of the eighth rolled around, both teams remained scoreless. Memphis had stranded a few runners, while we'd barely managed to put anyone on base. I was dancing with a runner on second, taking checks from our pitcher to keep him honest, when I lost my focus. It was a split-second thing. I'd glanced into the crowd where someone had snapped a photo with a flash. The runner had taken an extra step toward third and our pitcher whirled around, sending the perfect pick-off toward me. The ball zipped below my glove, bounded off second base, and sailed into the outfield. Our center fielder scooped up the ball and hurled it home, but his throw was wide and the runner scored.

That E gave Memphis the lead. My third strikeout a half-inning later finished us off.

"Hey, head up," Cal said as I slumped beside him in the dugout. "Team loss, remember?"

"Yeah," I said without conviction.

No one player won or lost a game. I knew that, but it sure felt like my suck-ass plate appearances and distraction in the field cost us this one. The cold stares I got as we headed into the locker room told me how the other guys felt too. By the time our hotel room door clicked shut and I flopped onto the wiry bed, I wanted to slip away and slink back to Nashville.

I hadn't even realized no one had mentioned Nick's absence, or a trade, or whatever had happened to him. None of the players brought it up, and none of the coaches bothered to explain. Laying there on my bed, staring at the peeling ceiling, I hoped the guy really was in a better place. This one couldn't get much worse . . . or so I'd thought.

The next night was a repeat of the first, only that time I had company in the misery box. Our team set two new franchise records: racking up eight fielding errors in a single game and allowing twenty-four runs by our opponents. Thanks to a dribbler by Santi in the third, we avoided a no-hitter—barely.

Coach shattered two clipboards that night.

Our third day of the roadie began at ten o'clock. We spent two hours taking ground balls like Little Leaguers while the coaching staff glared from the sidelines. They had subs brought in for lunch and gave us a generous fifteen minutes to down them before herding us back onto the field for three more hours of batting and fielding work.

By the time Coach called it quits, we were sweaty and exhausted.

"You have one hour to clean up, eat, and get your asses back here. Drop a ball tonight, and it might be *you* getting dropped tomorrow. Got it?"

Coach could be a real dick, but he rarely issued broad threats. Wide nets caught the wrong fish, so the proverb read. That day, he'd run out of fortune cookie logic and was tossing his net wherever he damn well pleased.

On our last night in Memphis, we pulled out a narrow win. There were no errors, and our batters racked up three runs. Not the impressive thrashing of our opponents we were used to, but a W was a W.

I'd entered the box four times that night. Two ended in strikeouts, but two sent me to first base, one on a walk, while the other was a solid hit over short for a single. There were no rousing speeches from Coach or his staff, but we avoided death stares on the bus ride home.

As good as that minor victory might've felt, none of us cared. We were all exhausted from three days on the road, two miserable games with one decent contest, and five hours of practice. We could do little more than pass out once our butts hit the seats.

Halfway to Nashville, the not-so-gentle buzzing of my phone jarred me awake. I rubbed my neck, unable to ease the throbbing of the bus-sized knot compliments of whatever angle my head tilted at while I slept. The knot resisted, so I surrendered to its pain and punched the screen to open Insta.

HawkEyeBB: Hey, you. How was Memphis? Run into Elvis?

I wanted to sulk, to maintain my miserable mood, but Coop's infectious grin flooded into my mind, and I found myself smiling at the screen.

NateStringerOfficial: It didn't totally suck . . . but it was close.

HawkEyeBB: Aww. Sorry. Want to talk about it?

NateStringerOfficial: Nah. Nothing to talk about. Some games it's just not there. How's your week? How'd that thing with the board go?

HawkEyeBB: Raj submitted the new report a few days ago, but he hasn't bothered to let me know how it went. I guess no news is good news, right?

NateStringerOfficial: Guess so.

HawkEyeBB: You're probably beat. I just wanted to let you know Ty, Gabe, Ben, and I are all set for the Mangoes tomorrow night. Miguel and Sam can't make it, so the box is all ours.

Memphis had been such a miserable trip that I'd forgotten our next game was the exhibition with the Mangoes. I should've been relieved. Those games were a lot of fun, and no one expected anything. The stats didn't count, and winning wasn't even an option. The Mangoes always won. It was part of the show.

But my heart just wasn't in it. I had to find a way to let go of the last three games, to wash the bad taste of Memphis out of my mouth and move forward. We had bad roadies—every team did—but this one felt worse than most. I wasn't sure why. It just did.

NateStringerOfficial: Sounds great. Should be a fun show.

HawkEyeBB: You sure you're okay?

My fingers hovered over the screen, almost typing the stream of consciousness that begged to pour out of me, to be heard and understood, to have someone soothe and comfort. But that wasn't what professionals did. We didn't sulk. We didn't wallow. We picked ourselves up and moved forward. Tough as iron. Hard as nails. Strong as . . . um . . . strong stuff.

NateStringerOfficial: Yeah, I'm good, just tired. See you guys tomorrow night.

Twenty-One

COOPER

I'd been on precisely one pseudo-date with my favorite minor leaguer, but the thought of seeing him again made my heart bounce around my chest faster than a squash ball rebounding off walls. Plus, I got to spend the entire night with Ty, Gabe, and Ben. I didn't know the guys well, and had never met Ben, the twelve-year-old deaf kid Ty had taken under his wing, but Miguel talked about Ty and Gabe like they were the most adorable couple alive, and *that* I had to see, especially since I was pretty sure Miguel and Sam were the cutest couple ever. Those two were saccharine covered in honey dipped in sugar topped with chocolate . . . with a candied cherry on top . . . and whipped cream.

And, just like that, I was hungry.

And nervous.

I knew Gabe and Ben were deaf, but from what Miguel said, Gabe lipread well enough that I likely wouldn't struggle to communicate. Ben was a different story. The kid barely lipread at all, and I didn't know a single sign. I wanted to get to know him, make him feel accepted, but couldn't figure out a comfortable way to navigate, well, anything. How was I supposed to even say hello? Something that simple felt like climbing an insurmountable obstacle.

The doorbell saved me from diving further down the rabbit hole of self-doubt.

I opened the door to find Ty, garbed in a Sounds jersey and jeans; annoyingly hot, as always. Gabe's floppy brown hair poked over his shoulder, while a towheaded youngster peered through the crook of his opposite arm. I could just make out the leather of a child-sized baseball glove on his left hand.

"Hey, handsome. You ready for a fun night at the park?" Ty pulled me into a hug, and I did my best to ignore his frustratingly hard body as it pressed into me. I wasn't into Ty, but I was breathing—and a guy—and his innate hotness was impossible to ignore. The fact he was so freakin' nice made him impossible to hate.

Darn him to the most festive level of gay hell.

Gabe took advantage of my complete immobilization in Ty's arms, leaned forward, and gave me a peck on the forehead like I was a toddler needing a sucker. Rather than demeaning, it was cute in the way only Gabe could manage. Cheeks full of dimples stared up at me as I pulled back.

"This is Ben," Ty said, stepping aside like a theater curtain to reveal an awkward, freckled youngster whose hair was actually more copper than corn. The glove flew to his face, covering everything except his eyes. Those bright blue orbs stared, unwavering, as I kneeled and said, "Hi, I'm Cooper," in an idiotic, exaggerated manner.

Ben glanced back to Gabe, who signed, I assumed, what I'd just said, though the giggle that escaped Ben's lips told me Gabe had likely added his own dimpled touch to the translation.

"He's deaf. Saying it slower won't help. Just talk normally and they'll figure it out. At least, that's how Gabe and I make it work." Ty's hand rested on my shoulder as his sympathetic eyes grinned down.

"Are you ready for the Mangoes?" Gabe asked aloud while signing to Ben.

The boy's face lit up, and his fingers flew. Gabe translated for us.

"He says he can't wait. He's heard about the Mangoes and all the crazy stuff they do, but hasn't ever seen them. Then he went on about some of their dances, and I got lost." Gabe winked at us. "His signs get a little frantic when he's excited."

"Sounds like every kid ever," Ty muttered, and we shared a chuckle.

We piled into Gabe's car and headed to First Horizon, each kid excited for different reasons—and different players they hoped to see.

As we passed the turnstiles, men and women in Sounds T-shirts wearing foam mangoes on their heads handed Ben his own mango head thingy and a mango-shaped baseball that was really a stuffed animal, er, fruit.

Ben's fingers barely stopped signing with Gabe as we ascended the elevator and entered our suite. His eyes were wider than his Mangoes hat as he strode down the line of gourmet stadium food splayed across the tables, then noticed the seats that peered down like the Royal Box at Wimbledon. Gabe's smile never faltered as he ushered the boy around and soaked himself in the excitement of youthful eyes. It was one of the most beautiful things I'd seen in a long time.

"He's good with Ben," I said, more to myself than Ty.

"Yeah, he's pretty awesome."

I turned to find the model-esque mechanic beaming at his boyfriend from across the suite. I watched a moment, sure he would shake out of his stare, but he didn't budge. There wasn't anything in the world that could've stolen his gaze from Gabe in that moment. Gabe, engrossed in whatever conversation he and Ben were having, must've felt Ty's eyes on him, because he glanced up, just for a second. When their eyes locked, I thought fire might bloom right there in the ballpark. In that one glance, that minuscule look, I understood what Miguel had meant about this unlikely pair. They might've been from different worlds, seen things differently, *heard* things differently, yet they were so clearly two halves of a perfectly matched set. In the blink of an eye, I watched hours of conversation pass between them, and my heart soared, and hoped, and dreamed.

"Ladies and gentlemen, it's time to welcome the most fun team in all of baseball to Sounds Stadium. Get on your feet and give these boys a Nashville welcome. Here are the Memphis Mangoes!"

A chorus of voices followed the announcer, most of whom were kids, cheering and screaming; but rather than hearing the *Rocky* theme song or some other equally inspiring tune designed to get competitive juices flowing, the theme from *The Greatest Showman* blasted through the speakers.

"Oh, oh, oh, oh, oh . . . Ladies and gents, this is the moment you've been waiting for!"

Ben ran to the railing and leaned over, pointing at the man in neon green from head to toe, topped off with a top hat somehow greener than the rest of his outfit. A pair of players in Mangoes uniforms stood behind him, waving their arms in choreographed motions to every word and note.

As the song built into the familiar chorus, Mangoes players streamed onto the field from every direction to the screams of thousands of youngsters. Some of them skipped, others pirouetted, while a few played leapfrog with their mates. Cannons boomed in the background, and fireworks blazed beyond the center field wall. In a flash of color and sequins, dozens of teenage girls in bedazzled cheerleader outfits, lime from feet to bow, flipped and flurried their way onto the field, forming a triangle behind the singing ringmaster.

When I thought it couldn't turn into any more of a spectacle, twenty silver-haired women shuffled their way onto the right field line, dancing and waving with every beat. Their uniforms matched the players' but read *Mango Mamas*. Not to be outdone, the Man-Goes filled in the third base line, an assortment of elderly men of every size and shape wearing helmets, everything from mechanic's goggles to *Star Wars* stormtrooper gear, all painted neon green to match their fruity theme. The grannies' dances at least attempted to match the music, while the Man-Goes simply wobbled and waved through their motions.

When the final chorus kicked in, a high school marching band strutted their way onto the field, adding percussion and brass to the festive insanity playing out before us. The players, dancers, grannies, and grandpas converged into a colorful chorus line of motion. Any hint of chaos had vanished, as perfectly choreographed waves and kicks hacked and slashed through the final refrain.

Ben laughed throughout the whole thing, waving his arms in time with the beat, while Gabe giggled like a three-year-old being tickled for the first time. I glanced over to catch Tyler beaming as he watched Gabe and Ben, pride pouring out of him, so strong and free.

It might've been the happiest, funniest, most ridiculous moment of my life.

Then the announcer stilled my heart with, "Now, give it up for your Nashville Sounds!"

The crowd, already hysterical, broke into pandemonium usually reserved for major league playoff games or the World Series. One by one, the announcer introduced the players. I don't remember when I stepped up beside Ben and started clapping, but by the time the voice cried, "Nate Stringer," my hands were smacking above my head and Ben and I were high-fiving.

The players took their positions and began warming up, so Ben and I bumped fists one last time, and I turned back, only then realizing Gabe and Ty had stopped cheering and were staring at me. Gabe, expert in all things requiring signals, crooked a finger and pulled me toward him.

"Uh, hey. Sorry, I got a little swept up. That was so much fun."

"Just wait. That was just the introduction," Ty said.

Gabe now had his arms crossed, never a good sign for, well, a signer.

"You cheered awfully hard for Nate," he said with a raised brow.

Heat flooded my face, and I was sure ten shades of red invaded my cheeks.

"Well, sure. I mean, he's the only player I know. I had to cheer for him, right?"

Gabe cocked his other brow. "Uh-huh. Right."

"Oh, look, they have egg rolls. Be right back." I darted away, hoping Gabe would forget that little exchange and focus on, well, anything else.

The warmth of his shoulder pressing into mine told me he never forgot anything.

"Is there something you need to tell us?"

Shit.

I didn't really know these guys. Why would I need to tell them anything? Whatever was happening with Nate and me was none of their business.

Or was it?

He was Miguel's friend, his little brother in baseball, or whatever they called it. And Miguel and Sam were besties with Gabe and Ty. Maybe they did deserve to know I was crushing all over their boy harder than a slushie machine crushing ice. God, my analogies were awful where Nate was concerned. He made me mushy, like a slushie with grape flavoring. Those were my favorite. They were sweet. Like Nate. He was sweet. But he didn't taste like grape. His lips tasted more like ChapStick, the unflavored kind. He'd have to work on that.

"Hi there." Gabe waved a hand in my face.

"Oh, sorry, I kind of got stuck in my head. What were you saying?"

He giggled. "You like Nate."

Damn. He just said it. It wasn't a question. How was I supposed to respond to that?

I stared down at my egg roll longingly. It needed me. I craved it. We were meant for each other. More importantly, it would keep me from saying something stupid, so I shoved the whole thing in my mouth.

Gabe spit his beer laughing.

When he came up for air (I was still trying to chew, by the way), he said, "I won't say anything. Just know you can talk to us, okay? We're family. If you want, you can be part of our family too." Then he grabbed his beer off the table and turned to take his seat with Ty, leaving me staring after him, speechless, unable to fully close my mouth thanks to having shoved all of China in it.

"Hey, Coop, come on, they're about to start," Ty called from his seat, so I grabbed a fresh beer and joined them to watch the game.

As the first Mango stepped out of the on-deck circle and headed toward the plate, Miley Cyrus's 'Flowers' played over the loud speakers while the batter sang into a long-stemmed white rose as if it were a microphone. When he reached the plate, he presented the flower to the Sounds catcher and gave him a faux kiss on his helmet. The crowd erupted with "Awww," and I got the immediate impression I was the only person in the place who didn't know how every single act would play out.

Crack.

Line drive straight into Nate's glove, a perfect out.

The batter snatched his rose back from the catcher and waved it angrily toward Nate, then stomped off the field toward his dugout like a jilted lover. Booster the Rooster, the Sounds mascot, waved a wing accusingly at Nate, like he'd had the gall to make a play on the poor batter's ball.

The *Footloose* theme song brought the crowd to their feet—and the entire roster of Mangoes out of the dugout to perform a dance number behind the impending batter. Even the umpire wiggled his butt back and forth to the beat as the batter set his stance.

Another inning and a half zipped by before it was Nate's turn to bat. We'd seen all sorts of craziness playing out as the Mangoes danced before pitches, flipped and tumbled around the bases, and even had one batter drop into a split and bat from that painful-looking position.

By the look on his face, Nate hadn't expected the pitcher to strip off his jersey and lead his entire team in a Mangoes version of the chicken dance before flinging a strike past him. By the time the second pitch arrived, the Mangoes had shimmied and thrust their way through a Lizzo tune, and poor Nate was doubled over laughing. With the third pitch, the Mangoes danced to a fast, Chipmunks-voiced version of 'Get Down on It.' This time, Nate was ready, saddling up to the catcher and adding a little spice of his own to their mango salad. He even managed a hit out of that at-bat, knocking that pitch over the second baseman for a single.

The Mangoes found their groove in the eighth inning, knocking in seven runs and lighting up the fans with their electric slide each time a runner touched the plate. Nashville's fiercely loyal home crowd didn't seem to mind losing to their fruity friends from the west, and kids' laughter could be heard from every corner of the parking lot as we made our way back toward the car. Ben barely stopped signing with Gabe, and the smile plastered across his face told me all I needed to know.

The Mangoes had been a hit—literally.

"Sorry we didn't get to go down and see the players," Ty said, his words dripping with barely disguised meaning.

I shrugged. "It's alright. This was so much fun. I'll talk to, um, the players another time."

Ty snorted. "I bet you will."

Ben gave me one last high-five as the guys dropped me off at my place, and we waved to each other as they drove away. It was remarkable how a smile on a little boy's face could warm my soul so much. As I turned to walk inside, my phone rang, and the screen announced an incoming call from *Private Number*.

I didn't usually answer calls from numbers I didn't recognize, but something made me hit the green button this time.

"Hello?"

"Hey, you. Did you have fun tonight?"

I did a happy dance right there on my doorstep.

Twenty-Two

Cooper

"Hey, you," I echoed.

"I saw you guys at the game. How'd you like the Mangoes?"

"Oh . . . my . . . gawd. Nate, that was the most fun I've had in ages."

His easy laugh drifted through the phone. "Yeah, they're a riot."

"And you, mister, shaking your booty with their music. What was all that? I mean, it's a nice booty and all, but really."

I swear I could *hear* him blushing. "What can I say? They're a lot of fun, and their catcher was egging me on. If you think they're silly from the stands, you should hear the crap they say to us on the field, baiting us to play along with their shenanigans."

Nate and I had talked several times, mostly via DM exchange, and he was usually reserved and understated. That night, his enthusiasm was off the chart. I'd never heard him so geared up.

"I know it's late, and you probably had a long day, but I really want to see you."

I nearly jumped through the phone . . . and passed out . . . and resurrected . . . all at the same time. He wanted to see me! He missed me. Holy cow and sheep and every other farm animal imaginable! Although, I'm not into farm animals. That's kind of sick. Though, whatever. Be free. Enjoy your bestiality, if that's your thing and you're not cruel but love your furry friend. Eww. Sorry. That still sounds terrible and sick. Maybe that's where my acceptance of others draws a line? Is there even a letter in the endless gay acronym for guys into sheep or horses? Is that what the plus stands for?

"Coop? You still there?"

I startled, shooing images of fluffy, well-satisfied sheep out of my head.

"Oh yeah, sorry. Drifted for a second. I'm not tired, not at all. Come over."

There was a heartbeat of a pause.

"To your place?"

"Yeah, why not?"

Another silent moment.

"Sorry, I'm not afraid of coming to see you, but . . . could people see me . . . you know . . . parking in your lot or walking in?"

Shit. He was freaked out about being seen visiting a guy late at night. I should've thought of that. Nobody wanted to snap my picture and plaster it on the front page of the sports section, but he lived his life in an ever-expanding bubble . . . or was that ever-shrinking? I was unfamiliar with bubbles and their properties.

"Well, I do live in an apartment complex. I guess someone could see you, but most of my neighbors are pretty low key. It'll be eleven by the time you get here, so I doubt—"

"Okay. Screw it. I really want to see you. I'll just be careful."

My heart did a somersault, then I gave him my address and directions for entering the gated complex.

Twenty minutes later, a tall guy in a hoodie, a Mangoes ball cap, and sunglasses stood at my door. I couldn't help the snicker that emerged as I turned the handle.

"You're not conspicuous at all," I said. "You've either just robbed the 7-Eleven, or you're here to rape me."

He whipped off his sunglasses as he slipped inside the door.

"I'd never rape you, but the thought of—"

"Nathaniel Stringer!" I said with mock offense. "I'm a gentleman. I'd never allow—"

And, continuing his streak of interrupting me with his lips, Nate grabbed me roughly by the shoulders, pulled my body into his, and locked our lips in a desperate, ravenous kiss.

I was too surprised to resist. As if . . .God, his lips were full and juicy . . . and tasted like cherries this time. I loved cherries. Their sweet juice oozed into my mouth as his tongue snuck its way inside me, probing, stroking, curling around my own tongue. My head spun, and I might've tipped over if Nate's strong arms hadn't been locked so tightly around me. I melted into his strength, into his passionate touch.

This man wanted me.

He wanted *me*.

I giggled through our kiss, breaking his spell, and he pulled back with a brow raised.

"Sorry." I couldn't stop giggling. "It's just . . . I just . . . I can't . . . You're here."

He raised my chin with a finger, forcing our eyes to meet. There was such warmth and joy in his gaze.

"Yeah, I'm here. I've wanted to be here all week."

"Really?"

He nodded. "I couldn't stop thinking about you on this roadie. It sucked so bad. I sucked. The only time it didn't feel awful was when I thought about you."

I opened my mouth to say something, though I don't know what would've come out if I could've spoken. My breath froze in my throat, and whatever thoughts rattled around in my head stilled. His eyes were all I could see or feel. I wanted to dive into those pools and never surface.

"I . . . um . . . I missed you too," I said, and his smile became the brightest sun.

He leaned in and kissed me again, this time gentle yet passionate, like a mother's hand stroking an infant's cheek, so soft and pure, so loving. I barely knew this man, yet he poured himself into that kiss and I felt he'd lived inside me my whole life.

How can moments feel like that? How can someone enter your life and, like the flip of a switch, become part of your every hope and dream? Damn, I was dramatic. It was a kiss—a really good one—but just a kiss. It was silly to think—

"I want to know everything about you, Coop." I shuddered as he traced a finger along my cheek.

"I'd really like . . . I mean . . . I want to know you too . . . but you can know me, of course . . . I mean, if that's what you . . . I'll tell you anything, everything . . . but you'll have to ask because I'll forget stuff and asking reminds me—"

His grin widened as I struggled with a bout of verbal diarrhea, then he ended my flailing with another kiss. His fingers tangled in my hair, pulling my head back, and fire bloomed across my neck as his lips, then his teeth, dragged across my tender skin.

"Oh god, Nate. Couch—now."

He grunted. "Bossy little thing, aren't you?" Then he lifted me off the ground and laid me on the couch. Holy shit. I'm not small, and he just picked me up and dumped me like a rag doll. That turned me on more than anything so far.

And then he laid on top of me, and the weight and heat of his body, and the hard throbbing beneath his jeans, sent my mind into a spiral of sensations I hadn't felt in years—maybe ever.

"Fuck, Nate!"

"Is that a statement or a request?" he growled.

"Shiiiiiiit!" was all my pea-brain let me say.

"Good. A request. I'm here to serve, m'lord." His terrible British accent mixed with his wolfish rumble made me chuckle again.

"Oh, now you've done it. Laughing at my accent is punishable by . . ." and he dug evil digits into my sides. My back arched and I howled as he found one ticklish spot after another. What am I saying? My whole body was one giant ticklish spot, and he took far too much pleasure in discovering how useless I became when poked . . . in the sides (not in happy places . . . yet).

"Wow. Feels like you've got some abs under there," he said, sitting up and giving me a moment to breathe.

I shrugged. "See for yourself."

Nate wasn't a guy you had to ask twice. He sat me up, grabbed the bottom of my T-shirt, and ripped it over my head. I barely saw it sail across the living room to land against the far wall.

"Holy shit, Coop." His eyes widened as he took in my torso. "I'm a pro athlete and I don't have a body like this. Hell, none of the guys on the team have abs on their sides. Fuck! Why didn't you tell me you had the body of a god?"

I think my toes blushed at that.

"I like to stay in shape, I guess."

He shook his head. "Cooper Hawk, you are way past *in shape*. Your body puts mine to shame, and I'm *in shape*. Holy crap, you're stunning." He ran a hand over my arm like he might break it if he pressed too hard. "I knew you were fit. I could feel it through your shirt, but damn . . ."

My blush deepened, and I had no words. Absolutely zero words.

I don't remember how long we sat there like that, me on my back, shirtless, with Nate sitting on my legs, touching my body, tracing the muscles of my chest and arms and abs. It was such a simple moment, free of expectation or sex or anything else. Just Nate touching me, exploring me, feeling me . . . and me giving him permission to find his way, any way he chose. Intimate didn't describe those moments. Sensual was an insult. They were everything at once, and only a prelude.

"I want to see you," I said, almost breathless as his fingers grazed my nipples again and again.

"It's your job to take what you want," he said, with mischief in his eyes.

So, I returned the favor, gripping his shirt, pulling it over his head, then tossing it to lie beside mine somewhere on the who-the-fuck-cares side of the room.

That's when I saw Nate for the first time. His skin, the color of walnut and cinnamon somehow melded into the perfectly rich flavor of sweet and savory . . . if one ate wood . . . which sounded strange when I thought about it.

I traced the outline of his pecs, and smiled as he shuddered as I had done with his first touch.

"Am I okay?" he asked, and I swear there was an insecure little boy staring down at me.

"Nate, you're beautiful," I said, with wonder in my voice.

His smile returned, and my soul glowed.

"Can I ask you something?"

He cocked his head. "Sure. Ask me anything."

"Your skin is so perfect. Where . . . I mean, are you—" God, how do I even ask this without sounding like an asshole?

He nodded, understanding. "My mom is Peruvian, and my dad is African American."

"Wow. That sure makes a handsome baby. I mean, you're not a baby. I didn't mean to imply—"

He leaned down and kissed me again. "Thank you. Your mom and dad didn't do too bad themselves."

I blushed again, and my eyes drifted away from his.

"What was that?"

"What?"

"You looked away, like you went somewhere else."

I wanted to sit up, to toss him off and run to the bedroom, anything but talk about my parents any more than I already had with this amazing man who probably wouldn't understand what it's like to not have the perfect family.

"Talk to me, Coop. What are you thinking? Is it your parents?"

He lowered himself beside me and wedged his body between me and the back of the couch, wrapping his arms around me while his hand gently stroked my hair.

I stared into his eyes, entranced by the gray horizon.

"You don't need to hear all about a sad little boy whose parents didn't want him."

I wasn't sure why I said that, why I chose to share something so bleak, so riddled with sadness and pain. I guess that's how I really felt about my childhood, but did Nate need to know that? What was I doing?

Nate didn't falter. "I want to understand."

So, I began to speak. And once I started, I couldn't stop, and the whole story of my early journey tumbled out. A few times, Nate reached up and wiped a tear from my cheek with his thumb, but he never interrupted. In fact, he never spoke, only held me as I painted on the canvas of my life.

When I finally ran out of words—and tears—we lay like that for eternal moments. His fingers entwined in my hair, stroking, soothing, offering comfort and compassion in ways I hadn't known, yet somehow instinctively knew were possible from him.

"I'm such a mess," I finally said, breaking our silence.

He wriggled his other arm free from beneath me and cradled my face in his palms. "You're a wonderful, amazing, incredible mess, Cooper Hawk."

And in those simple words, and the earnestness of his boundless gaze, something inside me knitted together. It sounds nuts, but I felt it. I believed him. For the first time in my life, despite all my success and accomplishment, I *believed* I was something special.

Nate helped me believe.

A tear rolled unchecked down my cheek as I leaned forward and kissed him, gently at first, trembling. His hands pressed against the sides of my head, and I felt his strength willing itself into me. My chest filled, and passion overcame pride as tenderness made way for desire. Our tongues met, and my skin tingled. Nate's hands fell from my face to my arms, then wrapped around me, pulling me into him, kneading my muscles and digging into my skin. I rolled to lie on top of him, rubbing our chests together, grinding my hips in sensuous circles as we both stiffened.

"Coop," he groaned.

I pressed my weight down on him, ground my cock into his through his jeans, felt it throbbing again. His hands slid to my ass, squeezing and pressing me harder against him. I could feel the slickness as pre-cum welled in my shorts, and the last of my resistance fell away.

I reached down, tore the button open, and unzipped his jeans. There was no underwear barring my access, so I gripped his cock and held it as he arched his back and groaned.

"Yes, Coop."

He grabbed the top of my shorts and yanked them down. I had to straighten on my knees, then wriggle out of them. He watched with widening eyes as my rigid dick slapped against my lower abs, milky moisture glistening in the lamp light, oozing over my now-taut uncut skin. He reached up and swiped it with his thumb, then smeared it across his tongue.

"Fucking delicious . . . and uncut. I'm gonna devour you, Cooper Hawk."

I stood and stepped to the end of the couch, then pulled his jeans from the bottom, sliding them off and adding them to the pile. Nate, freed from his clothing, sprang to his feet and wrapped himself around me, kissing me deeply while sliding his body up and down mine, grinding our cocks together. His teeth were on my neck again, then his tongue circled my nipples while his hands teased my sides.

When his mouth enveloped my cock, I thought the room might spin off into space. The warmth of his tongue swirling around my head sent shivers of pleasure up my spine. I gripped his head and shoved him down, forcing my whole length to the back of his throat. He gagged and pulled back, then dove again, undeterred, pressing me even deeper than I'd done a second before. His hand gripped my balls, squeezed, then tugged them down. A jolt of pain made me wince, then he squeezed again and pleasure radiated from that same place.

"Holy shit, Nate. You feel—"

A finger snaked its way around my hole, and all thought, all speech, anything but feeling and sensation and desire, sailed away. Somewhere in all the teasing and licking and biting, he'd coated his finger with my pre-cum, and it slid, almost effortlessly, inside me. I arched as he pressed, and my cock drove further into his throat.

"Oh, god, Nate. You're going to make me cum. God, please stop . . ."

But he didn't stop. His finger curled inside me, pressing into my prostate, slamming me with one hammer blow of pleasure after another, stripping all my control, my awareness, my thought, flooding my balls, spilling them out and into him over and over. I tried to pull back, but his hands gripped my ass, shoving me toward him, forcing us together as my body shuddered and emptied, and my world quaked.

I finally glanced down as he smacked his lips.

"You taste as good as you look," he said, a spark of devilry still swirling in his eyes.

"I need to take care of you now."

He stood and shook his head. "I got everything I wanted . . . for now."

"But . . ." I didn't want to be done. "Stay."

"What?"

"Don't go home. Stay tonight. Please."

He didn't even hesitate. "Only if you let me hold you all night."

And just like that, I died in his arms, the happiest, giddiest, giggliest death ever.

Twenty–Three

Nate

I woke around five thirty, bleary-eyed and disoriented, as was the case most mornings before drinking a bucket of coffee. My morning wood had the skin of my dick pulled so tight it threatened to bore a hole in the comforter. That, too, was fairly standard. What most mornings definitely did not include was the strange mixture of numbness and tingling in my right arm due to the weight of a grown-ass man laying on it. It took a second to shake my brain free of its fog and remember I was in Cooper's house, in his bed, with my arm still fast asleep beneath his body.

I managed to slide my lifeless limb free without waking my bedmate, then padded into the bathroom to relieve my throbbing bladder. When I returned, Coop's steady breath hadn't wavered, and his eyes darted beneath tightly closed lids. A few strands of rebellious hair curled across his forehead in the most adorable way. In that moment, I thought he might be the most beautiful man alive.

My eyes roamed his face, the gentle curve of his cheek, the chiseled set of his jaw, then traveled down to his chest. God, he was perfect. I'd seen plenty of hot bodies in my time in the minors, but Cooper was a statue . . . or should've been a statue. His rounded pecs flowed into a shredded torso filled with more abs than one man should possess. I pushed the covers back to see his manhood, shrouded in a hood of skin, perfectly curled like his resting body, in its bed of light brown curls. Even soft, he was perfect. I wanted to grab him, to cradle his cock, to take him in my mouth and let him live there.

I wanted all of this man, and I barely knew him.

How insane was that? How utterly, completely mad?

He shifted, and I held my breath, then he pressed himself against me, nestling his body into mine, as he'd done most of the night. His eyes never opened, so I wrapped my arm around him and nuzzled my nose into the crook of his neck. A moment later, I drifted off, more at peace than I'd been in years.

A couple hours later, my eyes fluttered open to find Coop propped up on one elbow, staring down as I'd done a short time earlier.

"Morning, handsome," he said, reaching over to trace my cheek with his fingertips.

I shivered at his touch.

"Morning." I ducked my mouth under the covers. "I have really bad breath."

He grinned, yanked the sheet away, and smothered my mouth with his.

Before I realized he'd rolled over, his weight pressed on top of me and his naked butt ground into my groin.

"Shit, Coop," I said, gasping for air. "Keep that up and I'll have to do a lot more than kiss you." His eyes flared, and I felt his hand reach behind him to grasp my cock, now fully erect. He shoved it against his butt, into his crack, teasing my head against his hole. He moved it back and forth, dragging my most sensitive skin against the part of his body I most wanted to enter. Every swipe sent my eyes rolling back. I reached down to grab his dick, but he grabbed my wrist and slammed it into the pillow by my head, leaning over me like he owned everything I was.

"You are mine now," he growled.

This was a man I'd never met, so full of confidence and strength, so sure of what he wanted—so determined to take it, to seize whatever he desired.

I stretched my other arm above my head, surrendering to his charge, and a grin parted his lips, like a beast pleased with the meal he was about to consume.

Still, he wiggled my cock against his hole. I'd never felt so many pulses, so many flames, as the veins in my dick bulged against his palm.

"Fuck, Coop—"

He kissed me, stopping anything I might've said.

"I want you inside me so fucking bad. You're going to pound me into tomorrow, Nate Stringer. You know that, right?"

"Uh-huh," I eked out.

He reached across the bed and slammed his palm on the pump of the lube bottle, filling his hand, then slathered my dick with slick warmth. He stroked my cock, and I had to squeeze my eyes shut to slow my heart, then I felt him press the tip of my head into him, ever so slightly.

"Ahh! Coop!"

He pulled back, and the look in his eyes was primal.

"I'm not doing that. Just playing a bit. Do you trust me?"

I nodded frantically. "Yes, sure. I mean, yeah. I do. I think."

And the tip slipped in again.

"Fuuuuck!"

And out.

He did that a few more times before producing a condom out of thin air and whipping it on me. I barely had time to register the rubber glove before it was slick and sliding deep inside him. I might've been the top, but I was clearly not in control. Coop was driving this train anywhere he wanted, and he was doing it like a man possessed.

His muscular ass gripped my dick so hard I thought he might yank it off as he bobbed up and down, driving me deeper into him with every press. He dug his fingers into my shoulders and kissed me with a reckless abandon caught somewhere between ravenous hunger and passionate lust. I tried to think, to see what was happening, but the music of our movement was too loud, felt too much. I could barely breathe, much less think. Cooper was everything. His body, his lips, his ass, the thrusting of my cock inside him, the grip of his muscles. My hands stroked his abs, making me harder as my mind envisioned this Adonis wanting me, desiring me, taking me for his own. All I could feel was his searing gaze and blinding touch.

"I want you to come, Nate. I want you to fill me. Pour yourself into me. Make me yours, Nate. NOW!"

His voice brooked no argument. It wasn't a request. It was a command.

I flipped him over with the skill of an acrobat, braced his legs over my shoulders and shoved myself into him with all the strength I possessed. He cried out, a wail of pleasure and pain, and his fingernails dug and scraped my back and butt. He pulled me into him, drove me to thrust harder and deeper. His moans and cries mixed with my sweat and tears, then the rush of adrenaline gave way to the flow of my body and I lost all control.

"Coop, I'm coming. Oh, fuck!"

His ass clenched like a vise, and my balls emptied into him, shooting over and over, so much and so long I lost myself in the thrusts. Somewhere in the midst of it all, I grabbed his cock and jerked him hard. We weren't perfectly in sync, but he showered my chest with a geyser of cream only seconds after I'd finished filling him with my own. I reached up and smeared it over my chest. He reached up and pressed his hand against mine, holding it against my heart.

"Holy shit, Coop," I gasped through ragged breaths. "That was fucking awesome."

His ass clenched hard.

"Ahh! You trying to drain me again?"

His brows rose. "You got another in you?"

"Fuck. And here I thought you were all sweet and innocent."

He batted his eyelashes. "I have no idea what you mean. I *am* pure and innocent . . . until you get my motor going."

I finally had enough breath to laugh and shake my head.

"You're trouble, Cooper Hawk. You know that?"

"Only if you want me to be."

I smiled and cupped his cheek, unable to think of a thing to say.

Twenty-Four

Cooper

"Guys, I didn't know who else to call, but I had to call somebody or I was going to explode all over Nashville."

Sam's gravelly chuckle grated against my ear. "Well, we can't have you doing that. It'd be our luck the city would find out we're friends and make us clean up the mess. I'm not into grime and gore."

I swear I could hear Miguel grinning through the phone. "Technically, dear, you are into grime. You own a mechanic shop thing. You're up to your elbows in grease every day."

"Not the same as scooping Cooper guts off the street."

"Oh, god, boys, enough. No more Cooper goop."

"Hey, Coop Goop. That could be a new lubricant brand," Miguel chimed.

"Love it. The logo could be a golden retriever with floppy red-brown hair—"

"Are you two done dragging me through the mud?"

"You started it by exploding all over us," Sam grumbled merrily.

I blew out a breath.

"Okay, no exploding. Although, I did blow a load—"

"Alright, son, Mom and I don't want to hear about your—"

"With Nate."

The line went deadly silent.

I couldn't even hear them breathing, which was unusual because Sam usually sounded like an overheated TV stalker who played Darth Vader in his spare time.

"Nate?" Miguel muttered. "Nate Stringer? My Nate? My little bro?"

"Um, yeah. But, I think, technically, he might be my Nate now . . . or at least . . . we're getting there . . . or going there . . . on our way there. Hell, I'm freakin' crazy over him, and I'm pretty sure he feels the same about me."

"Fuck me running."

"Are you asking? Was that an invitation?" Sam's grumble turned into a growl.

"Okay, got it. Mom and Dad like to do the thing. La, la, la. Not listening."

Miguel snorted. "You need to learn these things, son. You see, when a man loves another man—"

"Gah! I got it. In fact, last night, I got a lot of it, all the way up my ass!"

"Eww. Babe, did our little one just talk about shoving things up his bum hole?" For a second, I thought Sam might've actually been taken aback.

"Our baby's growing up," Miguel mock sniffed.

"Fuck you both. No, never mind. You'll take that literally and turn into horny rabbits on the phone. Just stop it! I'm trying to talk to you."

Miguel grunted. I think it was a chuckle. "Go on, son. Speak. I'll try to keep my eternal lust for your dad in check for the moment."

"You'll fail. You suck at keeping it in check," Sam muttered.

"Ha. You said 'suck.'"

"GUYS!"

Both of them laughed.

"Listen, seriously, Nate and I did the nasty last night, and again this morning. I mean, I guess last night was only a little nasty because tab A didn't go into slot B at all, but he sucked the ever-loving shit out of my cock, so that counts, right?"

"Uh, yeah, I think so. The Russian judge said 'no,' but nobody listens to her anyway," Sam deadpanned.

"We're still talking about Nate? The Sounds player? The guy I raised from a rookie college kid?" Miguel's voice had returned to disbelief.

"Yeah. Number twenty-three, second base, hot ass, big biceps, butt for days—"

"Got it. Same Nate. No further description needed."

"Babe, did you know he's gay?" Sam asked.

"Nope. Not even a little," Miguel said. "He never really dated, but a lot of guys trying to make it steer clear of relationships or dating while in the minors. Hell, most guys avoid distractions for the first couple years in the majors too, until they're established. I never really thought anything of it."

"He never—"

"Not a signal, no eye contact, no roaming gaze, nada." Miguel sounded more perplexed with every statement. "He never said anything to trigger alarm bells, never made a pass at me or anybody when I was around. I mean, the guy may as well have been a baseball monk."

"He's pretty stoic about most things," I added.

"Yeah, that's true," Miguel said. "He's always been kinda inside himself, but I never connected that to sexuality. He was just a serious kid consumed with making it to the bigs."

"Well, he was consumed last night. Or, more accurately, he did the consuming."

"God, I'm gonna hurl. He's my little brother, Coop. Really?" Sam and I both cracked up.

"Is it so bad? I mean, he's a great guy, and I'm not that bad once you get to know me and get past the fact that sometimes my brain sends me down paths and I really like long walks, especially on a beach with sand between my toes, the cool white sand, not the rough brown stuff, because that hurts and my feet are tender even though I abuse them a lot in tae kwon do.

Can you believe Nate was surprised I have a better body than he does? I think I was a little shocked too."

The line was silent.

I waited.

Still nothing.

Finally, Sam stuck his toe back in the water. "You have a better body than Nate? He's a pro athlete."

I giggled. Fuck me, I giggled on the phone with Sam and Miguel.

"Guess that answers that," Miguel said.

"What? What answers what?"

"Well, little one, we're guys, and we have eyes," Sam said.

"And cocks," Miguel added.

"And we knew you had a hot bod under there. Or we thought you did, and we were curious, like any self-respecting gays would be," Sam continued.

"But we respect you and feel kind of responsible and would never have asked to see it or anything because the ghost of your grandmother would haunt us for all eternity . . . and we're good like that," Miguel finished.

"Did you two just ramble in tandem at me?" I asked.

They grunted in unison.

"Guess we did," Sam said.

"Next time we're together, I'm taking my shirt off."

"No!" they boomed, again in unison.

"What? Afraid you can't see my abs and control yourself?"

Miguel snorted again. "Sam absolutely can't control himself. No, never. Not even a little."

"If you weren't Mom and Dad, I'd say let's have a play day, but I've never done a three-way, and you two are Mom and Dad, and I've kind of got my heart set on a certain baseball player we're supposed to be talking about instead of my eight-pack."

"Eight? Not six?" Sam breathed. "Fuck, fuck, fuck. Babe, we raised a porn star."

"Hey! I never said my cock was ginormous. Although, now that you mention it—"

"Stop! No cock talk. It's bad enough we know your abs put all of us to shame. The last thing we need is the image of you strutting around with a boner the size of Michigan—"

"More like California, maybe all of South America—"

"Cooper!"

I was almost in tears. These guys were killing me.

"Back to Nate. Guys, I really like him. He's amazing."

"Slow down," Miguel said. "Let's try starting over. How many times have you two been out? This little secret's been kept better than any I've heard in a while, and I'm a cop."

"Well, we hung out at the Bluebird after you guys left."

"We know that. Nothing happened—or so we thought," Sam said.

"No, nothing happened. We just talked a lot, got to know each other. I DMed him on Insta after that, and we started talking on there a lot."

"Aww, babe, is that how the kids do it these days? They DM on Insta?"

"I feel so old," Sam muttered.

"You are old," I said. "Now, continuing my story—"

"He's so feisty," Sam said.

"That's your influence. I raised an angel," Miguel quipped.

"Guys! Back to me." I huffed indignantly. "I didn't get to see Nate after the Mangoes game like we did that first night, but he called me when I got home."

"He called you? From his own cell?" Miguel asked, flabbergasted.

"Yeah. His number was private, but it was his phone. He texted me his number after we hung up. Then he came over to my place, and what started as a short visit ended up a sleepover. He woke up with me watching him from across a pillow."

"Well, damn," Miguel muttered.

"We kind of had sex again, then cleaned up and went to breakfast."

"Wait. Stop there," Miguel said. "He went to breakfast with you? In a public place?"

If he could've seen my eyes rolling . . . "Yes, that's generally where one finds breakfast, in a public restaurant. It wasn't fancy or anything, just the diner down the street. There wasn't any hand holding or kissing across a waffle. We were just two guys eating. Although . . ."

"Although what?" Sam asked.

"I may have had post-sex googly eyes. I'm not sure there was any way to hide them. And Nate kind of glowed."

"Nate *glowed*?" Miguel asked, incredulous.

"Yeah. Maybe glowed isn't the right word, but he smiled a lot more than I'd seen before. He has really white teeth. Did you know that?"

Sam grunted, and Miguel snorted.

"Anyway," I continued. "We went back to my place after breakfast, got naked one last time, then went to lunch."

"What? More eating?" Miguel asked.

"Sex makes me hungry. What can I say?"

"I don't know our child, Sam. Who is this boy?"

"Oh, he's *all* yours. This sounds very familiar," Sam's amused voice replied.

"Guys! Can we focus, please." The guys had become family almost from that first day, but damn, they were frustrating to talk with sometimes. "He called me after last night's game, and we talked for two hours. He kissed me through the phone as we hung up."

"Well, damn. Scarecrow has a heart."

"That's Tin Man. Scarecrow needed a brain," Sam corrected.

"Oh, right. My bad."

"Fuck me, Dorothy. You two are impossible," I said.

Two growly laughs replied.

Miguel finally settled and spoke in measured tones. "Buddy, I don't know what to tell you. Before this conversation, I thought

Nate was straight, if a little repressed. I never suspected him of being gay, not once in all the years I've known him."

"And I have a near-perfect gaydar," Sam interjected. "It never beeped around the guy. Not so much as a wobble of the needle."

Miguel picked up where Sam's sentence ended. "But I would advise caution."

"What?" That wasn't what I'd expected—or hoped for.

"Easy, Nate's a great guy, and he'd be lucky to have someone like you in his life, but he's been so far in the closet for so long . . . and he's trying to make it into professional baseball from a minor league team whose record on acceptance is less than stellar. All I'm saying is take it slow. You'll probably need a lot of patience if this is going to grow into more than a secret hookup."

"This wasn't a hookup—"

"Coop . . . I'm sorry, I didn't mean it to sound like that. Nate's not a hookup kind of guy, and neither are you . . . although it sounds like you are a bit more a demon in the sheets than we thought, so maybe we should be warning Nate—"

"Hey!"

"Right. Poor Nate, probably blew his ass out for the game last night," Sam guffawed.

"Guys!"

"I can just see him squatting down for a groundie and his uterus falling out, right there on the field," Miguel added, and they both devolved into fits.

"He fucked the ever-loving baseball shit out of me, thank you very kindly."

"Oh, hell. That's entirely too much info, son. Now I won't get the image of you with your ankles hooked over your shoulders in hoop earrings out of my head all night."

"And I'll hear you squealing like—"

"Miguel!" I begged into the phone. "I don't squeal."

"Pant? Grunt? Moan? Queef?"

"Queef!" Sam shouted through breathless howls.

"Oh. My. God. You guys are disgusting. I'm hanging up now."

"Go clean your drawers, son. I think I smell them from here," Miguel blurted.

Sam hollered.

I hung up.

Twenty-Five

Nate

Several weeks had passed since that first night sleeping with my arms wrapped firmly around Cooper. Save for a week-long swing through Ohio playing Columbus and Toledo, I woke up to his beautiful blue eyes nearly every morning. I never knew how long he'd been awake when my eyes fluttered open, but each sunrise was the same. His eyes greeted me first, then his smile, then his lips gently brushing against mine. I'd never been so happy than in those waking moments as he welcomed me to the new day with all its possibilities.

Days had never had so much promise as when they began with Cooper's kiss.

I knew I was walking on brittle, parchment-thin ice, but I couldn't stop seeing him. My heart wouldn't allow it. I needed Cooper, needed to feel him next to me, needed to hear his giggle and babble and beautiful sighs as he slept. I needed his warmth against my skin, and his hunger each time I stripped to shower or change or . . . anytime my shirt came off.

I'd never felt so wanted.

Or alive.

Cal never asked where I was spending my nights. That should've triggered alarm bells, or at least raised questions, but I was too blinded by contentment to care. In the span of a month, I'd gone from denying relationships existed—or could exist while I was in the minors—to craving the presence of a man I'd met only a short time ago.

I knew I was screwed when one of the guys in the locker room squirted a shampoo bottle in all directions, pretending it was post-championship champagne. The boys pelted him with towels and sweaty socks, but the damage was done. The scent had found its way to my nostrils—and it was Coop's brand and flavor. Twenty nasty, sweaty players morphed into my tall, muscular black belt, and I thought my chest might explode right there in front of them. Fortunately, the spotlight followed the shampoo squirter into the showers, and I was able to make a quick escape. I couldn't drive fast enough to Cooper's place. He squirted shampoo all over me, and we made love on the floor in his den for hours.

God, I love that smell.

"You ready?" he called from the den.

I was still in the bathroom, slathering my neck with sunscreen. "Coming. Almost done," I shouted back.

We tossed a cooler packed with fruits, cheeses, and meats into the trunk and pulled out of his complex. Edwin Warner Park wasn't too far away, but the hike we had planned would take most of the day, and we wanted to get back before dark. This was another rare day off without a game or practice, and we meant to make the most of it. Sam and Miguel were making dinner, and the last thing either of us wanted was to hand them shit-giving ammunition by being too late.

"What's in the case?" Coop asked as we emptied the trunk at the park's lot.

"My guitar. I figured it's time I played for you."

"Wow. He actually plays. I was starting to wonder." He bumped against me playfully.

"You'll see. Or hear, I guess."

He grabbed the cooler and threw its strap across his chest and shoulder, then slammed the trunk shut.

"We're a couple miles from the stopping point for lunch," he said. The hike was Coop's idea, something he said he did a few times each summer to clear his head. I'd asked what he needed to clear this time, but he just smiled and winked. My innocent little boy was full of mischief . . . and I loved every minute of it.

"Are you nervous?" he asked.

"Nah. I can handle you."

He chuckled. "I meant about tonight, goofball."

"Oh, uh, yeah, a little. I guess." I fiddled with my guitar strap, even though it was comfortably in place. "I don't know how Miguel will react. He's always been there for me, but he was a player. He knows how hard it is to make it. Shit, he didn't even make it."

"You think he'll tell you you're nuts? That you shouldn't date while you're in the minors? That whole thing?"

I shrugged. "Maybe. I don't know. It's what I'd tell a younger player."

Coop stopped and turned toward me. "Really? Even now?"

"I . . . well . . . no. I mean, yeah. Fuck. Why is this so hard?"

Coop waited patiently as I scratched my scalp and stared at a tree.

"Coop, I'm fucking falling for you, and that scares me more than anything I've ever done. All I've ever wanted is to play ball. It's all I've ever known. And here I am, putting it all at risk—"

"For me."

"No. No, Coop. Well, yes, for you, but not for you. You can't take that on yourself. You shouldn't . . . I mean . . . It's not your fault or anything. I'm starting to think I'd do anything for you . . . I didn't . . . Shit . . . I did mean that. I would. I mean, I will. Fuck!"

Coop closed the gap between us and cupped my cheek in that tender, loving way I'd come to relish. "I've already fallen for you, Nate Stringer. I know it's only been a month, but it feels like a lifetime. I know what's at stake, for both of us, and I'm willing to risk it all . . . for you . . . which means I'm also willing to step back and let you fly, watch you grow and succeed and rise . . . if that's what baseball has in store for you. I will never hold you back or stand in your way, only push and encourage and comfort. I'll do all of that for you, Nate, and anything else you need, anytime, no matter what."

I staggered back a step, my back pressing into a tree. Cooper stepped forward, refusing to let the gap between us grow again.

"Miguel loves you. He loved you yesterday. He'll love you tomorrow. Trust in that. Trust in us. Alright?"

I opened my mouth, but words wouldn't form. My pulse was racing, and the cool forest breeze suddenly sweltered on my skin. I wiped newly beaded sweat from my brow and tried to look away, but Cooper's gaze was a vice holding me fixed, unable to turn or move.

No one had ever said anything remotely like *any* of that to me . . . ever. I knew he was right about Miguel. He was the most stand-up dude I'd ever known. He would support me through anything. But that thought was fleeting. It barely registered. Faced with Cooper's unrestrained declaration, nothing else mattered. There were no sounds in the woods, no calls of birds or rustling of woodland creatures. There was nothing but Cooper and his fucking blue eyes, larger than the sun, deeper than the sea, peering into my heart and peeling layers away to leave my soul exposed and raw.

"Coop . . . I . . . my god, Cooper."

He stepped closer, his chest barely pressing into mine, and I tasted the sweet saltiness of his lips before the touch of his kiss.

I don't know how long he held that kiss, how long we stood frozen, with my back pressed against a pine and his hand cupping my cheek. I didn't care. Time didn't matter. The forest, the trail, the hikers who surely passed by—none of it mattered.

Only Cooper mattered.

"I think . . . I think I'm falling for you, Cooper Hawk," were the first words to escape me after his lips pulled back. I was probably more surprised by them than he was, though his eyes barely widened.

His eyes became watery pools, threatening to overflow.

"I'm so crazy about you, Nate Stringer. I love being together, being with you, seeing you, talking to you, texting and chatting at crazy hours of the night or when you're on a roadie or just when you think about me randomly in the middle of the day and are supposed to be focusing on baseball but you say my eyes flash into your head. God, when you say that, it makes my heart feel like a dragon laid an egg in my chest and it cracks open and the little baby claws its way out and its head pops out and it screams and that scream vibrates my whole body like an earthquake rocking the whole world. You tear me up, Nate. So fucking much."

My hands gripped his head and pulled him into my lips. I poured every ounce of passion and longing into that kiss, promising, giving, willing myself into him—and him into me. I thought my heart might burst, all over Cooper and the forest, raining down on every tree and blade of grass, coating the world in ecstasy and joy I'd never known before this beautiful man barged into my life. I couldn't hold him close enough, kiss him deeply enough. This wasn't the passion of sex or lust, but the exuberance of one lost in the rapture of another's being, hope-lessly—no, hope*fully*—immersed in another's love. I'd never felt so light and free.

"We'd better get going if we're going to make it to the lunch spot on schedule," Coop whispered through heavy breaths.

I reached up and smoothed his locks off his forehead. My smile was so wide my cheeks ached, but I didn't care. This was what living felt like, and I wanted to live forever.

"After you," I whispered back, then stole one last kiss.

Coop turned and took a step. I pinched his ass and giggled like a four-year-old high on Pixie Sticks.

His head whipped around, mock anger marring his features, and an accusing finger poked toward me. "Keep that up and I'll have to punish you."

So, being the masculine, mature man I was, I reached down and pinched him harder.

His eyes flew wide, then he chased after me as I darted up the trail, laughing all the way.

Somewhere between the apartment and his car, Coop had snuck a blanket in with the cooler. He spread it out with a flourish like he was setting a table for royalty. My gaze drifted from him to the insane view of the Tennessee Valley below. The hills in the park weren't the mountains of East Tennessee, but they did offer a clear, if heavily forested, line of sight across much of the region.

Our lunch spot sat at the end of a side trail on the peak of a hill I imagined Civil War scouts using for sighting enemy positions. Tennessee's role in that brother-against-brother conflict was pivotal, the last state to be ceded and the first to be readmitted, the state's capitol building was used as a headquarters and hospital for Union forces. As such, it was one of the few surviving state capitol buildings from those war-torn days.

There were no wars or battles or cannon blasts that day, only Cooper's innocent smile and dream-filled eyes—oh, and *my* swollen heart feeling like it might burst at any moment with childlike glee and an overwhelming sense of love and happiness.

I wasn't used to being happy like that. I mean, I wasn't generally *un*happy—baseball kept my mental and emotional state in balance—but there's a difference between being stable and well-tempered and being utterly, completely, insanely joyful. It felt so maddeningly out of control, like becoming a can of Coke someone shook so hard the aluminum bowed out, ready to burst, showering sugary goodness all over innocents unfortunate enough to be sitting nearby. Yeah, that was me: a can of shaken soda.

Being out of control wasn't me. It wasn't me at all. I was the guy who balanced everyone else. I kept the rookies' emotions in check when the game went haywire. I pulled guys aside and brought their feet back to the ground when Coach threatened to tear them a new one. I was the stabilizer, not the guy who got all giddy and silly—or whatever the fuck I was feeling right then. I'd never felt it before and had absolutely no idea how to identify—or handle—it. There was no handling it. It wasn't possible. The bubbles roiled and burst in my chest. I felt each one. And if I dared turn from the vista to watch Cooper's ruminations, the fates, with a cackle, shook my can even harder, and that out-of-control feeling welled into a hurricane of sweaty, silly, putty-in-his-palm goofiness.

I was so completely, utterly, totally screwed.

And I'd never been so happy.

"Hungry?"

I turned to find our lunch laid out, cheeses and meats in perfect patterns on pristine black plates. Three bowls of various fruits surrounded the charcuterie, and an uncorked wine bottle stood to the side.

I raised a brow and he filled our glasses. The liquid was thin and oddly blue.

"You have a game tonight. This is G2. Hydration is important, mister, but I wanted it to feel like a fancy picnic, so I put it in a wine bottle."

And just like that, Coop had me giggling like a Catholic schoolgirl in trouble. Damn it. I was a jock, a stud, a strapping young lad who didn't fucking giggle.

But I did.

And it felt so freakin' good.

Then Coop's smile nearly touched his ears, and I thought I might die right there on that hill.

"I might have a hard time eating anything but your mouth if you keep smiling at me like that."

The blush that invaded his face made him even more irresistible, so I raced around behind him, snaked my arms through his to grip his chest and dug my teeth into his neck.

"Damn, Dracula, getting anything back there?" He tried to squirm away.

"If I wanted to actually get anything out of you, it wouldn't be your neck I'd suck."

"Promises, promises." He didn't miss a beat. "Sit your fangs over there and eat up. We'll need to get back on the trail if we're going to make it back in time. We can't have Coach on your ass any more than he already is."

That was a mood killer. My fangs retracted as I rounded and sat across the blanket from him.

"That's for sure," my voice came out far poutier than I'd intended.

"Come on, every player has a slump. You've been on the team for five years. Just pull yourself out of it and everything will be fine." He took a bite of cracker layered with gouda and prosciutto. "How would you coach another player having this run?"

Run. That was one way to put it. I'd been hitless in eight straight games, and was on the verge of setting a team record for most strikeouts in a streak. It wasn't just physical, a quirk in my stance or the like. It had gotten into my head. I'd seen players get the "the yips" before, especially when fielding or throwing. World-class infielders would lose their ability to toss the ball anywhere near the first baseman, sailing balls into the dugout—or worse, deep into the stands—but I'd never experienced anything like that, certainly not at the plate. I was the guy the team counted on to get on base, to get things going. My slump was so bad Coach didn't start me in the last two games. My backup wasn't as strong in the field, so I slipped back into the starting rotation, but my batting didn't improve.

It had gotten so bad even my agent was calling to tell me to clean it up. She *never* called players . . . unless there was really bad news on the horizon.

"Let's leave baseball for the field today, okay?"

He eyed me over his glass of 2023's finest Gatorade vintage, but didn't say anything.

"What are you going to do about work?" The last thing I wanted was to take this day in paradise down a dark path, but he'd brought up baseball, and his work was the first thing I thought might distract from my own troubles.

Raj had become a tyrant. Dennis and three others of the team had been fired for the board reporting issue. While that seemed to ease the workplace tension always crackling across cube land, the company hadn't appeared in any hurry to replace them, dumping much of the workload on the one employee in the department they fully trusted. I'd hoped that would get Raj off Coop's back a little, make the guy realize how valuable and hardworking he was, but whatever humanity remained in Raj's crusty shell had burned off when the board scorched him for his people's errors. Coop worked ten or twelve-hour days and brought stacks of paperwork home every night. I loved spending nights with him, but most of those were consumed with cuddling a worn-out numbers genius, rather than diddling his abacus.

I really loved diddling his abacus.

"I've never hated a job." He set his glass down and stared across the treetops. "Nate, I can't keep doing this. If I thought it was temporary, that they'd hire someone else to help or at least recognize me for my effort, maybe I'd feel differently, but nothing's changing. They just keep piling on more. And Raj, wow, he's brutal. Even when he's giving me a compliment, he's insulting. That's a really hard verbal pretzel to form, but he's good at it."

"So, why stay there? The pay can't be *that* good."

Coop's stare intensified, as if he couldn't bear meeting my eyes while thinking about retreat or surrender—or however his mind thought of quitting anything.

"It's not the pay. Grammy, she . . . It's not the pay."

I wanted to ask a million questions. He'd told me about the impact his grandmother had made on countless lives across Nashville and beyond, but he'd never spoken a word about what she'd left him. He lived in the same apartment, drove the same middle-aged car, hadn't even bought a single new piece of clothing—and he needed some new clothes. I admired him for his frugality, his humility, but '80s chic wasn't nearly as in fashion as he thought it was.

But I kept my mouth shut. When he wanted me to know, he'd tell me. I got how personal that was, the loss of his grandmother wrapped in his own financial situation.

"Then what is it?"

"I don't know what I would do. I mean, I've thought about it. God, I've thought about it a lot. Grammy dying made me reassess everything I thought was important. It made me think about how precious and short life can be, even though she lived a full and long one."

His eyes misted, and I swear they traveled back in time. "I miss her, Nate, so much more than I tell anyone. Sometimes I think she visits me at night, whispers to me, kisses my ear like she did when I was little. I hated that when I was a teenager. It made me feel like such a little boy when I wanted to grow up and be a man. But now, I would give anything to have her lean up and kiss my ear, pinch my lobe, and make me squirm. I'd give up everything to see her smile just one more time."

I reached up and thumbed a tear from his cheek, letting my own roll down to my chin.

His chest filled, then bellowed out. Nearby birds whistled, and a stiff wind rustled through the trees.

"What would you do?" he asked quietly.

"What?"

"If you didn't have baseball? What would you do?"

"Shit. I don't know. Baseball is everything to me." I realized what I'd just said and traced my fingers across the back of his hand. "Almost everything."

He smiled weakly. "But if you got hurt and couldn't play, what would you want to do?"

"Huh. I have no idea, Coop."

"You've never thought about it?"

"Not really. Thinking about that felt like giving up, or not putting everything I've got into this shot. To make it at the pro level, you've got to go all in, no safety net, no outs . . . so to speak." Neither of us smiled at my weak attempt at humor. "Guess I've never let myself go down that road."

We sat in silence a moment longer, then Coop grabbed a pear and smeared goat cheese over it.

"Maybe I could do something with tae kwon do. I'd have to get my fifth degree before I could be called a master, but that's not too far out of reach. I'm past the minimum time requirement for testing, just need to put in more work, get more sparring practice." He shoved the last of the pear into his mouth. "I love numbers. Guess I could find another company needing a nerd."

"You're so much more than a nerd, Coop." It flew out of my mouth, sounding almost defensive, protective. His cheeks rose in an almost-smile. The tiny lines around his eyes definitely curled upward. "You're so amazing, Coop. You could do anything, anything you wanted. Don't put yourself in a box just because that's what you've always done or because it's comfortable. Push yourself. If you want to be the master of all tae kwon do everywhere in the world, do it."

He laughed, a carefree sound, finally unbound by the somber notes of our earlier talk.

"I'm pretty sure that position is taken by people far more skilled, older, and, um, likely more Asian than me."

"That's awfully racist of you, Mr. Hawk!"

He chortled. "Maybe, but it's also true. Tae kwon do is owned by the Koreans, and rightfully so. It's their creation, their national sport, their pride. The masters over there are so far beyond anything we have, in skill and understanding, in wisdom, in respect."

"Respect?"

"Not respect like you and I think, like Westerners think. It's totally different. How do I even explain it?" He scratched his head through his thick wavy mess. "It's like... they respect the idea of tae kwon do, not just the forms and sport. It's a way of life, not just a martial art. No, it's a way of *living*. That's more accurate, I think."

"Sounds complicated."

"It's simple, actually, just foreign to a Western mind."

"There you go, slamming my roots again," I snapped playfully.

He tossed a cracker at me.

"Throwing a cracker at the cracker. How rude!"

As quickly as that, we devolved into a wrestling match, scattering charcuterie and fruit, spilling aromatic G2, and staining our shirts and shorts with grass guts as we rolled about and on top of each other.

Twenty minutes—and a rock-star make-out session later—we tried desperately to ignore the boners that tented our shorts, tossed the last of our smushed food to the birds, packed up the cooler, and headed back the way we'd come. Lunchtime had burned through too much of our precious time to fully hike the intended trail, so we decided to head home and enjoy what little remained of the day naked and doing adult things that didn't involve cheese and crackers . . .

Except *this* cracker and his very excited sausage.

Twenty–Six

Nate

Summer's heat gave way to autumn's gentle breezes, heralding my favorite time of year: MiBL Playoff season. The minors didn't have the eternal series structure of the major leagues. Their playoffs took forever, as each round required teams to win best three-out-of-five or five-out-of-seven contests.

By contrast, Las Vegas hosted the two teams in each division, the International League and the Pacific Coast League, with the highest regular-season winning percentage for playoff games, which sent one of each to the league championship. The two league champions then met for one winner-takes-all National Championship game.

It was intense, everything-on-the-line, do-or-die baseball, and I loved every minute of it.

The Sounds had made the playoffs every year for the past eight seasons. With a dominant lead over the next best team in our division, we easily qualified for a ninth shot at the title.

On the last day of September, I jogged onto the field under the Las Vegas sun, ready to face whatever Memphis had to offer. We'd played them more times that season than any other team, and the blood boiled between us. It was somehow fitting we'd face off for our divisional crown.

My slump hadn't deepened. That was hardly possible, as I shattered goose egg and K records for batting and strikeouts, but my fielding had been stellar. Word on the street had me on the nominee list for a Gold Glove, something I'd never achieved at any level, and the one thing keeping my jersey on my back since my bat had abandoned me.

The ball whizzed around the horn as warm-ups concluded, and our pitcher tossed his final pregame throws. I glanced into the stands where Sam, Miguel, Gabe, Tyler, Ben, Annie, and Cooper sat. Annie was in the center of the gaggle, holding court, as was her right as the reigning queen of . . . well . . . the queens. Her hands flew, and I swore I could hear some Broadway tune drifting down to the field.

A moment later, as we lined up along the first base chalk for the national anthem and introductions, the sound of applause from hundreds turned every head in my team's line. Fans seated dozens of rows away were turned and giving Annie a standing ovation. She, in classic Annie form, bowed and waved like pageant royalty.

I shook my head and turned back toward the plate, focusing my mind on the task at hand. We had a game to win, then a championship.

It took just over two hours for us to shut out our nemesis 10–0, one of the widest margins of victory in Triple A divisional championship history. I managed to break my hitless streak at just the right time, smacking a double in the third and two singles in the fifth and eighth, sending home three of our ten runs.

The team celebrated together at Gordon Ramsay Steak, indulging at the franchise's expense for the first time all year. They might not pay for us to live, but they spared no expense when trophies were on the line.

Since I was tied up with team festivities, Sam and Miguel played host to the gang at one of the restaurants in the Venetian. Annie insisted it was the best hotel in town, so Sam and Miguel stayed in one suite; Tyler, Gabe, and Ben in another; while Annie had one all to herself, complete with a grand piano and eight-person hot tub. Cooper, the most diligent and organized of the group, had made all the reservations and, over the objections of everyone, footed the bill for the whole thing, claiming, "It's what Grammy would've wanted."

I still hadn't fully grasped the scope of her bequest to her grandson, but dropping thousands on luxury suites didn't make him flinch—at all.

All the lower levels played their version of playoff games on Saturday, while the boys from Nashville and Durham had the day off. Coach made us do a light practice, more for the mental fix than anything, but we had most of the day to sightsee or watch the doubles and singles vie for their trophies.

While I was at practice, the others, except for Annie and Ben, laid out by the pool. Our elder stateswoman insisted on taking the youngest pup in our pack on an adventure-filled jaunt along the Strip. She even surprised the lad by zip-lining down the whole length of Vegas's main drag. She hadn't picked up many signs, and Ben still didn't lipread well, but they found ways to make things work, only returning around dinnertime because Annie insisted the buffets were worth ten of the zip lines.

Coop and I had two hours together in the early afternoon. He'd spent days finding the perfect hiking tour, something called the Red Rock Canyon excursion. I'd never thought much of the desert, being more of a mountain and forest-loving guy, but there was a special majesty and beauty to the barren canyons, something timeless I didn't quite understand. Our guide told stories of the land and the natives' history, giving rocks and shrubs meaning and life I'd never known, giving me new perspective on the life before me, as Cooper glanced back and smiled my way.

We ate together that night.

Annie insisted I sit at the head of the table, since I was the player they'd come to watch and support. Ironically, that seat let me do most of the watching, and what I saw filled my heart beyond measure.

Tyler, Gabe, and Ben signed so quickly I could barely see their fingers through the blur. I struggled to believe Gabe when he told me Ty had only begun signing a year or so earlier. He looked so natural, so comfortable, communicating with his two deaf companions. And Ben, that happy boy, gazed at Gabe as if he were the only man alive. I knew he hadn't known his father, but to see him idolize a man I'd come to respect and admire was a beautiful thing. Poor Ty, the cover model mechanic, was so smitten he barely looked away all night. Every time Gabe flashed him a smile, the guy melted into a puddle of Jell-O right there at the table.

I'd half expected Sam and Miguel to have grown past their googly phase. They'd been together for three or four years, married for almost two, but they looked more stupidly in love than any pair of teenagers I'd ever known. It was oddly satisfying to see the gruff Sam so completely contort his body around Miguel's little finger. Cirque du Soleil acrobats could've learned a thing or two from him.

Annie sang 'Take Me Out to the Ballgame,' bringing the entire restaurant to a standstill. Every diner stood and joined in the chorus as she repeated the last refrain. Even the servers who appeared annoyed when she'd started were clapping and singing.

These were my friends. My family. They'd traveled across the continent *for me*. I could hardly believe it.

And then there was Cooper.

His hair had been frizzed and formed—or whatever fancy stylists in fancier hotels called it. Ty had taken him shopping, insisting his wardrobe wasn't appropriate for a star-studded dinner with his burgeoning major leaguer. It didn't matter that we couldn't tell anyone we were together, and that we sat a table apart to avoid random photos catching us in the same frame, Ty wanted him to look like dinner and dessert on a roll of butter and chocolate and diamonds.

That sounded weird, but it's what he said.

And fuck me running if Coop didn't look like the sexiest man alive.

His hair waved. The silky navy shirt Ty made him buy clung to every curve and bend, somehow tapering to his waist where the definition of his perfect abs poked through the fabric. And damn it, he must've been cold, because his high beams poked through in a way that made me want to bite them right there in front of everyone. And his jeans. Sweet baby Jesus. They were some fancy designer whose name I didn't recognize, but whoever the dude was, he knew how to make denim accentuate the perfectly round ass of a man whose muscles needed no help. I nearly passed out when he stood and walked to the restroom. Ty had to elbow me to bring me back to the table.

"Dude, you're gonna get caught staring," he'd whispered.

He was de-fucking-liciously fuckable . . . on a stick . . . with a cherry on top.

It was championship weekend, and nothing in the world could bring me down.

Twenty–Seven

COOPER

The Durham Bulls came to play.

No, that's not accurate.

They were out for blood.

As the team with the slightly higher regular-season winning percentage, Nashville was the home team, therefore took the field first on Sunday.

Our little family huddled together in the stands, chatting away at what we expected—what we hoped—would happen that day. I'd competed in a thousand martial arts competitions, and butterflies were part of the gig. They gave you that extra boost, that feeling of realness to a pretend battle that pushed you to give more, to do more, to drive your opponent into the dirt.

What I never truly understood was how nerve-racking it was for loved ones in the stands to watch helplessly as their baby (or baby doll, in this case) strode onto the field, or court, or whatever the fuck they played their sport on. How parents watched their children play sports was a wonder.

I was a complete disaster, and Miguel wasn't much better. The boys had wedged me in between them, each with a beefy arm hooked around my own. Nervous energy wafted off Miguel, through his arm, vibrating my soul. My own jitters-bordering-on-panic probably rattled his teeth. Together, we were a hot mess.

I wanted this for Nate so badly.

We all did.

The ump barked, "Play ball!" and the first pitch sailed toward the plate . . .

. . . and then out toward center field, where it slammed into the scoreboard, a dozen yards above the yellow paint marking the top of the wall.

I'd never believed in foreshadowing until that moment.

My stomach churned. It was a sea of discontent, swirling and frothing, battering my senses to the point of, well, senselessness.

I stood on the side of the road, watching cars whiz by, seeing a train coming, knowing it would slam into a tiny Fiat something or other, unable to stop the tragic disaster from occurring. I screamed, a full-throated, slow-motion cry of pain, helpless to do anything, to avert the oncoming death and destruction.

Okay, maybe that was a tad dramatic.

This was baseball, not air traffic control.

But it felt like it was.

Hit after hit, they kept coming. The scoreboard lights barely kept up with the count.

Then the pitcher got the yips, and walk after walk sent boys around bases.

I wanted to bring that imaginary scream to life right there in the middle of an ocean of fans.

I wanted to run out onto the field and snatch the ball out of the pitcher's hand. No, I didn't have a plan after that. If I threw the darn thing, it would more likely hit the dirt of the mound rather than the catcher's mitt, but I wanted to do something, anything. The ship was sinking. Hell, it was on fire, with sirens and lights blaring, and there wasn't even an iceberg to blame.

By the fourth inning, the Sounds were down 7–1, and the game hadn't been *that* close. Durham had racked up eleven hits already, which was more than most teams totaled in a whole night. The Sounds staff had sent three different pitchers to the mound, each receiving the same pummeling from the Bulls' batters. When a player gets in the zone, magic happens. When a whole team gets in the zone—all at the same time—they're unstoppable.

The Bulls were stampeding, and anyone in their way was getting crushed.

When the final out was called, bringing the championship to a blessed close, we'd been demolished 17–3 in a game that left no doubt who the best Triple A team in baseball was.

And it wasn't our boys.

My heart ached as I watched Nate walk off the field, his head hung low and glove slapping aimlessly at his leg. He'd wanted this, more than anything, for his team and for his future. He'd wanted to show the baseball world that he could bounce back from the depths of a serious slump and lead his team to victory, to a crown, to a national title.

Alas, that slump reared its horned head like a slumbering dragon that was thoroughly pissed off by some treasure-hunting hero who'd woken him from a thousand-year nap.

Not only did my man strike out a staggering *five* times, he committed two very uncharacteristic fielding errors, one of which involved hurling a ball so far over the first baseman's head that a woman in the stands had to duck out of the way, flinging her beer all over the row behind her.

Once everyone was showered and changed, the team demonstrated a world-class level of sportsmanship, publicly celebrating their division championship and congratulating themselves on fighting the good fight. Lingering fans and the media ate it up. They held their heads high and tried to show pride in their accomplishment, though I wasn't sure any of them felt much pride in the moment.

So ended another season.

Several weeks passed.

There were no practices or games, no drills or instructions.

It was officially the off-season, and Nate was bored out of his mind.

He and I spent most of his non-working time together. I tried teaching him basic tae kwon do forms, but he was too inflexible, and far too clumsy, to master them. It was funny. Nate was a professional athlete who could run circles around most men, but was unable to handle motions and stances any twelve-year-old with a colored belt could hold indefinitely.

I took it in stride, countering with how much I sucked at anything involving a ball; to which he made the obvious sexual retort; to which I disproved my own premise of sucking at balls by stripping him down and taking both of his balls as far into my mouth as my tongue would allow.

I was, indeed, a master with balls.

Sam and Miguel declared their house an asylum for all who needed a home for the Thanksgiving holiday. Tyler volunteered his culinary services, something for which we were all most thankful, because, while Sam's grilling skills had improved through meal after meal after meal after meal . . . after meal . . . none of us wanted another fucking grilled *anything*, possibly ever again, even at a cookout where grilling was wholly appropriate.

Oh, and Tyler was a genius in the kitchen.

That too.

Everyone promised to be there. Even Nate's parents, who had only been to Nashville twice since he'd started playing for the Sounds, bought tickets to dine with the gaggle. I could tell he was nervous about me meeting them, but he insisted he wanted them to know we were together. He didn't want to hide, not from them, not anymore.

Thanksgiving promised to be a fun, festive, family-filled feast . . . and that was a lot of Fs to give.

Nate gave the best Fs.

Twenty-Eight

Nate

The week before Thanksgiving, Coach called and asked me to come down to his office at the stadium. He made some excuse about paperwork, but my gut told me bad news was coming. In five years playing for him, he'd never once wanted to talk during the off-season. There'd never been any paperwork. My agent handled all that, if there was even anything to handle. Contracts were contracts. What more needed to be said—or signed?

After our weekend in Vegas, the team had slapped on smiles and shown pride in our championship run, but I'd struggled to enjoy any of it, not with how I'd finished *my* season. Except for the divisional championship, I'd stunk up the field for nearly four straight weeks, barely hitting the air around the ball, much less making contact with the darn thing. The few times I'd connected, it had sailed wide into foul territory, where it was easily fielded by an opponent—or, more embarrassingly, our batboy.

At the collegiate level, a long and deep slump like that would be troubling. As a professional, it was . . .

"Unforgivable," Coach Sabro grumbled. His voice wasn't raised. That was unnerving. The presence of Coach Eddelston and my agent in his office took the conversation to DEFCON 1. "Nate, you've been a solid player for this team for five years, but nobody makes a career in the minors. You know that. The goal is to play well here, then get a shot at the bigs. While your work at second has been great, one of the best, your consistency in the box has been shit, especially this season."

"I know—"

Coach raised a palm, silencing me. He then glanced to my agent, whose expression was that of someone who'd just put their favorite dog down.

"Nate," her voice was nearly breaking. "This is the end of the line."

"What . . . what? Back to Double A? Really?" I couldn't believe it.

She shook her head. "No. Not Double A. This is it, Nate. *Baseball*. It's over."

·I opened my mouth and froze. Everything—my body, my mind, my heart—it all seized. I couldn't breathe.

"But . . . but . . . we won the division. I was in the Gold Glove race. I—"

"Nate, I'm sorry." My agent's voice was soft, yet somehow steel at the same time. "I've called everybody, every franchise, majors down to Single A. Hell, I even pitched you for *coaching* jobs all the way down to the D-Two collegiate level. This season ended your dream. It's not going to happen. Every team knows it, so they want your slot for an up-and-comer who has a shot to make it. I'm so sorry, but your time in baseball is over. Today."

The two coaches stood.

Sabro nodded, as if he'd just concluded a deal, and they stepped out without a word. I felt my agent's hand squeeze my shoulder, then she fled, leaving me staring into Coach's teacher-style desk with my mouth still agape.

I wanted to scream.

I wanted to throw that desk into the fucking glass window that looked into the locker room.

I wanted to curl into a ball, to crawl under that desk and vanish.

I wanted to throw myself off the top row of seats, to never feel again, because what raged through me, the pain and anguish and embarrassment and anger and loss . . . and emptiness . . . I just couldn't . . .

My eyes wandered the length of Coach's wall, scanning one image after the next. One black-and-white shot showed a man in an old-time uniform with his arm draped around a boy's shoulders. I couldn't believe I'd never noticed that photo before. It was Coach Sabro as a kid. Holy shit, Coach had been a kid once upon a time. That might've surprised me as much as the picture, even though I knew, logically, it had to be true. We players just thought of him as perpetually old and crusty.

I stared at that little boy; the joy in his eyes, the way he held his glove to his chest with both hands, like it was the most precious thing in the world.

That's how I felt at his age. I remembered it so clearly, that first time I'd been handed a glove and ball—not as a toddler being goofy but as a five-year-old learning the game for the first time.

It was love at first sight.

The grass had been freshly cut on our raggedy local field. The dirt was dry and dusty, blowing in my eyes every time the wind kicked up. The summer sun was unbearable, and I was sweating through my cap and shirt. My parents stood off to the side, Mom fanning herself with some book she'd brought in case the practice droned on, as they tended to do. Dad hung on every word of our coach, like he was a baseball god descended from Mount Olympus to impart wisdom and error-free virtue.

He was just another dad who got stuck coaching, but he loved kids and he loved the game. His passion for the sport was infectious, and his venom raged in my veins as I trotted off the field for our post-practice McDonald's run.

Baseball became life.

In middle school, I was bigger, faster, and taller than the other kids. I was the stud, the kid everyone wanted on their team, the guy who got picked first. I wasn't just Nate. I was Nate the baller.

Nate the athlete.

Nate, the one who would make it one day.

Baseball became my identity, how I defined myself, how others saw me.

In high school, we were the best in the country, named a top ten team four years in a row. Teams dreaded seeing our name on their schedule.

I got sucked into the Vanderbilt pipeline as soon as NCAA rules allowed. They were among the best at their level too, and I couldn't graduate high school fast enough. The day I donned the black and gold was the proudest of my baseball life . . . thus far.

We didn't dominate collegiate ball the way my high school had reigned over the teenage diamond. While the best programs floated to the top each year, no one team wore the crown for long.

But we were good . . . really, really good.

And in my junior year, we did what few ever achieved: we hoisted the College World Series trophy.

The draft that followed was the icing on the cake.

I still remember buttoning up my Sounds uniform that first time. While I'd hoped to go straight onto a major league roster, skipping past the lower levels of the minor leagues was still better than most ever achieved. When I felt First Horizon's grass crunch under my cleats on day one, it was like my dad tossing me that first ball all over again.

Everyone should get to live their dream like I did.

Then my eyes moved back to Coach's desk; metal, dented, and starkly empty. There wasn't a single scrap of paper, not one folder, no knickknacks or trophies. Hell, there wasn't even a stray paperclip. It was utterly devoid of personality, of life.

It was my career staring back at me.

That was the moment I knew it was all real, that it was over, and the first tears fell.

Twenty-Nine

COOPER

Nate didn't stay at my place all week. He still had another year on his contract, so he'd have steady income for another fourteen months—such that MiBL pay was for a sidelined player—and that was some comfort.

But there was no comforting him over the loss of his dream.

Was it even possible to ease such pain?

I wanted to run to him, to drive to his apartment and wrap him in my arms, to tell him everything would be okay and we'd figure things out. The future would be bright and beautiful, as long as we were together.

But without baseball, he said his future was nothing but darkness and cloudy skies.

Nate was baseball. Baseball was Nate.

He tried to get out of attending Thanksgiving, but Miguel took his mentee firmly in hand and bitch-slapped him back into reality. I sat quietly and watched as the perpetually smiley cop frowned and schooled my guy.

"You were never dropped, Miguel," Nate deflected, sounding more like a pouty teen who'd lost a girlfriend than a professional sportsman licking his wounds.

"No, I never got to play at your level, not for a single day." He let that sink in, then continued. "I walked away on my own, because my family needed me on a different path, but I'll tell you something: the loss was the same. The hurt, the misery, it was all the same. I'd dreamed of wearing an MLB uniform since before I could talk, just like you. After I set down my bat, I *still* dreamed about baseball: the park, the grass, the sun on my face, the sound of the bat cracking against the ball, the clap of it hitting the mitt. I saw fucking baselines every time I drove. They were everywhere, those damn lines on the road reminding me of chalk. The worst was when I saw kids playing in the park, so happy and free, falling in love with the game, with *my* game, the one I'd just lost."

Miguel sucked in a calming breath.

"I get it, Nate. I get it all. Don't you dare doubt it. But I also get what lies on the other side of the baselines, what life can hold when you finally accept that no player, regardless of skill or level, plays forever. We all hang up our cleats and shelve our gloves, every one of us. You just did it sooner than you wanted. I know that sucks, but that's life sometimes."

He wrapped his arm around Nate and pulled him into a rough hug. "You'll be fine, bud. I promise. Sam and I—hell, all of us—we're here for you, no matter what. We're family. Even if you are an asshole."

Nate finally grunted an approximation of a laugh. "Fucker."

"That's my boy," Miguel said, his grin returning. "Now, stop being a dick to that man over there. He loves you, and he deserves a hell of a lot better than you've given him this week."

Nate's eyes drifted toward mine, and my heart swelled for the first time in a week.

"I'm sorry," he muttered. "Guess I've been—"

"Shut up and kiss me, asshole."

It took a second, but he did as instructed, crossing the few strides between us and settling into my lap for a long, welcome press of our lips. I hadn't needed his apology. No words were necessary. The emotion pouring through his touch told me all I needed to know.

When he came up for air, his first words caught in his throat.

"What am I going to do now?"

"I don't know, babe. We'll figure it out. Promise me we'll do that together."

"One hundred percent. Promise."

As our lips met again, Miguel stood. "When you two get done sucking the life out of each other, come into the dining room. I think Ty and Sam are almost done prepping dinner." He stopped in the doorway. "Oh, Nate, your parents arrived about thirty minutes ago. You might want to see them before they start to wonder if their boy ran away or something."

"You up for meeting my folks?" Nate whispered between kisses.

A smile bloomed. "One hundred percent."

Tyler lived up to his should've-been-a-chef reputation with the spread he created for Thanksgiving. Traditional turkey and dressing were surrounded by roasted and fried vegetables, cranberry sauce, and a handful of other side dishes one expected on Turkey Day. At the other end of the table, the Chef de Cuisine had arrayed less Thanksgivingy inventions, including duck breast in a caramel-orange-rum reduction, braised bananas with cinnamon and god-knows-what other spices that smelled like a tropical island had landed on the table, and a crown roast of pork with pearl onions and potatoes fondant whose crispy crusts made them look more like scallops than potatoes.

"I think I've died and gone to *Top Chef*," I whispered in Nate's ear.

He actually chuckled. There was hope, after all.

"Nathaniel!" a woman's voice soared above the din. A second later, a stunning Latina with flowing black hair and sparkling gray eyes barreled through the boys and nearly knocked Nate off his feet. I'd mastered many languages, but she began speaking in Spanish so quickly I could barely keep up. By the time she'd realized Nate wasn't alone and turned toward me, both of them had fresh tears flowing freely.

"And you must be Cooper. Nate hasn't bothered to tell me anything, not even your name, but that nice Sam spilled the pintos. Or is that peas? How does that go, Nathaniel?"

"Beans, Mom. It's beans."

"Oh, yes, spilled the beans. I prefer peas, by the way. Beans can be so mealy."

"Mom!"

She swatted Nate away, then gripped my arms with fingers of death and pulled me into her vortex of mommery that was a mix of strangulation, a hurricane of hands, topped with rapid-fire kisses and tears.

"You love my Nathaniel?" It was said more as a statement than a question, but her eyes begged for confirmation.

I leaned down and whispered in her ear, "More than life or breath. He's everything."

And her trickled tears became a downpour as she wrenched me to her breast once again.

"Hon, I think Cooper might want to breathe sometime in the near future. He's not supposed to be purple, is he?"

I gave Mr. Stringer a desperate glance. He was right; I was losing feeling in my extremities in her vice grip of an embrace.

"Welcome to the family, son," Mr. Stringer said, clapping me on the back.

"Um, Dad, let's not scare Coop away. We've only been together—"

"Fine, fine. When you're ready to come all the way out, let me know so I can be happy for you. Until then, I'll just pull for you,

Cooper, quietly . . . over there . . . in the corner. I might take one of those potatoes with me, you know, while I wait."

We laughed as he patted his burgeoning belly and snatched one of the fondants off the platter.

The arrival of Gabe, Ben, and Annie distracted Nate's parents long enough for us to clasp hands and join them at the front door. Everyone hugged, kissed, signed, and did whatever greeting friends did. Annie, never to be outdone by a gorgeous Latina who looked twenty years younger than she should have, sang her way into the house.

The gays applauded on cue.

I'd never felt more at home.

Thirty

COOPER

With the dawn of the new year, winter reached down and gripped Tennessee firmly by the balls with her icy claws . . . and tugged . . . and not in the gentle way that makes my spine tingle and toes curl and butt pucker. Yes, my butt puckered, like a doughnut whose hole hadn't quite been poked out completely. Wow, that was a bad analogy. Or was it frighteningly accurate?

Never mind.

No, this was not the gentle tug of a lover, but an angry bitch of a cold front screeching in from Chicago or some other winter wonderland that wasn't, in my humble opinion, very wonderful.

In keeping with the frigid state of our state, Nate still lived with Cal, though the first baseman had let Nate know he'd need to find a new place before his arranged-marriage roommate arrived for spring training. It was the last nail in the coffin that sealed away my man's baseball days for good, and, while it was a sad turning of the page, it was necessary.

He still had no idea what he would do next. Sam offered to let him work in the garage for a while, but he was more hopeless around cars than I was around ball sports.

Other balls, as we have established, were very comfortably in my wheelhouse.

I offered to let him move in with me, but he said he didn't want to rush that step between us. As much as I loved the idea of waking up next to him every morning, he was right. We needed to grow into that phase of our relationship without the pressure of outside influences, like teams dumping perfectly good players.

Sam and Miguel convinced him to set up camp in their guest bedroom when Cal kicked him out. He said he hoped it wouldn't come to that, but agreed to accept their kindness if there was no viable plan B.

He wasn't exactly mopey anymore, but he still hadn't returned to the carefree, if a bit stoic, Nate I'd come to love.

Time would heal, so we all hoped.

I stepped onto the mat, the maroon of the out-of-bounds area contrasting beautifully with the navy of the inner tiles. Three golden-robed members of the testing board glared from across the room. A royal blue silk fringed in gold was draped across the table behind which they sat, emotionless, unmoving, judges of my martial fate who wore more stripes than those to which I aspired that day.

Five bars.

Fifth dan.

Master.

All that stood between me and that title, those golden bands, were a series of demonstrations and the approval of those titans of tae kwon do who refused to acknowledge my presence with more than a fragile lift of a brow.

I bowed, slowly, respectfully, palms pressed against my sides, heart threatening to flee my chest.

"Begin," the master at the center commanded.

He hadn't told me what to do, hadn't given me a task or set a goal, so I did what came naturally at the beginning of a session with my own master back at home. I crossed the mat, displaying one form to perfection. Once my foot touched the red of the other side, I turned and began a new form. My hands flowed in graceful lines, then punched with a flutist's staccato. My kicks were precise, and the two times I shouted, my voice was commanding and crisp. They allowed me to pass them ten times before the master called out, "Halt."

I froze, planted my palms to my sides, and bowed once more.

"Target check," the master demanded, and a man I hadn't seen standing off to the side, also draped in gold and cinched in black, strode onto the mat. He stopped a few feet away and pressed his heels together.

I bowed toward him.

On one hand, he wore a blue padded target. He hefted the hand into the air at head height, and barked, "*Ap chagi*!"

My foot flew before I could think, a perfectly straight front kick smacked into the target.

"*Dollyo chagi*!"

My body twisted into a roundhouse kick that whirled and struck the target dead in the center.

"*Yop chagi*!" he shouted, holding the target a good foot above his six-foot height.

The side kick that followed nearly knocked him off balance. My own equilibrium remained still as a glacial pond. My eyes never wavered, lasers intent on the blue mitt on his hand.

"*Kodeup chagi*!"

A repeated kick. Good. We were finally getting to the fun stuff. I smacked the target four times before returning my foot to the floor and glaring at the master.

I would not bend.

I would not break.

What else have you got?

The master glanced at the table, and I caught a slight nod from the presiding judge. He turned back toward me and barked, "*Twio yop chagi*!"

Oh boy. Time to jump.

I took a step back, then leapt into the air and kicked forward with my foot turned sideways, striking the target now held as high above the master's head as his arms would allow. He actually stumbled back a step as I returned lightly to the ground and bounced on the balls of my feet.

"Halt!" came the order, and the master with the mitt withdrew.

Another bow.

"Creative routine. Begin."

I had choreographed this routine weeks earlier, practicing it for hours, reliving its steps, kicks, and thrusts each night in my dreams. When I began, my body danced with the grace of the ancient art. I was controlled and restrained, yet powerful. This test was mine, and I would not be denied.

When my routine ceased, and I offered the masters another bow, the room seemed to hold its breath.

The master at the center never flinched. "*Poomsae*!" his voice boomed.

My body followed his command without conscious thought. Forms flowing from limbs to palms, legs to feet. One kick speared the air a foot above my head, only to be followed by three, then four, then five more in rapid succession. I held each step, a gymnast holding his pose to prove to all, to prove to himself, the unwavering strength he possessed, both in muscles and within. Form after form, like water bubbling across stones, I laid myself bare for the golden eyes.

"Halt!"

I froze, spun, then bowed.

The master who'd challenged me with handheld targets returned to the mat with a stack of wooden squares clasped reverently in his hands. He stopped a few feet before me, and snapped his feet together. I bowed toward him as I had done to the others twice already. Then he held up the first board and cried, "Strike!"

Without hesitation, I wheeled, and my foot flew, splitting the board in half and sending a piece only feet from the judges' table.

He raised another board, then commanded a strike of a different form. I spun in the opposite direction and shattered the wood with perfect timing and force.

Then he raised two boards pressed together, and his mouth quirked at the corner. "Strike!"

I danced back, then shifted my weight, spun, and sent my foot through the target, hurling shattered pieces actually onto the judges' table, startling a thin man seated to the right of the presiding master.

"Halt!"

There was a moment of silence as the judges whispered, the central figure turning to one side, then the next.

"We have questions now."

I bowed.

"You have been a student for many years, but now test for fifth dan and the title of master. Your focus must shift. How will you turn from your own desires to help propagate the art?"

I knew there would be a question period, but had no idea what they would ask. This, however, was a logical foray into, "Why do you want to be a master?"

"As a student, my place was to follow and learn. As a master, I must lead and teach. My time in competitive sport provided me a unique platform that is still available today. Young people still remember when I made my Olympic run, and those who never knew of me could be easily reminded. I would use this as a launching point to teach existing athletes, as well as to recruit new talent to our sport."

The only female master on the panel shifted in her seat. "But how would you do this? Do you work in our sport? Are you active on social media? Do you do anything beyond train in your local dojang?"

I inclined my head, buying time to think. "I love tae kwon do. It's so much more than a sport, it's a discipline, an art, a way of life. It's a way of living. I want to inspire others in the same way my masters inspired me, but have yet to find the perfect path. I humbly ask your guidance."

I bowed slower and more deeply than before.

The masters whispered again, this time for what felt like an eternity. Beads of sweat that hadn't bothered me during the physical test now tickled my neck and forehead. For the first time that day, I felt nerves creeping in.

The presiding master rose, strode around the table, and stood at the edge of the mat facing me. Then he did the last thing I expected.

He bowed deeply and held it in the ultimate position of respect and deference.

I quickly dropped into a mirroring pose.

"Rise," he said, with a voice swelling with something other than the command I'd come to expect.

The other masters stood and joined him, as black-belted men and women rose from seats in the darkness and stepped forward, forming a pathway between the presiding master and me. He lifted his hand and motioned me forward. When I stopped before him and bowed, he issued only one word: "Turn."

Hands reached around and untied my belt. A second pair of hands held my *dobok* in place as the original weathered hands wrapped a stiff new belt about my waist. The shimmer of five golden bars caught my eye, and I wanted to shout at the ceiling.

Firm hands turned me by my shoulders to again face the presiding master, and we exchanged another bow. Then I heard the words I hadn't expected for years to come.

"Rise, Master Hawk."

Those around applauded, but no one moved from their positions in their lines. The golden-clad masters even remained in place. Then I noticed a small table that had been placed on the mat while I was turned, and a grin tugged at my lips.

Our tea ceremony was a custom very different from those treasured in Japan and other places throughout Asia. For one, the purpose was to celebrate the attainment of a new dan, and therefore required the newly "donned" (excuse the pun) athlete to take a drink for each level he or she had attained.

This wouldn't have been an issue had the tea ceremony actually served tea. Oh no. Our tradition used sake—and the "drink" I was expected to take was a shot from a large Korean drinking bowl.

Five celebratory tosses of the tea later, I felt no pain. Zero. Nada.

In fact, I was positively giddy.

And the masters were jumping into the bottle faster than my feet had flown in the test.

What had been a nerve-racking duel with the martial arts was now a rice-wine-fueled party.

"That may have been the most flawless test I've seen." A raspy female voice from behind me nearly startled the sake out of my hand. I turned to find the female judge from the panel staring up at me, shot glass poised at her lips.

"Thank you, Master Lina." I bowed.

"Oh, stop that. The test is over. You're in the club. No more bowing, at least for today."

"Yes, Master—"

She tutted me, so I slammed my mouth shut. Her eyes twinkled at my discomfort.

"I'd like to talk with you about your future," she said.

I took a sip, even though I was already well lubricated. "My future?"

"Yes. Master Wolen raised the question of your future as a master, your contribution to the art, and you threw yourself on our mercy."

"Um, technically, I threw myself on your counsel. I don't think mercy had anything to do with it."

She chuckled, like a villain in one of those old '30s movies who knew what was behind that door, you know, the one you never went into in a scary movie, but the idiot kids always did anyway because, if they didn't, none of them would die by chainsaw, and that was the whole point of those movies.

Maybe that wasn't in the '30s. What did I know? I was sloshed.

"Mercy, counsel, mentorship. They're all sides of the same coin."

"That would mean the coin had three sides, and that doesn't—"

She silenced me with a snicker and a palm.

"Talk less. Listen more. Grasshopper."

"Hey, that wasn't tae kwon do. That was—"

Another palm.

"I want you to buy me out."

I nearly dropped my tea.

She wanted me to eat her out? But she was so old. And I was gay. It didn't even make sense.

"I'm too old to teach like the kids deserve, and retirement feels right."

Oh. Buy her out, not eat—

"I think you'd be a wonderful master to carry on my legacy, and my dojang."

My head was spinning, and not just from the sake—or the proposition that wasn't actually a proposition unless you counted selling a business as a proposition, which, I guessed, it really was.

Hell, she *was* propositioning me.

While I was drunk.

"Just think about it. A move to Memphis probably wasn't in your plans, but I think this would be a good fit—and I would make you a very reasonable offer. I'm not looking to get rich, just to pass my kids off to a master who will make me proud. You would certainly do that, Cooper. It would be an honor for the dojang I built to carry your name."

And just like that, I was speechless. Completely out of words. Babble-less. Un-babbled. De-babbled.

Okay, maybe there were a few left.

"Master Lina, thank you. I am humbled and honored. I'm blown away, really."

She reached up and patted my cheek, just as Grammy used to do.

"You honor me, son. You honor me."

Thirty-One

Nate

I got to the restaurant ten minutes early, which was rare for me, because I was usually late to everything. At least, after getting dumped by the love of my life—baseball—I'd stopped caring about silly things like punctuality.

But that night was different.

Everything had to be perfect.

My agent had called a week earlier with a possibility that had sounded insane. Then again, I didn't exactly have the Yankees banging on my door, so anything dealing with sports was better than the barren wasteland that was my career currently. I asked her to get more details and get back to me, told her I'd give anything she put on my plate serious consideration.

Blah, blah, fucking, blah.

Well, fuck me running if she didn't call back with a solid offer.

I nearly shit my drawers.

That was two days ago, and I'd managed to keep the whole thing bottled up, not even telling Miguel or my parents or anyone. Miguel would kill me for keeping a secret from him, but then he'd break into a goofy smile the width of the Kansas sky and we'd end up wrestling like kids on the ground.

Cooper was another story.

I was scared to death of what he would think.

I mean, he'd want me to be happy, I knew that for sure. He loved me, and I loved him more than anything I'd ever known—maybe even more than baseball, which I'd never thought possible.

But for this opportunity to work, I'd have to move.

We'd always known that was likely at some point. If I'd made it into the majors, I would've had to go wherever the offer took me. Even in the minors, trades happened. So, we were well conditioned to the idea that someday, down the road, we might face the long-distance thing, even though neither of us could stand being more than ten feet apart.

We actually called that our "ten-foot rule." It was cute. It was our thing.

But "down the road" was quickly becoming "tomorrow," or very near to it, and the thought of packing my life and moving far from the man who held my heart . . . God, that sucked.

"Penny?"

Silverware clattered as my knees banged into the table bottom.

"Shit, you scared me to death." I held my hand over my heart in mock fright.

Coop grinned down, then leaned down and kissed me.

I couldn't help but glance around to see who might've witnessed the baseball player and his boyfriend exchange spit in public. After the Great Dumping, as Sam dubbed it, I'd stopped giving two shits what people thought. My public days were over, and if I wanted to tongue-wrestle Coop in the middle of a Chick-fil-A, fuck the owner and his homophobic, perfectly-brined-in-pickle-juice chicken sandwich that might've been handed down from a benevolent god to humanity because it was perfect.

What can I say? They really did have the best chicken sandwich, despite their man-tongue-spearing aversion.

"You okay, babe? You seem, I don't know, off somehow."

The Force was strong in this one. Fuck.

"No, I'm good. Fine. Great. I'm great."

He smirked as he picked up a menu. "That's reassuring. Very. Totally. A lot."

I blew out a sigh.

"Prosecution rests."

I tossed my head back against the chair and rolled my eyes.

"Okay, I have something—"

"And I want to hear it, but I have news," he said, cutting me off, which he *never* did.

"Um, okay. Great." I really wasn't sure how to broach my topic anyway. "You go first."

And right before my eyes, Coop turned into a gibbering puddle of nervous-as-hell mush.

"Okay, you're not going to believe any of this, because I can't believe it, and I believe most anything because I was raised to be trusting and innocent and I like to believe the best about people and situations, which often gets me hurt or disappointed, especially when I watch the news, because the news is always so sad and focused on death and kidnapping and rape and abortions that come from rape because some people want other people who got raped by evil people to carry little people to term and I just think that's nuts."

The waiter had stepped up to our table midway through whatever the fuck that was and was now staring, mouth agape, at Cooper.

I was pretty much doing the same.

"I did it again, didn't I?"

I nodded.

The waiter tapped his pen against one of our water glasses and said, "You need more water. Let me get that. Now. Before he speaks again."

And he fled the field.

I was torn between my own nerves from the news I had to share, and trying to translate Cooper into English, which was often impossible, even with an army of UN translators by my side.

"Why don't you take a sip of water and start again?" I said as soothingly as possible.

He did. Then he sucked in a deep breath, held it, then blew it slowly out.

"Alright. I'm good. I'm calm. I'm zen."

"I'll settle for calm."

"I'm fucking zen. Roll with it."

"Yes, sir. Master, sir." I held up both palms in surrender. He smirked.

"Okay, you know how I went to test for fifth dan?"

"Yeah." I nodded. "You were brilliant, just like I said you'd be."

"True," he said with a slight blush, "but my brilliance isn't the topic. Stay with me."

I rolled my eyes and grinned.

"Master Lina—she was one of the masters on my panel—approached me after the test. She's been around for a thousand years, runs one of the most prominent dojangs in Tennessee. Everyone loves her, and her kids compete at the highest levels. To say she's built a dynasty is an insult to dynasties, unless you're talking about *Dynasty* the TV show, because that was awesome."

I crossed my arms and leaned back.

"Sorry. Anyway. She pulled me aside while we were doing the not-so-tea ceremony and asked me to consider . . . get this . . . taking over her program."

Blink.

"She wants me to buy her out, which isn't what I originally thought she'd asked, which was actually quite embarrassing and horrifying because she's old and wrinkled and, well, a woman, and I'm not into women at all, but you already know that—"

"Coop!"

"Sorry."

"She wants to sell you her business? This is brilliant, babe. You love tae kwon do and you hate your job. You love kids, and there are a gazillion of them in a martial arts studio. I wouldn't even have to get pregnant. Such a relief."

He scrunched his nose. "You wanted to get pregnant?"

"No, babe, I was being silly."

"Oh." His mouth formed an actual O.

"Coop, I'm so excited for you."

"Us."

I froze.

"For us, Nate. This is for us. I want to do this together."

And my heart fell.

He still hadn't heard my news; my wonderful, exciting, thrilling news I'd been bursting at the seams to tell him for days . . . that would now crush us both.

"Please say something. I'm dying."

My head lowered, and I had to fight back emotions I hadn't even realized were hiding just beneath the surface. Coop was everything I wanted. Besides baseball, there was nothing else for me. I'd already reconciled with a life without baseball, but now one without Coop? I . . . I couldn't . . .

"You never said where the dojang was," I ventured.

He drew in another deep breath. "Memphis."

I nearly jumped out of my chair.

"Memphis? Really? Seriously? As in the home of Elvis? That Memphis?"

He nodded.

"Babe . . ."

Blink.

Then his voice turned into a pleading sound that made my heart crack right down the center.

"We can find something you love there. I know it. Babe, Grammy left me seventy-eight million dollars and five houses. We can afford for you not to work for a while. We'll make it work. Please say you'll come with me. I love you so much and—"

"Fuuuuuuuuuck!"

"Um, yes, please? Or was that a statement?" he asked.

"Did I miss something, or did you just say your grandmother left you over seventy million dollars?" I whispered the figure, afraid others might overhear the lottery-sized bomb he'd just dropped.

He nodded. "That was just the cash. There's stocks too, but I don't know much about those. Our guy at Goldman is getting a report together for me. He said the portfolio spits off over ten million a year in income, whatever that means."

My throat clenched.

How had he never known? From what he'd said, she never flaunted her wealth, but five houses?

For a starving baseball player who'd lived on Big Macs and Twizzlers for the past five years, having more than a few hundred in an account was cause for celebration.

The dojang thing made sense, and Coop would be an amazing instructor. It being in Memphis was something I hadn't seen coming, but the level of insane richness that was his grandmother . . . I couldn't comprehend all the zeroes.

How was I supposed to feel about dating a guy who could now buy out my contract a gazillion times over? I'd never be able to measure up or compete with that kind of wealth.

I suddenly felt small next to Cooper for the first time.

Would he still see me the same way? Would the money change us? Would it change him?

I glanced up to find pure innocence and love pouring out of his eyes. He looked even more rattled than I felt.

I knew, in that brief instant, my worries were ridiculous.

Cooper would never change. He would never be anything but the humble, lovable, somewhat goofy man I'd come to respect and admire.

I loved him. So damn much.

We could figure it out. I mean, hell, we were rich.

"Holy fucking mother of fuckery."

"What's with the potty mouth?"

"That's *fuck-off money*."

"Huh?"

"In baseball, when a guy gets a huge contract with a massive upfront, we call that *fuck-off money* because he can tell everybody to do just that with all that cash." I could barely think. "Coop, you have fuck-off money."

"I guess I do. It still hasn't sunk in." He glanced down at his fingers, then slowly looked up into my eyes. "I want to share it with you. I want to share everything with you, Nate. None of this means anything without you in my life. Please—"

"God, Cooper, you had me before I knew any of that. One hundred percent. Completely. Wholly. All my heart and body and soul. I'm so yours it hurts."

"It hurts?" His brows furrowed.

"Just an expression. Let's move on."

"Okay."

"It's just Memphis—"

"I know. Memphis. I get it. Nashville is home and the guys are here and we'd be starting over and—"

"Coop, stop talking, just for a second. I need to tell you something important."

He settled in his seat and gripped his sides with crossed arms.

"It's not bad news. God, it's amazing. Everything's amazing, babe." I felt like I could leap into the air and fly around the room. "I got a call from my agent. The Mangoes made me an offer to play for them. In Memphis."

Now it was his turn to blink.

And blink again.

And then a tear fell.

"The *Memphis* Mangoes? The funny team you loved so much?"

I nodded.

And his hand flew across the table and grasped mine, and squeezed, and dear lord, his grip was fucking iron.

"Killing me. Easy, baby. Please, glove hand."

Before I'd finished the last word, Coop was around the table and wrapped in my arms, bawling like a six-month-old who needed a bottle or a Binky or some other thing babies crave but don't know how to ask for.

"We're . . . we're moving to Memphis . . . together," he muttered into my neck, snot streaking my collar.

"Yeah, I guess we are."

Thirty-Two

Nate

"If we don't see you every holiday—"

"Yes, Mom." I hugged Miguel. This man had been my surrogate father and big brother and baseball sherpa since college. Saying goodbye to him was harder than I'd imagined.

Sam stood to the side, his hand rubbing circles on Miguel's back, and the big cop's chest heaved. I'd never seen him cry. Then again, he'd never sent his son off to see the world.

"My little Mango," he muttered.

I shoved him back to find a shit-eating grin splayed across his face.

"Don't be jealous of my juice."

"Eww, you're disgusting," Sam chirped.

"If you'd ever tasted his juice—"

"COOP!" all three of us shouted, ending whatever he was about to say.

"Just sayin', it's delicious." He smirked and strutted away, pretending to lick his fingers and wave them in the air.

"You're moving with him willingly? Now's the time to give us a signal if this is a kidnapping. Just wiggle your nose or do that tit dance you see muscleheads in the gym do if you need help," Miguel said.

"You've been a cop way too long. It's fried that pea-brain of yours."

"Be nice to your mother," Sam chided, smacking me with his grill spatula. He'd insisted we come over for one last barbecue before we hauled our overstuffed cars across the state to begin our new life.

"We're gonna miss you both, really," I said.

"We're a three-hour drive away. Besides, you can stay with us when the Mangoes come to town. That's an order, not a request. Plus, Miguel's right about holidays. This is where you belong, with us. I know Ty and Gabe would miss you boys if you weren't here. Annie would probably send the gay mafia to hunt you down and serenade you with show tunes until you made the drive."

I snorted. "Gay mafia?"

He cocked a brow. "You think I jest? Try her. Last guys to cross her suffered a drive-by landscaping. The neighborhood gentrified so fast that property values skyrocketed in a week."

I shook my head.

"We need to hit the road, babe. You have practice tomorrow," Coop called from the foyer.

I gave Miguel one last hug, whispering in his ear before he pulled back, "I love you, ya big jerk. Take care of Sam. You guys really are the best."

He surprised me with a kiss on the cheek, something he'd never done. "And I love you, Nate Stringer. You're the brother I never had, and I'd better hear from you before this week is up."

"You got it. I'll keep you posted on how life is as a Mango. I'm pretty pumped to learn all the dance moves."

"Sweet Jesus, he cares more about the moves than the baseball. Where has my baby bro gone?"

Sam doubled over. "He's been right there the whole time, dear. Trust me. That's him, bad dancing and all."

"Bad? Just you wait. Watch your social media for my Mango coming out. It'll be epic."

Coop's hands wrapped around my waist, and he poked his head over my shoulder, eyeing Sam.

"We love you guys. Come see us once we've settled in."

Sam and Miguel joined us in a group hug, then Coop pulled back suddenly.

"What?" I asked.

"I almost forgot. One of the things Grammy instructed in her will was for me to continue her work helping people, especially children in tough situations. She was a big fan of anonymous assistance, as she called it. Please let Ty and Gabe know that Ben's college tuition to Gallaudet University in Washington, DC is fully prepaid. It's the best deaf university in the country. That should be one less worry on his mother's plate."

"Babe, that's amazing," I said, turning to wrap him in a proper hug.

"Fucking awesome, Coop. I don't think Marjorie could have asked for a better living legacy than having you as her grandson," Sam said, and I swear there was mist in the burly man's eyes.

When we got in the car, I turned to Coop and gripped his face. "Babe, you really are the most amazing man I've ever known. I'm so proud of you, of who you are, of everything about you."

"Nate!" he tried to protest, but my grip was firm.

"I don't know where this road's gonna take us—other than Memphis—but I know one thing for sure: I don't want to spend one day, one minute, without you. I love you, Cooper Hawk, and can't wait to start our life together."

I kissed him with all the pent-up passion I could muster.

When I pulled back, our tears had mingled, and Coop's brilliant blue eyes sparkled. His smile filled my heart with a joy beyond any game or series or championship.

He reached up and cupped my cheek, and with tenderness and love, he asked, "Will you be my Mango?"

I hope you loved Nate & Cooper in The Batter's Box. If you did, it would mean the world to me if you would leave a review filled with stars. Your words help others discover my work (and make me feel all warm and fuzzy).

About Author

Casey Morales is an LGBT storyteller and the author of multiple bestselling MM romance novels. Born in the Southern United States, Casey is an avid tennis player, aspiring chef, dog lover, and ravenous consumer of gummy bears.

Also By Casey

Nashville Spicy series

Raised by Wolves series